THE QUEEN AGAINST
KARL MULLEN

MICHAEL GILBERT

THE QUEEN AGAINST KARL MULLEN

Carroll & Graf Publishers, Inc.
New York

This is a work of fiction. The characters and firms mentioned in it
are wholly imaginary. Certain offices and places which are mentioned do exist: which makes it all the more important to state that
no mention of the holder of such office or place has any reference to
the past or present holder.

Published by arrangement with the author.

First Carroll & Graf edition 1991

Carroll & Graf Publishers, Inc.
260 Fifth Avenue
New York, NY 10001

Library of Congress Cataloging-in-Publication Data

Gilbert, Michael Francis, 1912–
    The Queen against Karl Mullen / by Michael Gilbert. — 1st
Carroll & Graf ed.
        p.   cm.
    ISBN 0-88184-698-8 (cloth) : $18.95
    I. Title.
PR6013.I3335Q4   1991
823'.914—dc20   91-12124
                                                            CIP

Manufactured in the United States of America

Dedicated to Dr. J. L. Jenman, M.R.C.S., L.R.C.P.; and
to Peter Clarke, Barrister of Lincoln's Inn

1

It was half past five on an evening in early autumn and the City was disgorging its workers.

From the doorway of No. 10 Axe Lane, which is on the western fringe of the City, came two girls. Kathleen, large, fair and placid, and Rosemary, a small and lively brunette. There was nothing remarkable about them. Thousands like them were hurrying away, at that hour, from a day of office work to an evening of freedom.

There was nothing remarkable about the doorway either, except that, unlike its neighbours, it carried no plate to identify it. Only the handsome bronze springbok, on a pedestal in the front hall beside the porter's desk, suggested a South African connection. It was the Security Section of the South African Embassy. Its head was Fischer Yule, after the Ambassador and the Consul-General their most important functionary in England.

The two girls turned left outside the office. When they reached Cheapside they checked for a moment.

Kathleen said, "Off to school, is it?"

"That's right," said Rosemary. She was known by the other girls in the office to be attending a course of lectures at the City Northern Institute.

"So what are you on now?"

"Mediaeval hagiography."

"Rather you than me."

"And what are your plans for this evening? Jimmy, I suppose."

"You suppose right. He's not a ball of fire, but he's more fun, I'd say, than mediaeval what's-it." It had sometimes

7

occurred to her to wonder why an attractive girl like Rosemary should bother about what had happened five hundred years ago, when the present held so much interest and excitement. But she had not wondered about it for long. It was none of her business. She turned right towards St. Paul's. Rosemary headed down Cheapside towards the Bank underground station.

When she reached the platform her experience stood her in good stead. She knew exactly where to stand so as to be opposite one of the train doors and as soon as the door opened she could judge whether it was possible to insert herself into the crowded opening without suffering actual damage. On this occasion she was lucky. There was no question of getting a seat, but she was wedged, not uncomfortably, between an Indian student and a uniformed commissionaire.

By the time the train reached the Angel, Islington, the crowd had eased a little and she had no difficulty in getting off. All the same it was lucky, she thought, that she didn't suffer from claustrophobia. On one occasion the train had been held up for ten minutes and a woman standing near her had started screaming.

She showed her pass to the ticket collector, fielded the smile which ticket collectors usually gave her, and stepped out onto the pavement. Here she stopped to buy an evening paper from the old man who had his pitch at the station entrance.

Anyone watching her might have noticed that, whilst she was opening her bag and fumbling in it for the necessary coins, she had stationed herself so that she could look up and down the road. There were people on both pavements, but they were hurrying along, not loitering. She turned to the right down Goswell Road and followed two men who were arguing about football.

After about a hundred yards she swung off to the right. This was Winstanley Street, which led to the area known as New River Head. It was one of the curious backwaters of London. When the Metropolitan Water Board had constructed their tank farm they had acquired more land than they needed and since they had no plans for building on it, the land on either side of their tanks had long lain derelict, covered with a fine growth of weeds, head high to the brick walls around it. A few boys penetrated this jungle, but only by day. By night even the most daring kept clear of it. A woman's body without head or arms had been found there. That was fifty years ago, but the mythology, once established, had lingered.

None of these associations troubled Rosemary. From her point of view the road had two advantages. It was long and straight and it was almost always empty. By the time she reached the far end she was confident that no one was following her.

A further right turn took her back into civilisation. It was typical of the illogicality of all great cities that areas of prosperity and of desolation should exist side by side. Mornington Square, which she was now approaching from the south, was a quadrilateral of nineteenth-century houses which had risen in the world; slowly at first, but very sharply in the last twenty years as people had found it quiet and convenient for getting to work in the City. Houses which, just after the war, could have been snapped up for a few thousand pounds were now changing hands at fifty or even a hundred times that figure. Most of them were divided into tiny flats.

The house on the north side of the square which Rosemary was making for was one of the exceptions. It seemed, from the plate on the door, to be in the sole occupation of an organisation called the Orange Consortium. Londoners are incurious about their neighbours. Anyone who did think twice about it supposed either that it was concerned with the import and sale of oranges or it had some connection, possibly political, with the Orange Free State. Both these theories gained support from the fact that five of the seven occupants of the house were black South Africans.

Rosemary let herself in and climbed the central staircase to the top floor. This was the flat which belonged to the head of the Consortium. His name was Trevor Hartshorn. He was Rosemary's father and, in his own way, a remarkable man.

Joining the army in the ranks he had risen in twelve years from private to Regimental Sergeant-Major. Six years later he was Captain and quartermaster – and a widower, his wife having died of leukaemia. He had thereupon abandoned the army and taken a job in the City as office manager to one of its largest firms of solicitors.

Four years later a difference of opinion with the senior

partner had led him to abandon a job which he had carried out with striking efficiency and – still under forty – he had been snapped up by Andrew Mkeba to run the Orange Consortium.

It was an intelligent move. When he had joined it he had found it to be a group of friends prepared to talk, but unable to do anything effective.

He had changed it from a debating society into an action group.

His first step had been to put the finances onto a proper footing. There was plenty of money available from sympathisers and his time in the City had taught him how to approach the major fund-raisers. Once assured of the money he had reduced the number of the full-time members to four; all well paid professionals and all occupying self-contained flats in the Mornington Square headquarters. The remaining space, on the ground floor, was a communications room and office.

In charge of broadcasting and maintaining links with the African National Congress in Lusaka was Govan Kabaka, who had been called to the Bar at Lincoln's Inn, but had never practised. He also supplied a budget of carefully slanted material to the Radio Freedom Station in Addis Ababa. Raymond Masangi produced the movement's own monthly sheet, *Black Voices*, and arranged for its infiltration into South Africa via Mozambique and its distribution by COSATU, the Trades Union Congress, and Black Sash, the anti-apartheid women's group. 'Boyo' Sesolo, ex-athlete and world class weight-lifter, organised the boycott of individual athletes and sportsmen with South African connections. He ran the action section, the storm-troopers of the movement. Most of these were students or ex-students. Not from Oxford and Cambridge ('upper-class talking shops,' said Boyo) but from the robust and down-to-earth universities and polytechnics of London, Reading and Bristol. They acted as stewards for their own meetings and disrupters of their opponents' meetings, a function which they carried out with enthusiasm. A speaker from Andries Treurnich's Conservative Party, who had been billed to address the London School of Economics, had been lucky to escape serious injury. Certainly nothing had been heard of his speech after his opening words.

Last, and by no means least, was Hartshorn's second-in-

10

command, Andrew Mkeba. A thirty-year-old Xhosa from Johannesburg, he had been one of the leaders of the 1976 students' revolt in Soweto. He had been betrayed for his part in it and sent to the Robben Island Prison. He was one of the very few people who had succeeded in escaping from that establishment and, subsequently, from the country. He carried with him the stigmata of his preliminary examination: a fractured cheekbone, a damaged right eye and a broken and imperfectly reset jaw. The ruin of his face was compensated for by a smile which his crooked chin made uncommonly attractive.

Rosemary knew, of course, about all this activity. Her own hatred of the South African regime, though second-hand and founded on written reports in newspapers and books, was fervent and selfless. At that moment one idea was mastering all others. She was extremely hungry. Fortunately her father's thoughts seemed to be moving in the same direction. He said, "I thought we might eat out tonight. I've booked a table at the Chinese restaurant in Crawford Street. Are you ready?"

"Am I just. There's something I was going to tell you, but we can talk as we go."

"If it's something to do with your work, better not talk about it outside."

Rosemary sighed and reseated herself. She sometimes thought that her father's notions of security were unnecessarily rigorous. "It's just that we had a visitor this afternoon. Someone I hadn't seen before and obviously important."

"How was that obvious? You mean Yule deferred to him?"

This made Rosemary laugh. "Yule's an arrogant pig and he never defers to anyone. It was just that he gave him a ticket."

"Explain."

"There are these two passages opposite our front door. Harnham Court and Deanery Passage. They're both dead ends. They just run up to the back entrance of two large office blocks. Yule has made some arrangement with them. Their commissionaires allow a few of our people – they're all named and identified – to go through the building and out by the front door into Amchurch Lane. It's called being on the ticket."

Hartshorn, who had been following this on a street map said, "So then they can go either into St. Martin's-le-Grand or

11

Newgate Street."

"That's right. It's meant to be a terrific privilege. I could never see the point of it myself."

"Can't you? Well, I think perhaps I can."

"Anyway, this new man was taken straightaway and introduced to the two commissionaires. Therefore we all assumed he was a big wheel."

Hartshorn thought about this. He had considerable confidence in his daughter. If he had not had this confidence he would not have taken the risk – a risk not only for her, but for his own organisation – of inserting her into the centre of his opponent's machine. He said, "We'd better bring Andrew in on this." Noticing the look on her face he added, "After we've eaten."

It was nearly ten o'clock and Rosemary was feeling a lot happier and rather sleepy, when they knocked at the door of Andrew Mkeba's apartment, which was on the floor immediately below theirs. The room was more office than sitting-room and Andrew was at his desk, writing.

"Didn't want to interrupt you," said Hartshorn, "but I thought you ought to know about this at once."

Rosemary repeated her story. There was no need to explain about the 'ticket' system. Mkeba knew about this, as he knew every detail of the arrangement of Yule's office and its occupants.

He said, "Could you describe this man?"

"I'm not very good at describing people. He was about forty-five I'd guess. A powerful-looking brute, with one of those silly little beards under his lower lip."

"Would you recognise him if you saw him again?"

"Yes, I think so."

"Let's try." He went to one of the row of filing cabinets which lined two walls and took out an album of photographs. "See if you can find him here."

This was quickly done. There were a number of photographs which had been cut from newspapers. The clearest was a group at the opening of the new Pretoria race-track. There was also a candid-camera shot which had been enlarged.

"You're sure?"

"Certain, yes. When I saw him the second time, in Yule's

12

office, he had put on a pair of glasses, which made him look a bit different, but yes — I'm quite sure."

"Well, well, well," said Mkeba softly, "we are honoured."

"You know him?"

"Very well. Karl Mullen. The pencil man himself. A colonel from the military police headquarters at Daniel Malan Barracks in Pretoria. What can have brought *him* to England?"

"That is exactly what you must find out."

"Not easy," said Rosemary. "Mostly they speak in Afrikaans. From what you have taught me" — this was to Mkeba, who smiled encouragingly — "I can catch a few words. Fortunately, Yule sometimes likes to air his English. He is really very fluent. When his legal man's there he always speaks in English."

Her father said, "From the anteroom where you sit, how much can you actually hear?"

"If the door is open, everything. If it is shut, very little."

"And if anything of importance is being discussed," said Mkeba, "then, of course, the door will be shut. These are not the sort of people who shout their secrets from the housetops."

The two men looked at each other. It was clear that they had some project in mind, something they had discussed before, something which they were hesitating to put into words. To encourage them Rosemary said, "I suppose it might be possible to use some sort of device — "

Mkeba opened one of the desk drawers and got out a small box, about the size of a pack of playing cards. He said, "This is one of the latest transmitters. It is very sensitive. It operates to this pick-up." He laid on the desk beside it a tiny golden plug. "You wear it in your ear, like a deaf-aid. It will be quite invisible, particularly if you comb your hair forward a little. Would you like to try it?"

Rosemary slipped it into her ear. It fitted very comfortably and was easy enough to put in and take out.

"It's very odd," she said, "I can hear myself breathing."

"Everyone who uses a deaf-aid finds that to start with. I am assured that it is something you soon get used to. Now, I suggest you go out into the passage and up the stairs."

He opened the door for her, shut it behind her and listened to her footsteps as she climbed the stairs. When he judged

13

that she was far enough away he returned to the box and placed it on top of one of the filing cabinets behind a pile of books.

Then he came back, sat down and said in conversational tones, "Three blind mice. See how they run."

"They all ran after the farmer's wife," said Hartshorn. "She cut off their tails with a carving knife, or so I've been told."

"Did ever you see such a thing in your life," shouted Rosemary from the stairhead. She came clattering down, clearly intrigued and excited. "It was all beautifully clear. I could even hear you pushing those books aside on the cabinet."

"*If* we're going to use it," said her father, who sounded less enthusiastic than Mkeba, "you'll have to think of some place to put it."

"That's not too difficult. We all go in and out collecting papers and so on. Just a matter of waiting for the right moment."

"You'll have to hide it. That might take time."

"I'll think of something."

"Don't take any chances. It's not a game. These men are dangerous."

"Don't fuss, Daddy. Suppose they did happen to find the box, how are they going to know who put it there? It might have been any of us three girls, or his secretary, Mrs. Portland, or one of the cleaning women, or the commissionaire, or the girl who comes to disinfect the telephones, or a man who turned up unexpectedly last week to clean the windows. He'd be a very likely candidate."

"All right," growled her father. "All I'm saying is, watch your step."

"Certainly. And *my* next steps are going to be up to bed."

When she had gone, the two men sat for some time without speaking. It was the Captain who broke the silence. He said, "I suppose it is all right, Andrew?"

"I don't believe that eavesdropping is criminal," said Mkeba. "Even if assisted by mechanical devices."

"It might be some form of trespass."

"Possibly. But not something that would be likely to be taken to court, would you say?"

"I shouldn't think so. And as she said, unless she's caught

actually planting the receiver, no one would know that it was her. She might be suspected, of course. But one has to set against that the fact that by using it she might be able to provide us with most important information."

"There you speak like a professional, Trevor. You weigh up the pros and cons. You think matters out."

"It's a good thing someone does."

"Certainly. And the results of your thinking – I say this unreservedly – have been excellent. You have taken hold of our organisation – or should I say, of our disorganisation – and you have turned it into an effective machine. One which becomes daily more and more effective. Nevertheless, to you it is partly a business and partly, perhaps, a game. Yes?"

"A little more serious than that, I hope."

"But to us, Trevor – I speak for all of us – it is neither a business nor a game. It is a religion. Not a contest against opponents, but a fight against evil. Against the devil. He is a very strong and crafty opponent. Therefore we have to use every weapon to our hands, legal or illegal. There are no rules in such a fight. No limits, no holding back. That is what our young warriors think when they fight the casspir armoured cars with pea-shooters and stones. When you are in the middle of it, when you can see what is happening, even death is immaterial."

"And you're implying," said Hartshorn drily, "that since I'm *not* in the middle of it, since I can only read about it and see doctored television films, I can't feel strongly about it."

"Please don't think that I'm criticising you. But was it not the same thing with some people in your country before the war? You know what our great satirist, Pieter Dirk Uys, called them – 'Yes butters'. People who said, 'I never knew it was so bad, but if I had – ' People who'd heard rumours of the sort of treatment the Nazis meted out to their opponents, but didn't, or wouldn't, believe it. It was only after the war, when they could see the dead and living skeletons, when they could smell the death camps for themselves, that they realised the truth."

Hartshorn shifted uncomfortably in his chair. He was a post-war child, but he could still feel the sting of the years of appeasement.

"Can't argue against that," he said, "but I still think we're on the right track here. Feeling our way forward, carefully.

15

Avoiding pointless publicity. We can leave that to the cordon in Trafalgar Square. And the way things are going now, I've a feeling that soon, if we play the cards which are given to us, we shall land an arrow plumb in the middle of the target."

"Your metaphors are a little mixed, but I agree heartily with the sentiment."

Both men laughed.

"Speaking of which, one step we must take. We must have this new man – Karl Mullen – discreetly followed."

"City Detectives." Mkeba made a note. "Their men are all ex-policemen. A bit expensive, but very reliable."

"No shortage of cash," said Hartshorn. "Particularly after that concert. By the way, why did you call him the pencil man?"

"It was a nickname."

"Because he was always writing things down?"

"Not exactly. No. It was something else."

"From the way you're hedging, I guess it was something unpleasant."

"Not very pleasant. Certainly not the sort of thing I could have discussed with your daughter here. The fact is that he was an expert interrogator. He liked to used methods that left no outward mark."

"Electricity."

"Sometimes. But electricity was not brutal enough to appeal to the animal in him. So he used this implement. It was something he had copied from the methods of one Gestapo chief in the South of France. It was made of polished wood and looked like a pencil, but thicker and much longer. It was sharpened at one end. His victim was stripped and fastened, face downwards, on a bench. The pencil was pushed into him, slowly and carefully, right up until the point was several inches into the intestine."

"Obscene," said Hartshorn. "And horribly painful."

"Painful, yes. But that was not the worst of it. I told you it was long piece of wood. There would be six inches or more protruding. This could be hit with a heavy ruler. The first time he tried this torture he hit too hard. The shock was so severe that the man died. After that he was more discreet. A few gentle taps. No one could stand up to the excruciating pain. They would tell him anything he wanted to know. Some-

16

times making things up. Anything, anything, to prevent him hitting again."

Mkeba had picked up a pencil from the desk while he was speaking. On the last word he snapped it between his strong fingers.

2

Early on the following afternoon Fischer Yule said to Karl Mullen, "I had to spend most of the morning at King Charles II Street, being talked to by Max Freustadt, our Consul General. You know him?"

"I met him ten years ago. He was an up-and-coming man in the Foreign Department in Pretoria. Might have gone up further, and come along quicker, if he hadn't always seemed to be worrying."

"He's got a lot of things to worry him right now. You're one of them."

"Why's he worrying about me?"

"Because he knows nothing about you – officially."

"That's crazy. I know that our Foreign Department explained exactly what I was trying to do. And asked for full help and support."

"Sometimes people travel faster than letters. As soon as the official communiqué does turn up he promises he'll notify Whitehall that you're attached to my section."

"And until then I'm just a private citizen?"

"Presumably. But it needn't stop you working." There was a note in Yule's voice which suggested that he was not entirely enamoured of Mullen. "I'm sure there's a lot you can tell me. For a start, you might explain to me just exactly what you're up to."

"As I told you, I'm here to secure the extradition of one Jack Katanga to Mozambique."

"Why to Mozambique?"

"Because he happens to be a citizen of that country by birth and residence. Once he is back in Mozambique I can assure

18

you we shall have little difficulty in securing his transfer to Johannesburg, where he will stand trial for the murder of a member of the Transvaal security force."

"The second step won't be difficult," agreed Yule. "But I don't think the first one will be easy."

"Not easy, no. But we have one strong card. It seems that he has had the impudence to admit the murder, in print. In the book the British public are so eagerly awaiting."

"*Death Underground*? Yes. It's had a lot of publicity. I understood that it was a slashing attack on the mine-owners in the Rand."

"Correct. But it is also an account of his life."

"Have you read it?"

"No. It has been kept very carefully under wraps. No advance copies. No serialisation in the newspapers. Designed to explode with maximum effect on publication day, tomorrow. But inevitably certain extracts have leaked out. And there seems to be no doubt that among them is an account of his escape from custody five years ago. An escape which resulted in the death of one of his escorts."

Yule touched a bell on his desk and said to his secretary, the middle-aged, placid Mrs. Portland, "Would you ask Mr. Silverborn to join us." And to Mullen, "I thought we ought to bring our legal department in on this." As he spoke he was extracting a number of folders from the filing cabinet behind his desk. There was a bundle of three different-coloured folders, kept together by an elastic band; one buff, one red and one green. He slid out the buff folder and opened it. He said, "This is Katanga's personal history so far as it's known to us here. It starts five years ago when he got into the Vaal, through Swaziland, and helped to organise the big miners' strike on the Rand. That, as you know, was when he was picked up – Oh, Lewis, this is Karl Mullen."

Lewis Silverborn was tall and serious. His black hair was streaked with white. He nodded and lowered himself into a chair on the other side of the desk.

"I'll ask him to tell you what he was going to tell me. About Jack Katanga – "

"The *Death Underground* man?"

"About his book, yes. But I'd like him to let us have the earlier history. It may be relevant."

19

"Extremely relevant," agreed Silverborn. He had a note-book open on his knee.

"*Our* records," said Mullen complacently, "seem to go back a lot further than yours." He was on his own ground now and spoke with increased confidence. "To be precise they start in 1932. Katanga's grandmother was a Kikuyu girl from south Kenya. She was about sixteen years old, working in a Mombasa restaurant, when she was seduced by a Swedish sailor, who brought her south and set up house with her in Inhambane. When she'd produced a son for him, he dumped her and pushed off, presumably back to Sweden."

"I don't imagine we shall hear much about *that* in his book," said Yule.

"It doesn't reflect great credit on his grandfather. However, his grandmother was a woman of spirit. Lourenço Marques was a growing tourist centre and there was plenty of work in the restaurants and hotels. The son – let's call him Old Jack – married a local girl and took up the traditional Kikuyu occu-pation of farming."

"One of the traditional Kikuyu occupations," said Yule. "The other being brigandage."

Mullen did not like being interrupted, but had already sufficient respect for Yule not to demonstrate his feelings. He said, "At all events Old Jack became a farmer and a successful one. First with a plot he hired, then with a spread of his own, at Moamba. His son – Young Jack – seems to have been an exceptionally good-looking boy. His Swedish blood coming out perhaps. He caught the eye of a missionary, Simon Ramsay. His main mission was in Lourenço Marques, but he'd set up a number of local reading-rooms and libraries, one of them at Moamba. Young Jack, aged sixteen, became a protégé of his and was soon speaking excellent English and showing an interest in politics and economics – and in Ramsay's daugh-ter, Dorothy, two years younger than he was."

"Which she reciprocated?"

"Apparently. But it was at this point that things took an unexpected turn. You remember that there was an agreement between Mozambique and South Africa for the annual recruiting of labourers for work in the Witwatersrand mines. I always thought it was a gross misuse of language to describe it as slave-labour. The pay was reasonable and the work no

20

harder than the men were doing in their own country. The difficulty was that the government had to find a hundred thousand men every year and this involved a measure of conscription. Anyway. Old Jack was drafted. The term was three years. His wife was allowed to go with him. What happened next is a key to much that followed. Old Jack was badly crippled in a mine accident. He died soon afterwards, of his injuries. It was no one's fault. An independent enquiry completely exonerated the mine-owners. The family got a pension and low-cost housing for his widow and his daughters. Since the farm had suffered a forced sale they had no inducement to go back to Moamba. Young Jack didn't go with his sisters. He was taken in by Simon Ramsay. After a bit the inevitable happened."

"Absence," agreed Yule, "may make the heart grow fonder, but close proximity can be even more effective. What happened? Did Young Jack seduce the daughter of the house?"

"No. He proposed marriage. Father was horrified and made every effort to prevent such an unsuitable union. But Dorothy was firm. She maintained that she could help Jack in his work. To which her father is said to have replied, 'What work? He's simply a terrorist.'"

"Which was true."

"Certainly. His ostensible job was as a reporter on the *Lourenço Marques Gazette*. In fact a lot of his time and most of his enthusiasm was devoted to promoting and, ultimately, leading, the Anti-Forced Labour Movement. As soon as Dorothy reached the age of eighteen and parental consent was no longer necessary, the marriage took place. Simon Ramsay officiated, with horrified reluctance, and totally washed his hands of the pair."

"Is he still alive?"

"I believe so. He retired to England and when I last heard of him he had a living in Norfolk. Meanwhile Young Jack had moved on, from writing polemics, to actual intervention in the affairs of the Rand. The farm at Moamba had been sold, but he still had many friends there and it was, I imagine, a useful base of operations being on the southern border of Mozambique and a few miles from Swaziland. A no-go area for the police of both states."

"You surprise me," said Yule blandly. "Correct me if I'm

wrong, but under a recent treaty – the Nkomati Award it was called, wasn't it? – you know more about these things than I do – didn't the Mozambique authorities undertake to suppress *all* guerrilla activity? And wasn't there a similar agreement with the late King Subhuza of Swaziland?"

Mullen looked up sharply. He had more than a suspicion that his leg was being pulled, but Yule's face gave nothing away. He said, "Those agreements existed, yes. But as Shakespeare says, they were more honoured in the breach than the observance. I am reporting matters as they were. Not as they should have been."

"Of course, of course."

"The first undercover trip that Katanga made to the Rand seems to have been exploratory. On the second trip, with the help of Cyril Ramaphosa and his mine-workers' union, he succeeded in shutting down three of the largest mines on the Witwatersrand for a month. On his third and final expedition – "

"Right. That's where our records start," said Yule. "It seems to have been a startling success. I mean, of course, from Katanga's point of view." He was leafing through his file as he spoke. "The production of gold and diamonds was reduced to a trickle. Some of the smaller companies, that were facing bankruptcy, would have given in to the strikers, if they had been allowed to."

"Possibly. But since the government were men and not old women they weren't allowed to. Their backs were stiffened by a large reinforcement of police, backed by a few companies of special troops. The strikers were ordered to go back to work and many of them went. And Jack Katanga and others of the principal leaders were arrested. Unfortunately – "

"Very unfortunately," said Yule drily.

"The two policemen who were taking him by truck to Jo'burg bungled the job. Probably they underestimated their prisoner. They had handcuffed him, but with his hands in front. Not, as they should have been, behind his back. We don't know exactly what happened. Only the result. The driver of the truck heard a shot. By the time he'd slammed on the brakes and got round behind the truck, Young Jack was a hundred yards away, heading for open country."

"Still handcuffed?"

"Apparently. But the driver was too shaken by what he found in the back of the truck to do anything effective. One of the guards was unconscious, with blood pouring down his face. The other had been shot dead."

"Yes," said Yule. "I read the police report, which seemed a little evasive. And the report of the coroner's inquest, which was even less precise. However, we shall know all about it when we read the book, shan't we? What do *you* think, Lewis?"

"Think about what?" said Silverborn, surprised at being suddenly brought into the discussion.

"If we now get a detailed account, by the criminal, of his crime, won't that support an application for extradition?"

"Not an easy question to answer. The normal rule is that a country will extradite a person to stand trial in another country *if* there is prima facie evidence that he has committed a serious criminal offence there. And provided, of course, that there is a mutual extradition treaty between the two countries."

"Between Great Britain and South Africa."

"No. Between Great Britain and Mozambique. I'll find out about that. I rather think there is such a treaty."

"And surely a written statement by someone that he committed a murder must amount to prima facie evidence."

"I shall have to read the passage very carefully before arriving at any conclusion. And there is one thing that puzzles me. Why was an immediate application not made by the South African authorities to the Mozambique government to return Katanga to stand trial?"

"It was," said Mullen grimly. "But before anything effective could be done, he had skipped to England."

"And you have applied to the British government?"

"More than once. And they flatly refused to extradite him, on the grounds that his offence had not been proved to their satisfaction. And that the motive for pursuing him was primarily political. It soon became clear that we were deadlocked."

"And you think that this book is the key to open the lock."

"We hope so."

"You realise that it is going to involve an application to the High Court. An application which will certainly be resisted strenuously and will therefore be lengthy and expensive. The feeling of the Court will be against you and the attendant publicity will be hostile."

"I can assure you," said Mullen stiffly, "that we have counted the cost and are prepared to pay it, whether in hard cash or hard words."

"Then if that is your decision – "

Mr. Silverborn started to get up, but Yule waved him back. "One minute," he said. "I'd like to understand this. I have been out of the country for some years now and I can't pretend to judge the situation as accurately as you. Do I gather, from what you say, that you regard Jack Katanga as a serious threat to the stability of our country? I don't mean as an organiser of strikes on the Rand. I mean, in a wider sense."

Mullen, who understood the importance of what he was being asked, took time to arrange his thoughts.

"At the moment," he said, "the government has agreed to talk to the ANC. This gives it some sort of recognition. And great hopes are pinned on this. My own opinion is that these hopes may prove delusive. I do not think that they will lead to a grant of equal voting rights, one man one vote. Because that would be capitulation."

"The government may be forced to go down that road."

"So long as the army and the police remain staunch, they cannot be forced to go anywhere they don't wish. They will make concessions, no doubt. But I fear that disappointed hopes will lead to even greater trouble."

"Armed revolt?" said Yule.

"Possibly. There is a tremendous level of aggression. It is below the surface, but you can sense it, and feel it, and smell it. Not in the peaceful areas that visitors see; East Cape and the western seaboard. But among the homeland areas in Natal and in the industrial belt along the Vaal. It is like a fire smouldering underground, but liable to burst into flame at any moment."

"If it comes to active resistance the blacks would need a military leader."

"A military genius, I should say."

"Nelson Mandela?"

"No. He is an old man and in bad health."

"But Jack Katanga might take his place."

"He is young and vigorous. He writes articles and addresses

24

meetings. And he is bolstered by his romantic background of adventure and escape. Like the young Winston Churchill, yes? But at the moment his name is not widely known. Not yet. However, the blatant and unchallenged publication of this book could be an important step upwards. At the very least it will be a resounding propaganda success."

"Are you suggesting that its publication can be prevented?"

"Recent events," said Mullen with a wintry smile, "have demonstrated that any such attempt is the most effective form of advertisement imaginable."

"So. Being unable to suppress the book you are going to suppress its author."

"With a measure of luck, and a certain amount of resolution" – Mullen shot a look at Mr. Silverborn – "that should not be beyond our powers."

3

O eternal God, before whose face the generations rise and pass away, thyself unchanged abiding, we bless thy holy Name for all who have completed their earthly course in thy faith and fear and are now at rest.

Roger Sherman had come to the law later than most solicitors. After reading for a degree in history at Oxford he had spent some time wandering round the world before signing on for a short-term commission in the army. At the end of it, seeing few prospects in peacetime soldiering, he had entered into articles with Bantings, the well-known Lincoln's Inn solicitors, and although he had been qualified for less than three years was already tipped for a partnership.

On this fine October afternoon he had given up the opportunity of seeing his son play rugby football for St. Paul's, a treat for which he had been given leave of absence, and had come, instead, to the Temple church.

We remember before thee this day Marshall Fitzhugh, rendering thanks to thee for his life of devoted and fearless service. To him, with all the faithful departed, grant thy peace and work in them the good purpose of thy perfect will.

A great lawyer, thought Roger, and (which is not always the same thing) a great man; notable, among other virtues, for courage and integrity. He had defended the Chatham bombers, in the face of massive prejudice, securing a disagreement from two successive juries and the abandonment of the case against them. He had defied the wishes of the government when he signed the minority report on the sentencing of sexual offenders; and that at a time when his own elevation to the Bench was known to be under consideration.

When Roger was at law school he had heard Marshall Fitzhugh lecture – occasions when it was difficult to find a seat. He had seen him as combining in himself the finest ingredients of the English legal system; impartiality and humanity, lightened with a touch of humour. Now he had come to pay his last respects.

Bring us, O Lord, to enter into the house and gate of heaven, where there shall be no darkness nor dazzling, but one equal light; no noise nor silence but one equal music; no fears nor hopes but one equal possession; no ends nor beginnings but one equal eternity.

The Temple church was packed with people filling every seat and standing, two deep, against the south wall. Most of them were barristers and solicitors. Roger wondered whether it was possible, simply by looking at their faces, to make out which were which. A hundred years ago it would have been easy. The barristers superior in every way and conscious of it. Two world wars had changed that, as they had changed many things. And now that the solicitor was encroaching on the barrister's preserves, denied only the privilege of pleading in the highest courts, such differences as remained were fast disappearing. He wondered how long it would take before they adopted the more logical American system. Twenty years? Perhaps thirty. Things moved slowly in the law.

After the blessing the 'Trumpet Tune' of John Stanley ushered them out into the October sunlight; some conscious that they had fulfilled a social obligation; a few, perhaps, wondering whether, if all barristers and judges were of the stature of the Right Honourable Sir Marshall Fitzhugh, the law might have less reason to be self-critical.

Roger recognised the boy who was sidling through the crowd towards him as their newest office boy. He said, "Hullo, Charlie. Were you looking for me?"

"I was. Mr. Banting wants you. And my name's Cedric."

"You're wrong about that. Bantings is a very old-fashioned firm. *All* our new office boys are called Charlie."

The boy grinned and trotted ahead of him, past Dr. Johnson's Buildings, across the Strand and up Chancery Lane into Lincoln's Inn. The speed at which he went suggested that the summons from the senior partner was an urgent one. When he went into his office the man who was sitting in the client's chair got up, with a half smile on his face which

27

indicated that he expected Roger to recognise him; which he did, after a few seconds.

"It's Mullen, isn't it?"

"Right."

"Must be nearly twenty years."

"All of that. I went down the year after you did."

They had not been close friends at Oxford, but with rooms on the same staircase and attending some of the same lectures, they had necessarily seen quite a lot of each other.

"I was surprised when I happened to see your name in the Law List. I always thought you meant to go into the army."

"I did," said Roger. "In, and out again."

Mr. Banting smiled benevolently upon him. He did not regard Roger's deferred entry into the law as a drawback. Far from it. As a member of the R.N.V.R., he had found himself in the navy in September 1939, quitting it, after a number of exciting but satisfactory episodes, at the end of 1945. Whereupon he had got down to work and had rebuilt the firm, which had been founded by his grandfather and was tottering into senility. By forty-five years of intelligent effort he had rescued it from obscurity and it was now one of the leading firms in Lincoln's Inn.

He said, "It occurred to me, Roger, that since you knew each other, you'd be the appropriate person to look after Mr. Mullen. Take him along to your room and get him to tell you the story he was just starting to tell me. It sounds as though you'll need help from our litigators. Keep Palmer in the picture."

When they were seated in Roger's office, a tiny apartment at the back of the rambling seventeenth-century building, he said, "Bring me up to date a little. You went straight back to South Africa when you left Oxford?"

"Correct."

"And took up some official job there."

"I became a policeman. Or perhaps half a policeman and half a soldier. In our security forces there's very little difference between the two. My official rank is colonel. The nearest equivalent in your police would be chief superintendent."

"Let's settle for colonel."

Roger was trying to sum up his visitor. He realised that it must be something fairly important to have brought him to seek outside aid. His consulate would have its own legal department able to advise him on routine matters. The passage of time had certainly changed the rather lumpy young man he had known at Oxford. For better or for worse? Difficult to say. A security job in South Africa would be an emphatic moulder of character, in one direction or another.

"And it's some business connected with your job that has brought you over here?"

Mullen's mouth hardened. More used to cross-examining than being cross-examined, thought Roger. After a fairly long pause he said, "Yes. And since what happened this morning was connected, in a way, with my current job, I'd better tell you about that first."

When he had finished, omitting much but giving the essential points of his mission, Roger said, "It will be for better brains than mine to advise you about the extradition point. That's for counsel, who will make your application to the High Court. I could find the best man for you. But I imagine it's something else you want to consult us about just now."

"Yes, it is. I was taken, this morning, to one of your police stations and charged with shop-lifting."

Roger was experienced enough not to show either surprise or disbelief. He simply said, "Which shop?"

"It's called Lampards."

"I know it well. The big bookshop in Duke Street."

"They were making a great show of this book." Mullen opened the bag he was carrying and pulled out a copy and pushed it across the desk. It had a striking wrapper depicting a vertical cross-section of a mine. In a gallery at the bottom a skeleton was lying, with its knees drawn up and its arms extended as though in agony. On the surface, above the mine, a stout civilian was shaking hands with a grim-faced policeman.

"You'd hardly need to read the book to get the message," said Roger.

"Infantile propaganda. One of Lampards' windows was stacked with copies and the front room was crowded with people. I was told that the author was in a side room, signing copies. I managed to get through the scrum to the cash desk and paid for the three copies I wanted."

"I imagine you didn't get Katanga to sign them."

29

The hard lines of Mullen's mouth relaxed, for a moment, into the ghost of a smile. He said, "I thought about it, but considered that it would have been inappropriate. I was given this plastic bag for the three books and a receipt, which our legal people had told me I must keep, and then – you say you know the place well?"

"Very well. I've sometimes spent hours there wishing I had enough money to buy all the books I wanted."

"Then you'll remember how the place is arranged. You go down a couple of steps through an opening in the corner of the front room to get to the back part. That's split up into several smaller rooms, three of them, all opening onto a sort of central reservation where there's another cash desk. The room on the right is for limited editions in fine bindings, you know the sort of thing. I wandered in there to have a look at them. They were attractive, I agree, but too expensive for my purse."

"When you say you looked at them – ?"

"I picked one or two of them out and put them back again when I saw what they cost."

Roger said, "You were alone in the room at the time?"

He had a shrewd suspicion of what was coming.

"Yes. Unfortunately."

"What happened next?"

"I thought I'd go home. I didn't fancy fighting my way through the front room, which was more crowded than ever, but I'd an idea that one of the rooms on the other side of the central area had a door leading out to a side street."

"And so it has," said Roger. "I've often been in and out that way myself. Nineteenth-century classics in that room, as I remember it. Dickens, Thackeray, Trollope and such."

"I didn't stop to examine the books. I simply wanted to use the door, which had been left ajar by the last person who'd been that way. I pushed through, out onto the pavement and then – well, a lot of things happened rather fast."

"If they happened fast," said Roger, "let's take them slowly." He noticed that Mullen's face, normally a healthy brown was now red and that he was sweating.

"Well, the first thing was, I saw this man. He'd been standing at the corner, where the side road runs out into Duke Street. As soon as I saw him I knew that he was some sort of

policeman. Being one myself, I suppose I've got an instinct about it. I also knew that he'd been stationed on guard, where he was, so that he could keep both of the shop exits under observation."

"Quite likely," said Roger. He was not troubling to make notes. All of his attention was fixed on Mullen.

"I was carrying this bag of books in my left hand and at that moment I happened to put my right hand down to my jacket and I touched something in my right-hand jacket pocket which should certainly not have been there. It felt like a thinnish book."

"You were wearing the jacket you've got on now? And no overcoat?"

"Correct. And I was absolutely certain that my jacket pockets had both been empty when I went into the shop."

"So someone must have slipped this book – if it was a book – into your pocket."

"It was a book, all right," said Mullen grimly. "A copy of Oscar Wilde's *Salomé* with the Beardsley illustrations. And I knew very well how it had got there. Someone had slipped it into my pocket when I was pushing through the crowd in the front room. No difficulty about that. We were packed like sardines and there was a lot of jostling and pushing going on. And I realised exactly what was happening. There are people in this country who have no cause to love me. They guessed I should be at the shop and were ready for me. I was to be caught by that detective on the corner and charged with shoplifting."

"So what did you do?"

"There were only two choices. Move off and throw the book away. Or get back into the shop and replace the book before anyone noticed it was gone. I didn't fancy the first course. The man I'd spotted was a bulky brute and was already moving towards me."

"A chase and an undignified capture. Not an attractive idea," agreed Roger. "You might, I suppose, have gone back into the shop, insisted on seeing the manager and explained what had happened."

"Easy to be wise after the event," said Mullen sourly. "I can only say that such a proceeding never occurred to me. All I wanted to do was to get rid of the bloody book. As quickly as

possible."

"Natural reaction. So what happened?"

"When I got through the door I saw that the inner door was blocked. A man was standing, with his back to me, talking to someone in the central reservation. I saw that it wouldn't be easy to push past him and put the book back where it had come from."

"Which was?"

"The room with the fine editions. The one I told you about."

"Yes," said Roger, "but how did you know that the book in your pocket came from that room?"

Roger saw the colour spring up into Mullen's face. He said, "Look here. Do you believe me, or don't you?"

"Of course I believe you," said Roger smoothly. "But it's my job to ask you the sort of questions now that are bound to be asked sooner or later."

Mullen grunted. Then he said, "All right. I could feel that the book was thin and was in a slip-case. That meant it was one of the limited editions I'd been examining. It wasn't anything like a normal hardback or paperback."

"Understood. So then – ?"

"My main idea was to get rid of the bloody book. I couldn't put it back where it had come from so I just shoved it in between two other books, on one of the shelves near the door. Whilst I was doing that I saw the man in the inner doorway had swung round and was watching me. And I recognised him. It was Jack Katanga."

"Did he recognise you?"

"Of course."

"Then what?"

"He came forward with an unpleasant smirk on his face and examined the shelf. Then he said, 'Hadn't you better put that book back in the right place. I'm sure it doesn't belong between *Barchester Towers* and *The Warden*.' I said, 'I don't know what you're talking about.' He said, 'If you have got some explanation, I think you'd better give it to the manager.' I'd have walked out and left then, and I did make a move in that direction, only by this time the man I'd noticed outside was rather ostentatiously blocking the street door. So we all ended up in the manager's office. When we got there the girl from

the cash desk, who was some sort of superior assistant, said she'd seen me in the limited editions room and that the Oscar Wilde book belonged there. Katanga swore he'd seen me slipping the book back onto the shelf among the Trollope editions. And the man from the street, who turned out to be some sort of private detective and nothing to do with the shop at all, said he'd seen me coming out and had noticed me noticing him and diving back into the shop. He said he thought I was behaving suspiciously."

"And what did you say?"

"I said, O.K., I had been looking at their limited editions. Nothing wrong with that, was there? And yes, I had changed my mind after leaving the shop – I remembered that I wanted to look at their paperbacks, which were in a basement room. And as for the rest, why blame me if they kept their books in the wrong places?"

"I see."

"That worries you?"

"I'd rather you'd told them what you told me just now."

"Certainly not. It was up to them to prove that I'd taken the book. Not up to me to prove that I hadn't. Isn't that the legal position?"

"Yes," said Roger. "It's just that it may make things a bit awkward if it does come to court."

"Why? I shall tell them exactly what I told the manager. Just that and no more."

"I see," said Roger unhappily. "Well, we'll have to cross that bridge when we come to it. I imagine the manager wasn't satisfied and asked you to identify yourself."

"No difficulty. I had my passport with me. And I told him I was officially attached to the South African Embassy. And that he had no right either to question me or detain me."

"But that didn't stop him?"

"Stop him? Good God! As soon as he understood that I was a South African policeman he'd only got one idea, which was to make as much trouble for me as he could. By that time the constable he'd sent for had turned up and he told him – as though it was a proven fact – that I'd been detected stealing a very valuable book. I was then taken along to this police station and charged. They must have telephoned the Embassy by that time, because they said that, of course, I'd be given bail

33

and they warned me that I'd have to turn up at their stupid little court the next day – that is, tomorrow. Shall I have to go?"

"I'm afraid so. The proceedings will be formal. I shall be there and I shall ask for an adjournment, which will certainly be granted, so that the question of diplomatic immunity can be properly considered."

"You don't think there's any doubt about it?"

Roger said, with a smile, "It's not a branch of the law that I know much about. But don't worry. By the time the matter comes up I shall have briefed a barrister for you who has specialised in the subject and knows all about it. I'll fix a con for us."

"A con?"

"Sorry. A conference. He'll have one or two questions to ask you and it might help if you could bring your head man with you. Who would that be? The Ambassador?"

"He doesn't deal with matters like that. It would be either the Consul General, or the man I'm working with, the Head of Security."

"Excellent. Bring them both."

After Mullen had left, Roger took the copy of *Death Underground* and walked out with it into the garden which lies behind the hall of Lincoln's Inn; an oasis of peace, reserved for barristers and little used by them. Here he settled down on one of the benches, with his back to the high brick wall and opened the book.

When the curtain goes up in Grand Guignol, the theatre of horrors, the members of the audience lean forward in their seats, expecting to be shocked. From the lurid cover of the book and the reputation of its author Roger knew roughly what he would find in it. But even knowing this and making allowance for it, as he read he became conscious of disquiet and chill.

He was looking at a land of violence and hatred. A land where children were killed in the streets. A land ruled by the armoured car at the corner and the sjambok in the underground interrogation room. A land where people could be arrested and carried off as easily and as arbitrarily as they had been in pre-revolutionary France. A *lettre de cachet*, a midnight visit, and a man might disappear from human sight for years, or for ever. A land of slaves; yet not of slaves without hope. Rather of slaves working out ways to deliver themselves.

The two decisive episodes in Young Jack Katanga's life had followed close upon each other.

It was in 1975, when he was just sixteen, that his father had been crippled in that mine accident. 'You who wear bracelets on your wrists and rings on your fingers, count the cost of the gold, paid for in human lives and twisted limbs.'

His account of the enquiry which had followed the accident was satire worthy of Swift; the so-called independent tribunal, consisting of a senior police officer, a mining engineer and a junior member of the State Legislature, mouthing platitudes and congratulating themselves on safety precautions which existed only on paper.

If that episode had laid the fuse, the spark had clearly been applied by the Soweto massacre of the following year. From that moment Young Jack had been set on his course. If terror could only be met by terror, he must, in logic, become a terrorist.

Roger turned over the pages rapidly to get to the incident on which most of the publicity had focused. His third visit to the Witwatersrand, his betrayal, arrest and escape.

'I was sitting on one of the seats in the back of the truck with these two armed policemen on the seat opposite. My hands were manacled, but fortunately in front of me, not behind my back. They must have thought I was tame. I had already been beaten twice and the blood from the second beating was hardly dry on my face. I was suffering from shock and may have been partly concussed, but there was one idea in my mind. I knew that if I was to save my life, I had to act. A gun, a heavy police .38, hung in the unbuckled holster of the nearest of my captors. As the truck swayed, I swung forward and found that my hands were within inches of it. Next time the truck swayed I picked it out, using both hands, lifted it and brought it down on the man's head. It all happened so quickly that the other policeman took a second or more to register what had happened. Then I saw him reach for his own gun. I was holding the weapon awkwardly between my chained hands and I have no idea how my finger reached the trigger. There was no question of missing. The gun was touching his body. I must have pulled the trigger a split second before he fired. My bullet was already in him. His went through the floor. The truck jerked to a stop. I threw myself out over the tailboard, scrambled to my feet and started to run, as fast as I could with my hands fastened in front of me – '

Roger read the passage several times, carefully, as though he was in court, reciting it to a judge. If Katanga's captors had been terrorists or hijackers, then clearly what he did would not only have been justified, but laudable. He was fighting for his life. His opponent was in the act of drawing his own gun. He had acted in self-defence and in the only way open to him. Did the fact that he was dealing with so-called officers of the law make a lot of difference? Men who had already beaten him and were carrying him off to further beatings and possible death. He could not visualise an English jury bringing in a verdict of murder. Manslaughter possibly, more likely justifiable homicide.

When he had begun reading, the afternoon sun had been shining. Now it was starting to dim, behind the mist which often rolled up from the river on those autumn evenings. Lights were beginning to appear in the windows of Stone Buildings on the other side of the garden. He could see barristers sitting at their desks, hard at work, or making a fair pretence of it. The traffic sounds from Chancery Lane and High Holborn were muted by the surrounding buildings and came only faintly through the gathering mist.

It was too dark to read any more.

Roger looked down at the book in his hands with a sudden spasm of distaste. Its shrill, high-coloured violence was an intruder into the cloister in which he sat, cocooned by Law, as enswathed and protected as any learned clerk of old had been by the power and benevolence of mother Church. And a thought was scratching at the back of his mind, like a puppy asking for attention.

It was something that someone had told him and it was connected with the job he had taken on. Not just casually connected, but connected in a definite and important way.

In an endeavour to fix it, he cast his mind back over the main stages of his own life. Preparatory school, public school, university. Surely not as long ago as that. The next years were more difficult. He had visited many different lands in the course of his wanderings, but was unlikely to have encountered anyone connected with Mullen and his troubles. He had not been to South Africa. The army, then? Or his more recent years in the law?

More probable. But no light shone.

He clambered stiffly to his feet and walked back across New Square to his office.

4

"Laugh?" said Harold Ratter. "I'm telling you, I nearly split my sides. Really, I did."

Mr. Ratter was a mountainous man, large in every dimension. It was the increase in his girth that had driven him to leave the ranks of the Metropolitan Police and join City Detectives. If he did split his sides, thought Captain Hartshorn, the results would be dramatic.

"The moment he laid eyes on me, and it was not surprising he did, me being what you might call a conspicuous figure, I could see he had something on his mind. A guilty conscience. With the practice I've had I can spot a guilty conscience a mile away, in a manner of speaking."

"Excellent," said Hartshorn. "Then what?"

"I thought, there's something on here, so I followed him up. I didn't atcherly see him pushing that book – the one he'd nicked – back on the shelf."

"Pity."

"However, I saw him by the shelf. Next best thing."

"It would have been even better if you'd seen him putting it back," said Hartshorn.

Mr. Ratter considered the suggestion that he should commit perjury and rejected it regretfully. "The way it was, I only got to the door after it was all over. Lucky I did though. He seemed to be thinking of making a break for it, but he couldn't get past me."

It was clear that when Mr. Ratter was standing in a doorway no one was going to get past him at all easily.

"Then, I suppose, the police were called and he was charged and taken off."

"Speaking personally, I was a bit surprised at that. Usually, I mean, normally when someone who's pretty well-known gets involved in something not too serious – like it might be a member of parliament being done for careless driving – he'd be warned to expect a summons and when it arrived he'd turn up at the court, or instruct his solicitor to do it, and everything would be handled, as you might say, discreetly."

"But in this case Mullen was charged?"

"Well, you see how it was. I had to tell the constable that I thought he'd tried to bolt. So, from that point of view, he didn't have much option. Any old how, he could see what the manager wanted. A funny little character he was, with a white beard. Like one of them dwarfs in *Snow White*. The manager, I mean. Well, as soon as he heard that Mullen was not only a South African, but a South African policeman, he was so excited he nearly lost his top set. Charge him! Why, what he really wanted was to have him taken away in chains."

"Interesting reaction," said Hartshorn. "So Mullen was led off to the police station. I don't suppose he cared for that."

"I should say not. He started blowing off about international something or other and diplomatic something else. Would have done you good to hear him."

"I must congratulate you. You did an excellent job and when I speak to your head man I won't forget it. However, since I fancy Mullen would recognise you if he saw you again, you'd better put a different man on his tail. Can I leave you to fix that up?"

"You want us to stay on the job?"

"More than ever," said Hartshorn. "Lots for everyone to do."

When Mr. Ratter had rolled away he turned to the other men in his office. Even Kabaka, normally pessimistic, was smiling.

"What do you think, Govan?"

"Not bad," said Kabaka. From him this meant 'very good'.

"I wonder if you appreciate exactly how good this is. You realise, of course, that the time has come for us to change gear."

Mkeba clearly understood him. Kabaka and Masangi tried to look as though they did. Sesolo was baffled.

Hartshorn said, "So far as the South African government

are concerned, apartheid was always a black card. It gave their opponents a moral edge against them, and was, anyway, unenforceable. So – they have proceeded to dismantle it. The Mixed Marriages Act, the Pass Laws and the Immorality Acts have all been repealed and the Homeland strategy has been abandoned. The recent announcement by de Klerk that he was opening the Nationalist Party to black and white alike knocked away the last plank. Apartheid is dead."

"So what you're telling us," said Mkeba, "is that anti-apartheid is dead, too."

It was Boyo Sesolo who took this most hardly. He was a simple soul, and enjoyed combat. He made a grumbling noise deep in his throat and said, "Then who do we fight?"

"The people who matter," said Hartshorn. "The only people capable of turning the clock back. The South African police. And one of them has been delivered into our hands."

"How do you suggest we go about it?" said Masangi.

"Let's think it out," said Hartshorn. "He'll appear in court tomorrow morning. But the proceedings will be formal, so we don't want to get people steamed up. Just a tip-off that this could be the start of something exciting."

"One evening paper, one middle-of-the-road daily," said Kabaka.

"That sort of thing. Then, by the time he appears on remand they'll all be waiting for him with their tongues hanging out."

"I wouldn't bank on it," said Kabaka. "He'll plead diplomatic immunity and ten-to-one he'll get away with it. *And* the defence will ask for a reporting ban on the hearing. That won't stop them commenting, of course. But they'll have to watch their step."

Mkeba said, "We might be able to help the prosecution. I don't think, from what your daughter's told us, that he's got an open-and-shut case on the diplomatic immunity angle. He's not an official on a proper posting. Just a visiting fireman."

"Nothing to stop them saying what they like about him," said Kabaka. "They've got all the cards in their hands."

Hartshorn wasn't listening. He was lying back in his chair with the look of a child to whom Father Christmas has presented a wonderful unexpected present.

40

He said, "Just suppose he *can't* wriggle out under some sort of diplomatic cover. Suppose he goes for trial, with Jack Katanga as the main prosecution witness. They're very hot on shop-lifting these days. Why, he *might* even get a prison sentence."

"It might snow krugerrands," said Govan Kabaka.

Fischer Yule was not amused and he took no trouble to hide his feelings. He said, "That was a bloody silly thing to do, wasn't it?"

"I don't see how I could help it."

"Perhaps you didn't know – as now seems to be the case – that the detective on the corner was nothing to do with the shop. He'd no status in the matter. So all you had to do was to walk off and drop that stupid book into the river. Trying to put it back was simply childish panic."

"If he wasn't the store detective, who was he? And what was he doing there?"

"I'd have thought you could have guessed the answer to that. A private detective, no doubt, whose job was to keep an eye on you. Probably hired by our friends in Mornington Square, with instructions to see what you were up to. And, of course, he wasn't going to turn up a chance of getting you into trouble if the opportunity was presented to him on a plate. As it was."

Mullen disliked both the matter and manner of Yule's comments and in the ordinary way he would not have hesitated to demonstrate his feelings and answer them in kind. Two things restrained him. The first was that he realised that he was in a fix and that Yule and his organisation were probably the only people who could get him out of it. The second reason was disconcerting. In the past his position and his powers had enabled him to frighten a great number of people. Now he was faced with someone who frightened him. If Yule did return to Pretoria as chairman of the prestigious State Security Council, a position for which he had been tipped, the first head to roll might be his own. And heads which rolled in South Africa rolled an uncomfortably long way.

"We're getting repercussions from this book, already," Yule went on. "Copies have been distributed secretly in the Rand.

41

Now it will be required reading for everyone who has any connection with the mines, employers and employed. Katanga's own boys in the Anti-Forced Labour Movement are busy organising a one-day lightning strike. When the news of what's happened here reaches them, I doubt if it'll be confined to one day. It could even have repercussions beyond the mining-belt. I'm sure you understand what I'm saying, Colonel."

"Yes," said Mullen unhappily.

"*So it's got to be stopped.*"

"By claiming diplomatic privilege, you mean? What do you think the chances are?"

"Silverborn's working on that now. We'll see what he has to say about it in a moment. There's something else I wanted to tell you first."

He brought out the three folders that Mullen had seen before, but this time he selected the red and green ones. He said, "I agreed, you remember, that your historical record of Katanga started sooner than ours and was more detailed. But history, to paraphrase Mr. Ford, isn't everything. This" – he laid his hand on the green file – "deals with personal affairs. Katanga's household in Putney, his wife, his wife's father in Norfolk and like matters. The red file, however, is in some ways the most interesting of the three. It contains medical information. Now, if I have gathered the facts of that unfortunate bookshop incident correctly, the one essential witness for the prosecution is Katanga himself."

"That must be right. He's the only one who claims he saw me touch the book."

"So that if, for any reason, he was unable or unwilling to come forward, the case would fall to the ground."

"Of course he'll come forward. Why not? He'll make a meal of it."

"Because it's just possible that he might die before the case comes on."

Mullen stared at him. If this statement had been made to him in South Africa he would have understood its implications. But in England?

Yule, who had read his mind said, with a slight smile, "No, Colonel. I was not talking about – what is the cant expression? – expedient demise. What I meant was that he might die at any moment from natural causes. Basically, he is a very strong and healthy man, but there are certain precautions he has to take. The details are all in the folder. It seems that, about two years ago, he had an accident. He was, by that time, a regular, possibly a fairly heavy drinker. His preferred tipple was whisky. Sometimes he poured it out himself. Sometimes his wife poured it out for him. On this occasion he came in hot and tired, picked up a glass that was on the table and took a large gulp of its contents, which unfortunately for him, consisted of disinfectant, slightly diluted with water. It had been got ready by his wife to dress the paw of their dog. The result was serious, but not fatal. When he reached hospital it was discovered that his gullet was badly scarred. His windpipe, was not, of course, affected, or not directly. You'll understand that better if you look at the sketch our doctor drew for me. The red one is the gullet, the blue one is the windpipe. Food down one, air down the other."

"I'd no idea they were so close to each other."

"Not just close, actually touching. That's the whole point. Katanga was warned that the scarring in his gullet could lead to oedema."

"Come again."

Yule, who was enjoying the opportunity of displaying medical expertise, said, "Oedema is the technical name for an unhealthy mass of swollen tissue. If it was allowed to accumulate around the gullet it would not only make swallowing difficult, it *might* start to exert pressure on the windpipe also."

"And that is what it is doing?"

"Not at the moment. Because, as I said, he is taking precautions. Every two or three days he uses a bougie. That is a plastic affair which can be swallowed and brought up again. It can't be a very pleasant operation. To help it slip down I understand that it's dipped into a bowl of olive oil, which is kept handy in the sideboard for this purpose. You get the picture?"

"I understand what you're saying," said Mullen. "What I don't understand is where you got all this information from. Not from his doctor, surely."

"Not from his doctor, no." Yule closed the red file gently and opened the green one. "The information came to us in the course of our routine enquiries. You must not imagine that we sit about all day doing nothing. No, no. When Katanga arrived in this country five years ago, by a most irregular route, incidentally, and with no proper papers, we naturally devoted close attention to him. Our first endeavours were directed to getting him sent back to Mozambique."

"Mine, also."

"Quite so. We have been working on the same lines. With an equal lack of success. Our next step was to find out as much as we possibly could about Katanga himself. If we could deflate his popularity, both within establishment circles here and with the general public world-wide, that would be an important step forward. And we had one piece of luck. For the first three years of his stay he lived in a small rented house on a road just south of Hammersmith Bridge. The housework was shared between his wife and a worthy widow called Mrs. Queen, who lived next door. Two years ago, for some reason – possibly an upsurge of anti-black feeling in the locality, who knows? – he decided to move. An increasingly busy programme of writing and speaking was putting a fair amount of money into his pocket. I suspect, also, that he was being handsomely subsidised from Mornington Square. Anyway, he took a step up the social ladder. He rented a small house in the Putney area. It was a somewhat isolated property on the fringe of the Heath. The move meant that he had to look elsewhere for help in the house. This was our chance. We were able to supply him with just what he required."

Yule paused to locate the paper he wanted in the green folder. Mullen could see that he was enjoying himself. He did not grudge him his pleasure. He had a feeling that this development would be to his advantage.

"So. Let me introduce you to Anna. Full name, Anna Masai, a Basuto girl from Maseru in Lesotho. Her 'father' – I use the word in inverted commas – is Leon Macheli, a professor of applied science at Durban University and a world expert in physical crystallography. A certain unfortunate event in his home town – you may know the incident I'm referring to – "

Mullen did indeed know about it. It was a cross-border attack into Lesotho in search of ANC supporters.

"It decided him to cut adrift and come to England. In view of his fine academic record he had no difficulty in getting a residence permit for himself and his wife and for Anna, who

44

was included by him as his daughter. Our information was more accurate. She was neither his natural nor his adopted daughter. Simply a girl in whom he had taken an interest and who had adopted his name. Pretty enough, in a snub-nosed immature way and intelligent. He had taught her some English. In short, she was his protégée. He wanted her with him in England and in getting her there committed himself to the mis-statement that she was his daughter. A criminal offence in both countries."

"I see," said Mullen. The possibilities of the situation were becoming increasingly apparent.

"I interviewed her myself and made the situation quite clear. Either she did what I told her, or she and the Professor – to whom, I fancy, she was sincerely attached – suffered the consequences. It did not take her long to make up her mind. We equipped her with excellent references and told her to be prepared to accept a very reasonable wage. Before long she was installed in the Katanga household. To the satisfaction of Dorothy Katanga, because Anna was a hard worker, and to Jack Katanga for – possibly – other reasons."

"You mean – ?"

"I mean what you're thinking. Katanga was by now a virile, forceful, mature man. I can easily suppose that his little missionary-reared wife had lost most of the original attraction she had for him. You will have noted that they had no children."

"So he seduced the hired help."

"If he did – and it is only a presumption – he was both careful and tactful. His wife, with their newly acquired wealth, was able to enjoy long shopping mornings in the West End. And the house, remember, was isolated. Also he did not make the mistake that some men have made – read your criminal cases – of degrading or insulting his wife. On the contrary, he behaved more courteously to her – particularly in public – than he had, perhaps, done before."

"Are you suggesting that Katanga's wife welcomed the importation of a mistress into the household?"

"I don't know whether she welcomed it. She may not even have known what went on when she was out shopping. However, that is not the real point. What we have to look at" – he had touched the bell on his desk and said to Mrs. Portland,

"Would you ask Mr. Silverborn to step in? Thank you. – What we must look at very carefully are the chances of keeping this deplorable case out of court altogether. Ah, Lewis, you have some news for us."

"Views, not news," said Mr. Silverborn. "I find that we are in a curiously unexplored field of the law. Most of it stems from the Vienna Conventions of 1961 and 1963 and there are very few decided cases to help us. In fact, most of the decisions and statements are American. Not binding on our courts, of course, but since the Americans have adopted both Conventions on almost exactly the same lines as we have, they could be regarded as persuasive."

"And what is the answer at the end of the day?"

Like all lawyers this was the sort of question that Mr. Silverborn disliked. He said, "The only answer I can give you is that *if* Mr. Mullen can be regarded as a diplomatic agent, then he would be totally immune from the criminal jurisdiction of our courts."

"And how would it be decided whether he was a diplomatic agent or not?"

"That is a question for experts in international law. I have already had a word" – he turned to Mullen, who was showing signs of impatience – "with your English solicitor, Mr. Roger Sherman. He fully appreciates the difficulties of the position and, no doubt, has already sent a set of instructions to Counsel. If we are denied the protection of diplomatic privilege in the Magistrates' Court, we should have to appeal to a Divisional Court. Indeed, if the Divisional Court found against us, we might have to take the matter on to the Court of Appeal. In either case Counsel will be needed. In the end, senior Counsel."

Mullen, who had been coming quietly to the boil, now exploded. He said, "For God's sake, how long do you think this legal hurdle-race is going to take?"

"The court will usually expedite such matters if there is a valid reason for doing so."

"Valid reason! Do you realise I only came here to try to get Katanga extradited? I've got to be back in Pretoria by the end of the month to give evidence at the U.D.F. terrorist trial. I never anticipated being here for more than a few weeks at the outside."

46

"I promise you that we'll waste no time," said Mr. Silverborn. He tried not to let the fact that he disliked Mullen colour his reactions.

In the room next door, Kathleen was saying to Rosemary, "You've been scribbling very busily. What's it all about?"

"Something I'm getting up for the big white chief," said Rosemary. She had stopped scribbling, but her pencil was still poised.

"How's the hag-ography going?" said Mavis. A big, cow-like girl she was secretly rather impressed by Rosemary's pursuit of learning and therefore missed no opportunity to make fun of it.

At this point Mr. Silverborn came out of the inner office on the way back to his own room. He beamed vaguely at the three girls. Rosemary put down her pencil and shut her shorthand notebook. She said, "Yesterday evening we got to the point where the Pope decided that St. George couldn't keep his sainthood, on the grounds that he never really existed."

"The Pope actually said that?" said Mavis.

"About *our* St. George," said Kathleen.

"Apparently so."

Mavis said something very rude about the Pope.

5

In the early evening of that Friday a cabinet meeting was being held at No. 11 Mornington Square. Captain Hartshorn was in the chair, with Andrew Mkeba beside him and the three departmental chiefs opposite.

Hartshorn said, "You will all have seen copies of the cable which I sent to the press chief at the ANC. It went through the Eastern Tourist Agency and will, with luck, have reached Lusaka by now."

"I noticed," said Govan Kabaka, "that you didn't ask them to take any particular action."

"There was no necessity. They are not stupid. They will appreciate the possibilities of the situation as clearly as we do. The publishers managed to supply them with nearly a thousand copies of Katanga's book. I am told that the open demand through Mozambique, Zimbabwe and Botswana, coupled with an even larger underground demand in South Africa – particularly in the Transvaal – has already forced them to ask for a further two thousand copies. The book has, of course, been banned by Pretoria and possession of a copy is a criminal offence. That won't stop people reading it."

"On the contrary. Splendid publicity," said Govan.

"I agree," said Hartshorn, "and it puts us on our mettle. Our job is to see that this case gets as much publicity as the book."

"If Mullen is convicted," said Kabaka, "the publicity will be self-generating."

"Maybe. But this is no time for relaxing. We may be winning, but we haven't won yet."

"In a tug-of-war," said Sesolo, in his deep voice, "if you stop

48

pulling, you find yourself on your back."

"We've been presented," said Hartshorn "with a wonderful chance of demonstrating, to the people of this country, just what sort of characters are running your country. And it's a two-way chance. If Mullen is convicted, a senior police-officer will have been found guilty of a mean piece of petty thieving. If he wriggles out under diplomatic privilege, that's not going to make him popular, either. Far from it."

"It would be better if he was convicted," said Kabaka. "It's just that I don't quite see what we can do about it."

"I think we may be able to help the prosecution. I've had two reports from my daughter. You all know what she's doing and are all, I hope, aware of the need for absolute discretion."

This was aimed primarily at Sesolo. Discretion was not his strongest point.

"The first report is of a conversation on Wednesday afternoon. You must understand that when Yule is talking to Mullen, the conversation is in Afrikaans and my daughter can only pick up a general idea of what is said. There was something about an accident with a drink and treatment in hospital and she picked up the name Anna Masai. The second part of the conversation, which started with the arrival of their legal man, was all in English. My daughter took it down in shorthand and you have seen the transcription."

Four heads nodded.

"I'd like to draw your attention to something which comes at the end of the morning's transcript. It's not long. Please read it, to see if you get the same impression that I did."

There were a few minutes of silence, broken only by the rustle of pages and the hard breathing of Boyo Sesolo, whose grasp of English was not on a par with that of his colleagues.

Mkeba, who had finished a lap ahead of the others, said, "What I make of it is that this legal chap – what's his name? – Silverborn – doesn't know what the hell the answer to the diplomatic point is. And like all solicitors when they don't know the answer, he's going scuttling off to Counsel.

The others nodded. Hartshorn said, "So you've all missed it. I did, the first time I read it. Look at what Mullen says right at the end."

"You mean when he's getting annoyed about the law's delays?"

49

"Right. His exact words are, 'I never anticipated being here for more than a few weeks at the outside.'"

"I think I see what you're getting at," said Mkeba, slowly. "The best chance Mullen has is to make out that he's come here on some sort of diplomatic posting. But *if* he was only planning to be here for a week or two at the outside, that knocks out any suggestion that he's come here to take up a post. Right?"

"Exactly right. I don't say that it's conclusive. But if it was sprung on him in court it would give Mullen a very difficult question to answer."

"*If* it was sprung on him," said Govan. "How do you intend to arrange that?"

"I don't know," said Hartshorn. "Not yet. But I'm going to find out."

On that same Friday and at about the same time Bantings were shutting up shop for the week. The younger members of the firm were chattering happily as they went down the steps outside the senior partner's window and headed for the delights of the weekend. Filing cabinets were being slammed and word processors and fax machines locked away. Complicated, expensive and superfluous toys, thought Mr. Banting and smiled when he suddenly remembered that his grandfather had said exactly the same when typewriters had first been introduced.

He was in no hurry to leave the office. Since the death of his wife he had lived in a set of chambers above Old Square and returning to them had no particular attraction for him. His eye was caught by a headline in the *Evening Standard* which his secretary had brought in with his five o'clock cup of tea.

SOUTH AFRICA – MAGISTRATE'S ATTACK

When he had skimmed through the item, which was not as exciting as the headline (had he visualised, for a moment, one of the more pugnacious London stipendiaries piloting a bomber over Johannesburg?) he dialled Roger Sherman's number on the office line. Roger said, "If you'll give me five minutes, sir, to finish signing my letters, I'll be right along."

"Take as long as you like," said Mr. Banting.

As has already been suggested, he approved of Roger, and

this for a number of reasons unconnected with the law; because he was easy to talk to and had a sense of humour; because he had married an attractive girl called Harriet whom Mr. Banting had monopolised at the last firm's dinner; above all because he had lived a chunk of his life in very different surroundings before coming into the law. Mr. Banting was honest enough to admit that it was only the happenstance of war breaking out in 1939 that had enabled him to do the same himself, but this did not affect his outlook on the matter. He realised that not all of his partners shared his feelings.

When Roger arrived he, too, had a copy of the *Evening Standard*. He said, "We all knew that the hearing this morning was a formality. We were up before Lauderdale, in the South-West London Court. As usual he looked as though his breakfast had disagreed with him."

"Gastric ulcers, I'm told."

"Is that right? Anyway, there was really no need for anyone to do more than apply for an adjournment, which he was bound to grant. The Branch Crown Prosecutor was a man called Totten – "

"I remember him. Face like a King Charles Spaniel."

"He was a very worried spaniel. When we were having a chat afterwards he wasted a quarter of an hour telling me that he was so overworked that he hardly had a moment to sit down. I must say, it does sound as if he's got a considerable workload. He has to look after cases from West End Central and Horseferry Road, as well as South-West London – "

"My heart bleeds for him," said Mr. Banting. "But how did the Press get in on the act? I thought you'd applied for a reporting ban."

"So we have. And if Mullen had kept quiet we'd have been in and out in a couple of minutes. But what did he have to do but stand up and shout his mouth off."

"Indeed. What did he say?"

"He said that he objected to all this dillying and dallying. He was a man with a lot of work to do, even if they weren't. Why couldn't they simply take note of the undeniable fact that he was entitled to diplomatic privilege and kick this misconceived prosecution out of court?"

"He said that?"

"In so many words."

"To Lauderdale! Well, well. What happened?"

"I thought, for a moment, that the old boy was going to blow up. Then he took a deep breath and said, 'You committed this alleged offence yesterday, Mr. Mullen?' Mullen grunted something. 'And you were charged on the same day and have been brought before this court on the following day. Did it not occur to you that it might be an improvement if alleged offences in *your* country were dealt with as expeditiously?'"

"Good," said Mr. Banting. "Very good."

"Of course this was lapped up by the press boys. They were barred from reporting the case itself, but there was nothing to stop them dealing with off-the-cuff remarks made by the Magistrate. There were only two of them there and they were both scribbling like maniacs. It was a bit of a scoop for them. I can tell you one thing. When this comes up next week it'll be standing-room only in the press-box."

"Yes," said Mr. Banting thoughtfully. "I'm sure you're right. This case is going to make a big splash. What are your ideas about the next move?"

"We shall have to ask for the diplomatic point to be taken first. Totten more or less admitted that he was out of his depth and I'm sure next time we shall see someone more effective on the Crown side. They'll probably produce an expert on that sort of question."

"Which means that we have to do the same. Who had you in mind?"

"I've taken a few soundings. The general view seems to be that Martin Bull is the man we ought to get. Something of a specialist in international law and a good fighter."

"Whose chambers?"

"De Morgan's."

"Is he, though? Well, that gives us some fairly heavy metal if we have to go higher. Tell me, suppose we go down on this point and have to fight the case on its merits. What do you think the chances are?"

"I'm not too happy about that, sir. Mullen has told me one story and wants us to tell a different one to the court."

"That does happen," said Mr. Banting. "Counsel can usually wriggle out of it somehow. But it brings me to what I really wanted to say. We had a partners' meeting this morn-

52

ing. The normal one we have on Friday mornings, to moan about how little money we're making. But John Benson did say that he'd heard from someone or other about this case and that he wasn't absolutely happy about a firm like ours being involved in police court wrangling and particularly not when we were acting for a South African thug."

"Did he actually say 'thug'?"

"Either thug or bully. I can't remember which."

"Wasn't he rather prejudging the issue. What does he know about Mullen?"

"He knows that he comes from South Africa and is some sort of policeman and that's all most people in this country need to know in order to make their minds up."

"You mean, in order to be prejudiced."

"Don't take it out of me, my boy. I'm older than John and more broad-minded."

"Then you don't want me to tell Mullen to go somewhere else? There are firms in the City who would jump at the case."

"No doubt. Particularly since Mullen will have South African government money behind him. No. All I'm saying at the moment is, cross the first bridge first. The diplomatic point is a very interesting one. No one could blame us for pursuing that, and Counsel will make a meal of it."

"I'm glad you're not ordering me off altogether," said Roger. "I've had a six-page letter from my son, at St. Paul's. Harriet must have told him about the case. He was tremendously bucked that I was acting for a character like Mullen. He said that it showed that the law of England was old enough and steady enough to stand up for unpopular people."

"That sounds like a quotation."

"It is. I got it from one of Marshall Fitzhugh's speeches and put it in one of my letters to him. Now he's played it back to me."

"It's a curious thing," said Mr. Banting, "how children are always far to the left of their parents."

The headlines in the *Evening Standard* had caught the eye of other, more influential, people.

The News Editor of the *Sentinel*, that bible of the radical intelligentsia, said to his deputy, "What's all this about?"

"South Africa," said the deputy.

"Explain."

"Old Lauderdale had obviously heard that Mullen was a South African policeman and therefore naturally a Beast of Belsen and took the first opportunity of tearing a strip off him."

"Will it develop?"

By this the News Editor meant, as his deputy well understood, will there be a fruitful fall-out from which subsequent stories can be garnered, one leading to another, until it finally peters out in the correspondence columns having fulfilled the destiny of News which is to occupy the maximum amount of space with the minimum of readership boredom?

"I think it might come along nicely," said his deputy. "Anything to do with police brutality is news."

"You think so?"

"Well, isn't it?"

"It's news of a sort," said the Editor, "but is it *vital* news? Is it the sort of thing that stirs the heart of the great British public? Because in my experience the heart of the great British public is about as difficult to stir as my grandmother's Christmas puddings."

"Then you think that it's only category 'B' stuff?" He was disappointed, but willing to learn.

"The top of category 'B', certainly. But you'll soon find out that category 'A' news – the stuff that gets right home to readers – has to be something that worries *them*. A lot of people are interested in South Africa. I'm not denying it. They read about the sort of things that are going on in there and they say, 'bloody bad show, killing women and children', and then they get on with something that really interests them, golf or bridge or whatever. Dean Swift had the right of it. What a newspaper man he'd have made, if he hadn't happened to be a clergyman! You remember his poem about the old ladies chatting over their cards? 'My female friends . . . Receive the news in doleful dumps. The Dean is dead *(and what is trumps?)*'."

"Then what *do* you put in category 'A'?"

"Well, take the King's Cross disaster. That *was* news. After all, any one of our readers might have been on that train and could be on the next one. Or the two planes which collided outside Heathrow. That sort of thing. I was a boy in the thirties and I can tell you this. Every single thing that Adolf Hitler said or did was top news. Why? Because young men could see it leading them straight back to the Somme and Passchendaele."

"I understand that," said his deputy reluctantly, "but surely if people in this country aren't worried enough about South Africa, isn't it our duty to do something about it? Oughtn't we to be leading public opinion, not following behind it?"

He was not long down from Cambridge and still retained some of his light-blue idealism.

His opposite number on that popular sheet, *The Comet*, saw the headlines. He said to his deputy, "Lauderdale had better be careful. He'll be in trouble with the Lord Chancellor if he starts shooting his mouth off."

The matter was also under discussion at West End Central Police Station, where Chief Inspector Ancrum had received a visit from Chief Superintendent Baron, Head of the Special Branch.

Ancrum said, "Sheridan is a very experienced officer. I don't think he had any option. Once he heard that Mullen had nearly made a break for it he had to take him along. Of course, he was given bail as soon as the formalities were finished."

"Who said he nearly made a break for it?"

"That was old Ratter. He works for City Tecs now."

"Ratter? Do you mean a fat chap who used to be in 'V' Division at Wimbledon?"

"That's the one. They got a new Assistant Commissioner in No. 1 District — as it was then. He was dead nuts on physical fitness. Mile runs before breakfast. The Monty touch. Ratter didn't go for that at all. He said if he tried to run a hundred yards he'd die, so he got out."

"But apart from his weight problem, you'd say he was a reliable man?"

"Reliable and experienced."

Baron said, "I'm not criticising what Sheridan did. I don't think he had any option. What I'm saying is that when a case has a political angle to it, you have to be dead careful."

"If there is a political angle," said Ancrum, "the case goes straight to you. It's the sort of thing you're paid to look after."

55

6

On the following morning Captain Hartshorn walked down from Mornington Square into the City. It was lovely autumn weather and he was in no hurry. He enjoyed the City at weekends when the streets were almost empty, when the towering business blocks had been deserted by the black-coated, striped-trousered lemmings and the shops and cafés which catered for them were mostly shut.

Of set purpose he directed his course more to the west than he need have done. Crossing Smithfield Market and steering by the dome of St. Paul's he came out at the point where Newgate Street meets Paternoster Row. He had heard a lot from his daughter about Fischer Yule's office, but had not yet seen it himself. His present intention was to fix its location in his own mind and to see whether it would be possible to have it watched.

As he swung into Cheapside he noticed, ahead of him, the trim figure of a black girl. He slowed his pace and kept his eye on her until she turned left into Axe Lane. By the time he reached the corner she was on the point of running up the two or three steps which led to the front entrance of what he guessed, correctly, to be the headquarters of the South African Security Section. He knew that it was open on Saturday mornings, though only for the convenience of the top brass. Typists and secretaries were not expected to attend. This meant that he had no means of finding out what went on there on that day. A pity, he thought, since discussions held in such circumstances could well be important.

He decided that it would be imprudent to show himself in Axe Lane and continued on his way down Cheapside towards

Basinghall Street.

The legal firm of Angel and Auchstraw had its modest office on the top storey of a building in Basinghall Street, with its back windows overlooking the Mansion House. Though small, its name was well known to a number of the people who worked between Temple Bar and Aldgate Pump. They referred to it as the Angel Orchestra. Its activities had been commented on more than once by the police in private; and publicly by judges who are, of course, privileged. The firm was Roland Auchstraw. No one had ever met Mr. Angel and it was generally believed that Auchstraw had invented him, in order to give a certain euphony to the title.

Captain Hartshorn knew the firm well. Describing it to a friend he had said, 'Well, all I can tell you about it is that it's the sort of firm where the partners are always the last to leave in the evening. Before they go they lock up all their records in a safe and put any loose papers through a shredder.' He might have added that they were one of the few firms that retained the pre-war practice of opening on Saturday mornings since some of the people who visited them preferred to do so when the streets were empty.

"Nice to see you again, Captain," said Roland Auchstraw. He was a short, tubby, guileless-looking man who had deliberately cultivated a resemblance to Phiz's Mr. Pickwick. He had even taken to wearing a pair of small steel-rimmed glasses modelled on the ones shown in these illustrations, though since they were of plain glass it is difficult to see how they assisted his eyesight, which was, in fact, remarkably keen. His opponents in court had learnt to keep their own papers covered after he had won a case by reading the first paragraph in one of their documents that had certainly *not* been intended for his eyes.

"Nice to see you, too," said the Captain. "How's business?"

"Slack, very slack. Hard to turn an honest penny these days. I hope you've brought me an interesting job. I take it you're still with your Orange boys."

"Certainly. And you can regard them, for these purposes, as your client."

Mr. Auchstraw said, "Splendid. Splendid." It was agreeable when clients came to him well provided with money. This was not always the case, for many of them were legal-aided, but he had acted for the Orange Consortium before and knew something of the ways in which it was financed.

"I have two immediate jobs for you. May be more to come, as the situation develops."

"The situation?" said Mr. Auchstraw thoughtfully

Hartshorn knew that it was no use running an ally like Roland Auchstraw in blinkers. He told him the whole story, not even omitting the part played by his daughter and the information he had had from her. Auchstraw listened carefully. The possibilities were clear enough to his observant eye.

"You'll appreciate," said Hartshorn, "that it's no use having this information unless we can pass it onto the prosecution to help them knock down the plea of diplomatic privilege."

"I understand that. But it's going to need devilish careful handling. If we pass it to some white-wigged junior who's still wet behind the ears, he won't have thought out the angles. He'll just blurt it out and when he's asked how he got the information he'll fluff and no one will believe a word he says."

"It's an important case. Do you think they'll risk giving it to a new boy?"

"Not probable. But possible. Between you and me, the Crown Prosecutions Service is in a mess. It's overworked and understaffed. When you think that one Branch Crown Prosecutor has to look after the cases in three busy courts, it's not surprising that he hardly knows whether it's Wednesday or Christmas. He's got a couple of assistant B.C.P.s to help him, but they're really only office boys. And if," he added handsomely, "they were half as clever as *my* office boy, they might be some use to him."

"But he can ask for help."

"Yes. If he's modest enough to admit that he's out of his depth. There's a stable of barristers available. They class them as Category 1 to 4. Category 4 can be quite hot. Might even be Treasury Counsel."

"And since you don't yet know who's going to take the case, you can't prime him."

"True. But as soon as I do know I'll get it to him, I can promise you that. The Crown Prosecutions Service is what you might call a rambling edifice. Thirty-five area branches and all their underlings. And being a rambling edifice it's got a lot of side doors and back doors. You understand me?"

"I understand you perfectly," said Hartshorn. "And I've every confidence in you. Now for the second point. I want the headquarters of the South African Security Branch kept under observation until further notice."

"Fischer Yule's outfit."

"Right. And I'd guess that he's chosen his office with an eye to making it difficult to watch. Difficult, that is, without the watchers being noticed. Axe Lane is not the sort of place someone can hang about in all day. He'd be noticed inside five minutes and reported in ten."

"Not easy," agreed Mr. Auchstraw. "Needs thought."

From one of his cabinets he had extracted a street guide and a section of the excellent plan which is produced by the Land Registry. It was on a scale large enough to show individual buildings. He said, "Two turnings off Axe Lane. I see. Harnham Court and Deanery Passage. Both running up to big office blocks. They must employ commissionaires."

"I don't think it's any use approaching them. They've already been bought." He explained the system of alternative exits devised by Yule.

"Cunning bugger," said Mr. Auchstraw in tones of warm appreciation. "You know what it means, don't you? On a weekday, if you wanted to be sure of following anyone coming out, you'd need a team of four permanently on duty. And if you're wanting to organise permanent observation you've only got two options. You could use someone employed in one of the other buildings. Trouble is, the ones on either side are banks. They're apt to be holier-than-thou. Then there are three buildings on the other side of the road lower down. Numbers 15, 17 and 19. According to this guide they're all of them occupied by dozens of small outfits. All right. If money's really no object, I might be able to take a room in one of them on a short let. Say three months. It wouldn't be cheap, though."

"It might not be cheap, And I realise it will involve you in a good deal of work. But if you could manage it, that would be ideal."

"We never object to trouble and extra work," said Mr. Auchstraw, "as long as it helps our clients." He sounded so benevolent when he said this that Captain Hartshorn found himself listening for a choir of angel voices.

Other parties were on the move on that fine Saturday morning. Roger set out after breakfast from his top-floor flat in Osnaburgh Terrace, walked the short distance to Warren Street underground station and took a Northern Line train in the direction of Edgware.

He was impelled by the thought that had been worrying him, on and off, for two days. Overnight it had taken more definite shape and now he fancied that he could track it to its source.

Nor was he displeased at getting out of the flat. His son, Michael, was home from St. Paul's for the first long weekend of the autumn term. He had arrived with a split lip and a black eye. ('Playing against Dulwich. Dirty crowd') and the conversation had been mostly about rugby football, but Roger had an uneasy feeling that shop-lifting was soon going to surface. It was partly on account of this that he had decided to devote a whole morning to trying to lay a ghost.

He did not know that he was being followed. The idea had not crossed his mind; nor was there any reason that it should have done.

The train pottered northward, coming out into the open between Hampstead and Golders Green and finally depositing him at Colindale. He had been worried about getting into the Newspaper Library and was relieved to find that his British Museum reader's ticket passed him in without trouble.

The nondescript man who was following him was not so fortunate. Having tried, without success, to sidle past the commissionaire on the door he was forced to hang about outside.

A helpful assistant dealt with Roger's enquiry.

"Oxford," he said. "City or University?"

"Could be either."

"Then I suggest you consult *Willing's Press Guide*. It's on the shelf over there. It will give you all the names. Do you know the date?"

Yes, he knew the date. Mullen had said, 'I came down a year after you did.' So that must be the year when it happened; if it did.

He filled in a form and composed himself to wait. His thoughts were not entirely comfortable. Was he, he wondered, behaving like the younger son in the fairy story, who persisted in asking questions, when knowledge was dangerous and ignorance would have been bliss?

When the heavy, yellowing volumes of old newsprint arrived on a trolley and were lifted onto the table in front of him he hesitated for some time before opening them.

The attendant, coming up behind him, said, "I hope those are the ones you wanted, sir."

"Yes," said Roger. "Those are the ones. Thank you." He started to read. It took him an hour to find what he wanted.

When he got back to the flat, still unaware that his movements were of interest to anyone but himself, he found his wife on her own. Michael was at Twickenham, watching the Harlequins play Leicester. This naturally brought them to the subject of black eyes and split lips, but Harriet could see that he was not really interested in mayhem on the rugby field. He had been uneasy when he set out; now he was more than uneasy. He was worried.

She would dearly have liked to know where he had been and what he had been up to, but unless he chose to tell her she wasn't going to ask. It was on this basis that a happy marriage had been built during the last eighteen years.

When Roger was drinking his after-lunch coffee he said, apropos of nothing that had gone before, "I went up to Colindale this morning. The Newspaper Library. It's an amazing place. They've got copies of practically every newspaper that's been published anywhere in England during the last hundred years and more."

"It sounds wonderful," said Harriet.

"I'll tell you what I was looking for. I was trying to run down a memory of something one of my Oxford friends had told me."

"Did you find it?"

"I'm sorry to say I did. It was a single paragraph hidden away in the *Oxford News and Journal*. A report that an undergraduate of Worcester College called Mullen had pleaded guilty to a charge of stealing a book from Messrs. Harmsworths bookshop. In order not to jeopardise his career the court had shown clemency. It had simply bound him over for one year."

"Meaning what?"

61

"Meaning that provided he did not offend again for one year, no further action would be taken. Anyway, it was his last year at Oxford."

"And who was Mullen?"

"Charles Mullen. Whilst he was at Oxford he preferred to use the English form of Karl."

The implications of this were slowly dawning on Harriet. She said, "My God. Yes. I see. Awkward."

"If, as seems likely, the news was so unimportant that the national press ignored it and, anyway, the Christian name was different, the chances of this being noticed now are a hundred-to-one against."

"A thousand-to-one, I'd say."

"But it puts me in an extremely awkward position. In the ordinary way, in a case of this sort, you can present the accused as a man of spotless reputation, who is totally unlikely to have committed the offence. It's a very strong card."

"Which the prosecution can trump if they happen to read the *Oxford News and Journal* of twenty years ago."

"That's right," said Roger. He finished his coffee, which was now cold, in one gulp and looked as though he wished he could swallow the *Oxford News and Journal* with it.

Harriet said, "I suppose it's occurred to you that there's a simple way out of this. Couldn't you ask Mullen to use another solicitor? Someone who wouldn't be burdened with this awkward knowledge. You're not the only solicitor in London."

"I'm the only one Mullen knows. But I think I'll have a word with Counsel first."

"But if you tell Counsel, won't he be bound to tell the other side?"

"Certainly not. The prosecution is supposed to supply the defence with all relevant facts – though often they don't. The defence is under no obligation whatever to help the prosecution. In fact, if he chooses to take the risk, he could ask his opposite number for the defendant's antecedents and get back a 609 with 'nil recorded'."

"A *what?*"

"Sorry. A 609 is a police document."

"Please let's stick to the King's English. I'm confused enough already. You mean that if the prosecution don't know about this earlier matter you can trap them into giving Mullen a clean sheet?"

"Right."

"It doesn't seem right at all. It seems unethical."

"A lot of criminal procedure is unethical. In a case like this the only thing Counsel can't do is use the words 'of good character' about his client and that's such a normal thing that the other side might notice the omission and guess that something was up. But they'd hardly have time to dig it out."

"You make it sound like a game," said Harriet crossly.

"It's not Counsel I'm bothered about. He's paid to deal with dicey situations like this. It's Mullen. I shall have to tell him."

"And then," said Harriet hopefully, "surely he'll go to another solicitor."

Like most women she was equal parts idealist and realist. The idealist told her that it was absolutely right for her husband to take on this unpopular task. The law, if it was to function properly, must be equally available to the popular and the unpopular. But realism was saying something quite different. Roger was over forty. He had got himself, by good luck, into a firm which suited him and which had seemed, so far, to approve of him. Very probably he would soon be offered a partnership.

If he upset them, there would be no partnership for him. He might have to go somewhere else, without prospects. He might even, perish the thought, become a local authority solicitor. Possibly she was prejudiced, but she had sat next to one at a dinner party and he had lectured her on rating law from the soup to the savoury.

Roger said, "You realise that none of this may happen. If he succeeds in his plea for diplomatic immunity the case will be slung out and that will be an end of it."

"Speriamo," said Harriet in her best Italian.

The News Editor of the *Sentinel* said to his deputy, "By the way, one of our men who's just back from South Africa said that Mullen is quite a well-known character out there. He's got a nickname. They call him the Pencil Man."

"Meaning what?"

"Stoddart didn't know. He thought perhaps it meant that Mullen was a back-room boy. The sort of policeman who sat in his office writing minutes instead of getting out on the street and doing his job."

The deputy thought about it. He said, "If we could find out what it means – if it's some sort of insult – we should be able to make something of it."

"We could let our cartoonist have it. Might give him some new ideas. He'll have to give up his grotesque cartoons of Maggie now."

7

The list of names painted inside the doorway of No. 7 Dr. Johnson's Buildings was headed by Leopold de Morgan. In accordance with convention, there was nothing to indicate the fact that he was a Queen's Counsel and a Member of Parliament; or that he had held the office of Attorney General in the Socialist government.

Martin Bull had joined the Chambers sixteen years before and his name was now halfway down the list of twenty-two. At this moment he was in conference with Roger Sherman taking what he described as 'a preliminary canter over the course'. He and Roger had been friends since the time, many years before, they had been members of the same bob-sleigh team in the run-up to the Winter Olympics.

"One thing's clear," said Bull, "You'll have to bring Mullen along here. Also his boss. Who would that be?"

"It depends. Theoretically, the Ambassador. But, if he's holding some sort of consular post it would be the Consul General. In fact, I doubt whether he comes under either of them. If he's attached to anyone it's either the Security Section, in Axe Lane, or a separate outfit in High Holborn – "

"Stop, stop," said Bull, pushing his hand claw-wise through his hair. "Stop and start again. This is where I rely on you."

"I thought you were the expert. I told Banting you knew all there was to be known about international law."

"Then I hope you're aware that you were talking out of the back of your neck." He spoke with the familiarity to be expected between two men who had descended an ice-slope at seventy miles an hour on a fragile saddle of wood and steel, clasped together in a more than fraternal embrace. This was because they were alone. In conference, with strangers present, they behaved with a Victorian formality of language and deportment. "How much I know about international law is beside the point. What matters is the application of that law to these particular circumstances. So stop fluffing and let me have everything you've found out so far."

"All right. Here goes. There's the Embassy, on the east side of Trafalgar Square, maintained, I suspect, largely as a front, and there's the Consulate in King Charles II Street. That's a pretty busy place. It deals with members of the public. People who want passports or visas or to complain about their aunt having been insulted by the police in Johannesburg. Then you've got the technical outfit in High Holborn. Commercial Attaché. Scientific Officer and bods like that. They've all got their own in-house security men – "

"I don't follow. If all these outfits have got their own security men, where does the other section fit in? The one you called the Security Section."

"A good question," said Roger. "And it's something that puzzled me. It's run by a man called Fischer Yule. It's practically autonomous, and extremely secretive. I suppose the true description of Yule's outfit would be counter-propaganda. Passive and active. There are one or two newspapers that are not entirely hostile. He can supply them with facts about the extent to which South Africa is being misunderstood. And they keep tags on known dissidents. People like Jack Katanga, who's just produced this book."

"*Death Underground*. Rather good stuff, I thought. I suppose it was ghosted."

"I don't think so. It's his first book, but he's been churning out articles for the press for years."

Martin Bull thought about this for a minute in silence. Then he said, "Do you think it really was a coincidence that Katanga should have been the one to spot Mullen putting the book back?"

"Always bearing in mind that your instructions are that he never took it in the first place."

"Certainly. And it's a great pity. If he'd allow us to run the line that the whole thing was a set-up – that the book was planted on him and Katanga being where he was and this mysterious detective happening to be outside was all part of a skilful fix – I think we'd have a very good chance. Particularly since their vital witness is Katanga and he could hardly be described as unprejudiced. But if he insists on sticking to straight denial – 'I never touched the bloody book and I defy you to prove it' – then, if you want my honest opinion, I think he'll go down."

"Even without this additional tit-bit of the earlier conviction."

"If they had that, he'd be sunk. Our only real hope would be to get the case thrown out under diplomatic immunity provisions."

"And what are the chances of that?"

"I'll give you an answer when I've seen Mullen and his superior officer. It won't be a walk-over. Oh, I hear they've dumped poor little Totten and taken in Dudley Lashmar."

"Never heard of him."

"You will. He's a young man on the way up."

"I gather you don't like him."

"I don't dislike him. He's clever and hard-working, but not generally popular. I think it's because he's too fond of demonstrating how clever he is. He enjoys arguing unarguable propositions, like nothing exists until someone sees it, or how do you know that the world isn't flat. And shouting down all your counter-arguments."

"I see," said Roger. "An undergraduate who hasn't grown up. Whose Chambers does he fascinate with his sparkle?"

"He's one of Sir Humphrey Belling's boys. And what's the joke?"

"It's just occurred to me. If this case goes to the Court of Criminal Appeal, or even higher – which it might – we'd have the present Attorney General fighting a sham battle with one of his predecessors. Tweedledum and Tweedledee."

"So far as Sir Humphrey's concerned, it wouldn't have been a sham battle, I assure you. He loathes de Morgan's guts."

"Because one's a hide-bound Conservative and the other's a dangerous Radical?"

"I don't think politics comes into it. Or not a lot. More a personal matter. You may remember that the Attorney Generals under the Socialists all refused knighthoods. When Humphrey eventually got the job, under the Tories, Leopold wrote him a letter, with his tongue in his cheek, congratulating him on his eminence and saying he supposed that Humphrey would follow the excellent example of his Socialist predecessors. Upon which Humphrey wrote back, thanking him for the first part of his letter and pointedly ignoring the second. The truth is, he wanted that K badly."

8

"Money down the drain," said Hartshorn.

"Do you mean to say," said Boyo Sesolo, "that he trailed behind this lawyer feller all the way up to the library, then sat outside, picking his nose, then follered him home again? What use did he think that was?"

"No use at all."

They were in Sesolo's flat, which was on the first floor of the Mornington Square house, facing the Communications Room and immediately above the Administration block which occupied the whole of the ground floor. This isolation of Boyo had been deliberate. He was an exuberant character, who often hosted parties of his old athletic friends, or of members of his student army; parties which were apt to continue, with musical honours, into the early hours of the morning.

"Why didn't you use some of my boys? They're stoodents. They'd have a card to get into any library. Or if they hadn't, be sure they'd have found some way round it."

To call Sesolo's helpers 'boys' was misleading. They were students or ex-students, in their twenties or early thirties. A few of them were, no doubt, motivated by a genuine dislike of South African police brutality. But to most of them it was a game. A rough game, in which, since they were playing for the popular side, their violence was condoned, or even approved of. Descendants of the Mohocks and the Tityre-tu, they had substituted for the old aristocratic ruffianism a colder and more deliberate brutality. Most of them were tolerably well-off and none of them asked for money for their services. They were paid by the squeals and humiliation of their victims.

"I've been thinking about that," said Hartshorn. "I don't see much future in trailing round after that solicitor. Whatever he went up to Colindale to do, he's done it. We had our chance and we fluffed it. And I don't think he'll give us another one. Because, normally, he's a very wide-awake character."

"You know him?"

"Not personally. But our paths, as you might say, crossed. He was a company commander in the Royal Warwicks when I was R.S.M. in the Buffs. We were brigaded together for training and I heard a good deal from my friends in the Sergeants' Mess about Captain Sherman. He was quite a lad. Always ready for anything that was going. They were sorry to hear that he was handing in his chips at the end of camp. I remember thinking at the time, here was I, sweating my guts out to get a commission, which he was chucking away as though it was so much waste paper."

"That's life, isn't it?" said Sesolo. "Reverting to what we were discussing, I've got two or three boys wouldn't say 'no' to a little action."

"Then there is something they could do. It wouldn't be exciting, but it might pay dividends if they could keep an eye on Katanga. He's got this little house – it's called the Homestead – in a side road off Putney Park Lane, opposite the Convent. I don't mean picket the place. There's Putney Heath alongside, so they've plenty of chance to keep out of sight. What they've got to do is keep their eyes open. Remember, he's the star witness for the prosecution. You can bet the defence will be going flat out to get any dirt they can on him."

"Or if they can't find any dirt, to manufacture some, eh?"

"I wouldn't put it past them. Either way, it's going to be useful for there to be a friend or two at hand. Their main job is observation. Make a note of anyone who visits him. Particularly lawyers or policemen. And, of course, if anyone tries to get rough with him, they could butt in."

"They'd enjoy that," said Sesolo. "They're great butter-inners."

Six men were crowded, rather uncomfortably, into Martin Bull's room. There was Max Freustadt, the Consul General, with his Head of Chancery, Dieter Langenhoven. Fischer

70

Yule had brought his legal man, Silverborn, with him. Roger and his client, Mullen, were squeezed together at the end of the table. The air was thick with tobacco smoke.

"I think that's as far as we can go with the main charge," said Bull. "We'll be up before Lauderdale. His stomach makes him a bit irritable, but he's a sound enough lawyer and he'll listen to arguments. I intend to take the diplomatic privilege point before the case is allowed to go any further."

"I entirely agree," said Freustadt. "The less anyone hears about this deplorable business, the better for all concerned."

His opinion of Mullen was clear from the look which accompanied this statement. Before the silence which it provoked could become uncomfortable, Bull continued smoothly, "I won't trouble you with the purely legal points, though I'd be delighted to discuss them afterwards with Mr. Silverborn. Quite simply, what I shall seek to establish is that Mr. Mullen came here to take up a diplomatic post. The only fact which seems, at first sight, to tell against this is that he spends most of his time with your Security Section in Axe Lane."

This statement, which seemed to have a question mark at the end of it, was directed equally to Yule and Mullen. It was Yule who fielded it. He said, with a slight smile, "The frequent visits which Mr. Mullen pays to No. 10 Axe Lane can be very easily explained. I have managed to accommodate him with a flat at the back of the building, pending the time when he can acquire more permanent accommodation."

"Not easy to get digs in London, today," agreed Bull. "Well, so much for that. What we have to keep our eyes on is Article 31 of the Schedule to the Diplomatic Privileges Act, 1964. That is the Article, as I expect you know, which gives diplomatic agents immunity from all criminal proceedings and exempts them from any obligation to give evidence."

Everyone except Mullen nodded sagaciously as though they had known all about Article 31. Mullen contented himself with grunting.

"So, quite clearly, what we have to do is to establish that Mr. Mullen is a diplomatic agent. That is to say, a member of the Ambassador's diplomatic staff. And the person who can give the best answer to that is the Ambassador."

"I feel certain that His Excellency will be glad to give us

whatever assistance he can," said Freustadt. "We have informed him of the unfortunate – the most unfortunate – circumstances of the case. Mr. Langenhoven and I will draft a carefully written statement and we will obtain his signature to it."

Langenhoven nodded agreement to this. He said, "We should welcome Counsel's advice as to what particular points he feels it would be useful to cover."

It seemed to Roger that what he was asking was, 'What particular lies do you want us to tell?' but it did not appear to worry Bull, who said, "I rather gather from what I have been told that Mr. Mullen is an expert in all aspects of anti-terrorism. His job would therefore be to advise His Excellency on such matters."

"An anti-terrorist adviser," said Freustadt.

"Just so," said Langenhoven.

Much nodding of heads.

Bull said, "I trust that His Excellency is in London at the moment. You realise that time is short. It's Wednesday today and we have to be ready by next Monday."

"His Excellency is available," Freustadt assured him. "And will be informed of your advice. I am sure that he will be delighted to help."

"Good. A statement by the Ambassador, signed in his own hand, must carry a lot of weight, but it will have to be supported by the oral testimony of Mr. Mullen."

"Me give evidence?"

"Yes."

"But I thought you said that this Act, or whatever it was, laid down that I shouldn't give evidence."

"You are not compelled to give evidence. But if what you are able to tell the court helps us to establish diplomatic immunity, then there is nothing to prevent you doing so, if you wish."

Mullen grunted again. A shark trapped in shallow water being tormented by shrimps, thought Roger.

The appearance, during the course of that week, of a small notice indicating that the Westminster Novelties Company had opened an office on the third floor of No. 15 Axe Lane excited little comment among the eleven other firms occupying that building. Some of them had been there for many years, some were birds of passage.

The junior employees of Ferryman & Lazenby, Average Adjusters, had noted the arrival of the two men who seemed to constitute the entire staff of Westminster Novelties. Since one of them was stout and looked amiable and the other was thin and looked depressed they had named them Laurel and Hardy and referred to them as such when they had occasion to speculate on exactly what sort of novelties they dealt in.

One curious point about the new tenants was that they seemed to receive no mail at all. Maybe as Christmas approached things would look up. But they were workers. They arrived early and departed late and the office was never left unattended. When one went out to lunch the other remained at his post. Also it seemed that they had made some arrangement with their landlords which allowed them to work on Saturdays.

"My clients," Roland Auchstraw had told them, "regard Saturday morning as a very important period for observation. And should a young coloured girl appear, she will have to be followed."

"One to follow, one to stay in observation," said Harold Ratter.

Auchstraw thought about this. He had already spent a good deal of his clients' money on securing the office so quickly. To put in a third man would add a further charge.

He said, "No. I understand that identifying this young lady is one of the main objects of the operation. If she appears, she must be followed. It will need two of you to do it. Fortunately, being a Saturday, the alternative exits will not be available to her."

"Leave it to us," said Ratter.

It was a job which suited him very well, since it consisted of taking turns with Chris Woodray, an old associate from 'V' Division days, at sitting in a comfortable chair observing the visitors to No. 10 as they came and went.

They were soon able to identify the staff, the secretaries and typists who arrived first and the more important male members who followed them. Also the regular callers, the postman, the milk delivery-man and a hopeful character who had visited all the offices in the Lane endeavouring, with little

73

success, to sell them typing and carbon paper and other office requisites.

A careful note was kept of all these and a report went at the end of the day to Captain Hartshorn. He did not seem depressed by the negative nature of this information. He was interested mainly in one man, whom the watchers had identified, from a photograph, as Karl Mullen.

"He's in and out half a dozen times a day," said Ratter. "And since the first time we saw him he's coming *out*, it's a fair guess he's staying there."

Hartshorn agreed that this was probable. His daughter confirmed it. She said, "He's always here in the mornings when we arrive. I guess he's tucked away in a flat somewhere up at the top. Probably an old commissionaire's pad."

On Saturday morning, as eleven o'clock was striking from the City churches, Ratter said, "There she is, Chris. A neat little black packet as per specification. Going in now."

No time was wasted. They switched off the electric fire and the lights and went out, locking the office door behind them. Being the only Saturday workers they had been entrusted with a key of the street door and they locked this too, before setting off, one up the Lane to Gresham Street, the other down it into Cheapside.

When they had turned the corner and were out of sight, all they had to do was to wait. The girl was bound to emerge at one end or the other. The second watcher, noting which way she turned, had then to circle round by St. Martin's-le-Grand as quickly as possible and join his colleague. This manoeuvre was carried out without difficulty, helped by the fact that the girl had stopped to do some window-shopping in Cheapside, before making for St. Paul's underground station. There she boarded a Central Line train for Tottenham Court Road, switched to the Northern Line and emerged finally at Tufnell Park.

Both of the men were experts at their job and it did not appear to them that the girl was aware that she was being followed. However, now that they seemed to be nearing the end of the chase precautions had to be taken.

They left the station ahead of the girl. One turned to the left, the other to the right, both swinging off as though they had some urgent job in hand. The girl turned right. As soon as he saw this, Woodray turned round, crossed the road and advanced along the opposite pavement. The two men now had her as firmly held as a plane in the beams of twin searchlights.

It was not a long chase. A few minutes later the girl was running up the steps of one of the terrace houses, halfway along a road of mixed houses and shops. They noted that she had no key and had to ring the bell. The door was opened by a middle-aged man with a white beard, wearing gold-rimmed glasses. He seemed glad to see her.

"Also Basuto," said Woodray. "Her father, do you think? Uncle, maybe."

Ratter offered no opinion about this. He was busy examining the shops on the far side of the road.

"We'll try this one," he said, selecting a small shop bearing the sign Sundridge Tobacconist and Newsagent. On such occasions he had found that it paid to come quickly to the point. He produced his professional card and showed it to the man behind the counter, who said, in tones of surprise and alarm, "Detectives! Wassit all about? Criminal stuff, eh."

"Not criminal this time," said Ratter, in a voice which suggested that he spent his working day pursuing armed robbers. "Civil work this time. Divorce. That girl we saw go in the house opposite – three doors up, the one with the green blinds – she's a witness in the case. Our client thinks she's a bad character. You know what I mean."

"All the same these black girls," said the newsagent. "No more morals than a monkey."

"What we've got to do is watch the house. See if any gentlemen-friends come to call. If by any chance you were able to give us the use of an upstairs window" – he drew out a fat wallet – "our client would expect us to recompense you – appropriately." The five syllables of this last word, drawn out impressively, were accompanied by the deposit of five five-pound notes on the counter. Any scruples which the tobacconist may have entertained were melted by the sight.

"I've an upstairs room I don't use myself. Would you be wanting it for long?"

"That depends on what you can tell us about the young lady."

"I don't know a lot about her, not really."

"About her habits."

"Oh, her habits. Yes. Well, most Saturdays she arrives about this time and stays home – I call it her home, because I think the old pair are her father and mother – anyway, she stays put until after lunch on Sunday, then she pushes off. Seems like she must have a job somewhere and gets weekends off."

"Sound thinking," said Ratter. "Then one other thing. If so be you've got a telephone, I could keep my client informed. Another fiver should cover any calls I make. I shan't be ringing up Timbuctoo, I promise you."

Mr. Sundridge agreed that an additional five pounds would be satisfactory.

"Excellent," said Captain Hartshorn when they telephoned him. "I don't think you need stop the night there. Turn up in good time on Sunday. And bring a camera with you – one of those ones with a telescopic attachment. I expect you can raise one. Yes. Splendid. Then see if you can get a shot of the girl *and* the old man. If he's a recent import we can probably identify him."

Ratter and Woodray were back on duty soon after breakfast. They had brought supplies of food and drink with them and were glad of them as the hours passed. It was nearly five o'clock before the house they were watching showed any sign of life.

When the front door opened they got two excellent snaps of the man and the girl as they stood together on the steps chatting. The camera was packed up and they were out in the street before the girl had reached the end of the road.

Once again the first part of the chase was by underground and presented no problems. Back down the Northern Line to the Embankment station, then a switch to the District Line. When the girl disregarded trains for both Richmond and Ealing it was clear that what she wanted was a Wimbledon train.

"Looks like a home run," said Ratter with satisfaction.

Being old 'V' Division men the area of London south of the river, between Putney Bridge and Surbiton, was familiar territory.

"Depends which way she goes," said Woodray. "That bit by the Heath's too bloody open." Ratter agreed with him. He, too, had worn out more than one pair of regulation boots on the long hard pavements of Wimbledon, Kingston and Malden.

The girl got out of the train at East Putney station and set off via Charlton Drive and up Putney Hill. She was walking more briskly now.

"Horse smelling the stable," said Woodray. He swung along easily on his long legs. Ratter was not so happy. He was carrying too much weight. In this stretch it was not difficult for the pursuers to remain unobserved. The pavements were reasonably crowded with Sunday strollers. It was six o'clock, but still quite light. The girl turned right at the top of the hill and took the road which skirted the north side of the Heath.

This did present problems. On the right-hand side, what had once been half a dozen large houses, was now the Ashburton Council Estate. On the left lay the Heath, but part of this section had recently been fenced off by hurdles to form a pasture for sheep. The hurdles presented no difficulty, but the sheep, if they got among them, would certainly stampede and draw attention to them.

"Bloody animals," said Ratter. It was a long straight stretch of road and, as it happened, almost empty of pedestrians. He could have wished it was an hour later, but the autumn sun hung with perverse brightness in the western sky. "You better keep up behind her, Chris. See which way she turns at the end. I'll fall back a bit."

The girl had now reached the corner where Putney Park Lane ran down to the Heath. There was a well-populated section ahead and Ratter was beginning to breathe more easily when the girl stopped and swung round, apparently to look at the sheep. Woodray, who was twenty yards behind her, had no option. He had to keep going. If he, too, had stopped he must have been noticed. As he passed the girl she gave him what started as a casual glance, but suddenly became more fixed.

Woodray knew what was coming. It had happened before. He had found that if you followed a person for some time, even though they took no apparent notice of you they were unconsciously registering a picture. Something glimpsed in a shop window, on a station platform, on a crowded pavement. Then, if you were brought face to face, the picture would come into focus. I've seen that man before! More than once!

Alarm bells ringing!

Since Ratter, also, was unable to stop he had done the next best thing by crossing to the other pavement. But his was not the sort of figure that was easily forgotten, even across the width of the road and in the gathering dusk. After a single scared glance the girl took to her heels.

At this moment three young men joined the party. It was difficult to say where they had come from. Two of them seemed to emerge from the cul-de-sac ahead. One might have been on the Heath itself.

Their leader and spokesman, a large fair-haired youth wearing corduroy trousers and a roll-neck sweater, said to Woodray, "Am I wrong, chum, or were you annoying that girl?"

The other two young men had closed up. Ratter also. Three to two looked like bad odds, but appearances were deceptive. It was three amateurs against two professionals.

Ratter walked straight up to the large young man and, without giving any indication of what he was planning to do, swung the heavy, hardwood, walking-stick which he was carrying. It was a scything blow which caught the young man behind his right knee and sent him rolling onto the ground.

Woodray's action was even more decisive. He had caught a flash of blue further up the road. He pulled out a police whistle and blew a shrill blast on it. Its effect was immediate. The patrolling policeman swung round, the sheep on the common raised their heads in alarm and windows were jerked open. The other two young men, evidently deciding that discretion was the better part of valour, vaulted the hurdle and made off across the Heath scattering the already alarmed flock. The large young man had tried to get up and when he found that his right leg no longer worked had fallen back groaning.

"What's all this about?" said the policeman. "Well, well. If it isn't old Ratty. I thought you'd died long ago."

"Might have died this evening if you hadn't turned up. Attempted mugging. Three of them. Maybe more. Had to defend ourselves."

"Who's your friend? Chris Woodray, isn't it? You're a nice pair to get into trouble, I must say."

The man on the ground called attention to himself by

trying to sit up and groaning.

"Looks like we shall need some transport," said the policeman. Front doors were opening and a small crowd was collecting. "Soon as possible." He was about to use his bat-phone when Ratter stopped him. He said, "We don't want a squad car. We want a taxi."

"You're not pressing charges then?"

"Charges," said the young man indignantly. He had managed to hoist himself onto one leg by clinging to the lamppost. "He hit me, not me him."

"Are *you* making a charge?"

The young man was about to say, 'Yes, I bloody am', when discretion prevailed. He said, "No. Leave it alone."

"In that case," said the policeman patiently,"one of you kind people might ring for a taxi and then I suggest you go home. All of you."

"For God's sake," said Captain Hartshorn. "What is this? Civil war? We're not going to get very far if we start fighting each other."

"I've had a word with young Jepson," said Sesolo. "He's a good boy, but apt to jump to conclusions. And this time, I'm not sure you can blame him. His orders were to watch the Katanga household and see no one tried to interfere with them. Right?"

"And just because this girl was black, I suppose they assumed she had something to do with Katanga."

"Assuming didn't come into it. They'd been watching the house, on and off, for a week. They knew all about Anna. She's the household help."

"They're sure about that?"

"Certain sure. She's a trim little piece. Very easy on the eye. Like all young men they've got minds like sewers and they naturally thought she might be something more than just a help about the house – "

"Never mind about that," said Hartshorn. "What's important is what she does on Saturdays and Sundays."

"Seems likely she has her weekends off. Quite a normal arrangement."

"Indeed," said Hartshorn softly. "But what isn't so normal is how she spends her Saturday mornings *before* she gets back

79

to her father's house in Tufnell Park." He was handling the report, in Ratter's laborious handwriting, that lay, with two photographs clipped to it, on his desk.

"You tell me," said Sesolo. "What does she do?"

"It seems she has a date – a regular Saturday morning date – with Fischer Yule's security outfit."

Sesolo absorbed this information slowly. His mind did not work at the same speed as Andrew Mkeba's. Andrew had been sitting quietly in the corner. Now he said, "It's odder than you think, Boyo. We've identified the old man. He seems to be the girl's father. He's Professor Leon Macheli, from Maseru in Lesotho. He came over here after the December massacre. As a matter of fact, we're already helping him. So you would hardly expect him – or his daughter – to have any sympathy for the South African establishment. Yet she trots off on Saturday mornings for a heart-to-heart chat with Yule. Which means that this interesting little piece has got a foot in both camps. So clearly she's got to be watched. But we don't want her watched by two different lots of our people, who start fighting as soon as they meet."

"I was thinking the same thing," said Hartshorn. It was like being back in his old job as Regimental Sergeant-Major. The most difficult job in the army, at the mid-point in the organisation, holding the balance between officers and other ranks. In the present case, he knew the value of Sesolo's private army and did not want it discouraged.

He said, "I think, on the whole, we'll sign off City Detectives. For the time being, at least. Give young – what's his name – "

"Ronnie Jepson."

" – give him a pat on the back from me and tell him that the information he's given us about Anna was worth a knock or two. I gather he's out and about again."

"He's back on his legs, yes."

"Excellent. I've a feeling that the time is coming when he and his friends may be very useful indeed."

9

"Number 27 on your register, sir," said the Police Sergeant. "Karl Mullen."

Mullen had spent the last hour sitting at the end of a bench in the Court anteroom, the other occupants of which appeared to be prostitutes, pimps and drunkards. He had been outraged by this treatment and saw no reason to hide the fact.

Nor was Mr. Lauderdale feeling at his best. He had come to Court early to prepare for the difficulties which he anticipated, and this had meant curtailing the quiet half-hour after breakfast which his doctor had prescribed. He looked with distaste at the crowded press benches and the overflow of the public at the back of the Court. Everyone had waited patiently while he dealt with his regular customers. Now, at last, they could see, in the flesh, the South African whose fingers had been so surprisingly trapped in the machinery of justice.

Rising quickly from his seat, Martin Bull said, "I appear for the defendant and my learned friend Mr. Lashmar appears for the prosecution." He got this out a beat ahead of Lashmar, who had also stood up, evidently considering that he had the priority.

When Bull remained standing, the Magistrate shot a look of enquiry at him. Surely it was for the prosecution to begin?

"Before we start," said Bull, "I have an application to make. It has no connection with the merits of the charge. It relates solely to the question of jurisdiction."

Mr. Lauderdale said, "I have considered that question and it will have to be decided sooner or later. But should it not wait until a decision has been reached as to whether the evidence supports a committal or not? If my conclusion is that

81

it does not, then the question of jurisdiction does not arise."

"I feel," said Bull, "and I am sure that I have my learned friend's support, that unless we take the jurisdiction point first, a great deal of the Court's time may be wasted."

Lashmar nodded agreement. In fact, he was not ready for the hearing of the case.

"Oh, very well," said Lauderdale testily, "if that's what you both feel, perhaps you would enlighten me, Mr. Bull, as to why a properly constituted Court of this country is unable to hear what appears, on the face of it – I offer no opinion as to its validity – to be a very simple charge of attempted theft?"

"I must start, sir, by referring you to the Vienna Convention on Diplomatic Relations of 1961, which was incorporated into United Kingdom law by the Diplomatic Privileges Act of 1966."

"You may assume," said Mr. Lauderdale, "that I am not entirely unacquainted with these two measures." He had studied them both for the first time that morning.

"Then if, as I trust I shall be able to do, I can demonstrate that the accused is, without question, a diplomatic agent, in the sense that this term is used both in the Convention *and* the Act, then might I draw your attention at once to Article 29 of the Convention. According to this Article, the person of a diplomatic agent is inviolable. He is not to be liable to any form of arrest or detention and the State that receives him is enjoined to take all appropriate steps" – here Bull spoke more slowly and with increased emphasis – "to prevent any attack on his person, his freedom or his dignity."

His dignity, thought Roger. Save and preserve us! How can he be expected to be dignified sitting behind an iron railing on a bench recently vacated by a garrulous pimp? Or is he detached enough to reflect that what he is being subjected to now is a great deal less painful than what he has sometimes inflicted on people in his own country who had been charged with no offence at all. One look at Mullen's face answered that question. He was not making any attempt to be detached. He was alight with hatred and frustration.

"It seems to me," said Mr. Lauderdale, "that your whole submission can be expressed in half a dozen words. *Is Mullen a diplomatic agent or not?* If he is, I would concede, without the necessity of any further argument, that, under Article 29, he

82

is immune from the criminal jurisdiction of this country."

"I am obliged, sir. That is the precise point that I was approaching."

Meaning, thought Roger, that we should get there much quicker if you didn't keep interrupting.

"We are helped by the fact that the words are defined in the Convention. A diplomatic agent is either the head of a State's Mission – this would normally mean the Ambassador – *or* a member of the staff of that Mission having diplomatic rank. I therefore propose, first, to produce to the Court a written statement, signed by the Ambassador himself – "

It was observed that Lashmar was on his feet.

"In my submission, sir, this document cannot be considered by the Court."

"On what grounds, Mr. Lashmar?"

"On the grounds laid down by the Lord Chief Justice in the case of the Romford Urban District Council against Walliker. Put quite shortly, a written statement will not be accepted by the Court if the person making that statement is available to give evidence in person."

"Mr. Bull?"

"I agree that my learned friend has given us an accurate statement of the practice of the Court. The point is that, in this case, His Excellency is *not* available to give evidence."

"You mean he is out of the country?"

"No, sir. I mean that he cannot give evidence in person. It would be an intolerable breach of protocol. His Excellency represents the government of South Africa. He could no more be expected to give evidence in an English Court than our own Queen could be expected to do so in a South African Court."

Mr. Lauderdale considered this. He was aware that he was treading on dangerous ground. He decided to compromise. He said, "In view of what you say, Mr. Bull, and without endorsing its validity, I am agreeable to the document being read. I shall have to make my own mind up as to its evidential value when I have heard it."

"I have copies for you and more for my learned friend. If I might ask the clerk to hand them in. Thank you. I need not trouble you with the first part, which simply establishes the position and authority of the Ambassador. It is the central paragraph which is relevant. He says, 'In view of the many difficult problems which arise as a result of the activities of terrorists in this, as in many other countries, I felt that it would be of assistance to my Mission to have a man with experience in such matters to act as my adviser.' With respect, that seems to me to dispose of the matter."

"I must confess," said Mr. Lauderdale, "that I should have been happier if His Excellency had been a little more specific as to the precise functions which he expected Mullen to carry out."

"In that case," said Bull, managing to look happier than he felt, "I propose to ask the accused to give evidence. It is true that he is not a compellable witness, but his immunity in the matter can be – and has been – waived. Mr. Mullen has expressed himself as glad to assist the Court in this matter."

He didn't look in the least glad, thought Roger, as Mullen removed himself from the dock to the witness-box, mumbled the oath and glared round the Court.

"Tell us first, Mr. Mullen, when did you arrive in this country?"

"On October 1st."

"And what are your functions in this country? Would I be right in thinking that you have available, in your own files, background material about terrorists which would be useful to the authorities here?"

This was so clearly a leading question that the Magistrate shot a look at Lashmar. However, he seemed relaxed and indifferent.

"Certainly," said Mullen. "I found that my files, in certain cases, were considerably fuller than those kept here."

"It would, I think, be helpful if you could give us a specific example."

"Very well. One matter in which I was concerned was the presence in this country of a citizen of Mozambique called Jack Katanga. A notorious terrorist, a stirrer-up of trouble in the Transvaal and a self-confessed murderer."

The Magistrate, who had been studying his papers, said, "I don't wish to embark on the substantive charge, but I can't help noticing that one of the witnesses in that matter – in fact the principal witness – is named Katanga. Is that the man you are talking about?"

84

"If I might clarify the point," said Bull. "He is the same person. He was in the shop, primarily, in order to sign copies of a book he had written, called *Death Underground*. Mr. Mullen was also there to purchase copies of it, since he felt it might be effective to change the mind of the authorities here, who had steadfastly refused to extradite Katanga."

"Why should a book – ?"

Before the Magistrate could complete his sentence Mullen interrupted him. He said, in a voice which frustration had raised to little short of a raucous shout, "Seeing that forty-two pages of this precious work are devoted to a detailed description of a cowardly murder which this man had committed we thought that the British authorities might conceivably agree that there was evidence of an extraditable crime having been committed."

When he stopped speaking there was a moment of complete silence. Then the Magistrate, looking at Mullen over the top of his glasses, said, "Thank you," and made a note.

Since everyone had been expecting an explosion this was curiously deflating.

"Please continue, Mr. Bull."

"I have not much to add, sir. Tell me, Mr. Mullen, which of the many departments of the Embassy have you been mainly in touch with since you arrived?"

"With their Security Section, naturally."

"At Axe Lane, in the City."

"Yes. I am also lodging there. I am co-operating with the head of that section, Mr. Fischer Yule, in all cases known to us of persons in this country who are working against our State."

Bull sat down, Mullen tried to leave the witness-box and was restrained by the clerk, who pointed out that Lashmar was on his feet.

He drawled, "A few points, Mr. Mullen. You have explained the nature of your job here. Might we look for a moment at your duties – your very important duties – in your own country. Is it correct that you – how shall I put it – keep an eye on people who do not support the current regime?"

"Put it any way you like."

"And bring them before the Court."

"In certain cases."

"In certain cases, yes. For instance I read in the papers that

85

the preliminary hearings are shortly to begin in what they call the U.D.F. terrorist trial."

"Yes."

"Also – again I rely on the papers – that an application has been made for reopening the trial of the Sharpeville Six on the grounds that one of the State witnesses was assaulted by the police and coerced into giving false evidence."

Mullen, the blood mounting in his face, said, "That appeal is coming shortly before the Court. The grounds of appeal are the usual rigmarole of nonsense put forward by all terrorists when they are caught."

"It was not my purpose to go into the rights and wrongs of that, or any other case – "

No, thought Roger. Your purpose was to annoy the witness and make him lose his temper.

" – it was simply this. With all these complex and important matters requiring your attention at home, how comes it that the authorities have released you for what is almost a non-job in this country?"

"I am a soldier. I go where I am ordered to go."

"What I am questioning is the reality of those orders."

"I don't follow you."

"In answer to my learned friend you said that you had a good deal of information about South African terrorists in this country in your files which you could pass on to the appropriate authorities here."

"That's what I said."

"I wasn't aware that postal communications between this country and South Africa had been permanently suspended."

"What are you talking about?"

"He means," said Mr. Lauderdale, "that this information could equally well have been sent by post."

"If we trusted the English postal authorities."

"Do I understand by that," said Lashmar, "that you were afraid that your letters would be intercepted and allowed to fall into the wrong hands?"

"You can understand whatever you like."

"Surely, if the letters had been enclosed in the diplomatic bag – "

"Everyone knows that your security people regularly rifle our diplomatic bag."

"If when you say 'everyone' you mean to include me," said Mr. Lauderdale sharply, "I must ask to be excluded. I understood that the privacy of the diplomatic bag was strictly observed."

Since it was clear that Mullen was about to say something very rude indeed, Bull rose swiftly to his feet. He said, "I submit, sir, that my learned friend's present line of questioning is straying rather far from the point at issue."

"I am sorry if that is so," said Lashmar. "One or two further points then. You mentioned that you were advising about other terrorists in this country. Could you let us have some details of them?"

"Of course I can't." The contempt in Mullen's voice was clear. "I mentioned Katanga since he has been indiscreet enough to advertise himself in his book. To mention any other names would be a palpable breach of security. Surely even you understand that."

"If you can't mention names, perhaps you could tell us how many such cases you are currently investigating."

"Certainly not."

"Then leaving aside these other – er – shadowy figures which you can tell us nothing about, might I suggest that the real truth of the matter is that you had one reason only for coming here and that was to attend to the extradition of Katanga."

"You can make any unfounded and nonsensical suggestion you like. I can't stop you."

"My suggestion was, in fact, based on two statements made by you yourself. The first was in this Court last week. If I have the record correct you informed the learned Magistrate that you had a lot of work to do, even if he hadn't."

"Work in this country."

"You did not say so. However, your second statement was more specific. You are reported as saying" – Lashmar looked down at his papers and drew a deep breath – "that you only came here to get Katanga extradited and that you never anticipated being here for more than a few weeks."

It was clear to everyone that this shot had hit Mullen between wind and water. For a moment he seemed to have lost his aggressive self-possession altogether. Then, with an obvious effort, he recovered his balance.

"And who am I supposed to have made that asinine remark to?"

"Will you please answer my question? Did you make this comment or not?"

"No."

"You did not make it?"

"That's not what I said. I said, No. I won't answer your question until you answer mine."

Lashmar looked at the Magistrate, who said, "In our Courts, refusal to answer a question properly put to you by Counsel is a serious contempt of Court, for which you can be punished."

"It's not a proper question. How can I be expected to remember every casual comment I've made in the last ten days?"

"If you can't remember, then that is a perfectly proper answer to the question."

"What I'm saying is that *if* I could be informed about who I said it to, then I probably *could* remember it."

The Magistrate said, "I think that's not unreasonable, Mr. Lashmar."

A hurried conference followed between Lashmar and the Crown solicitor. Neither of them looked happy.

Mullen took the opportunity to snarl at them. "If you made the whole thing up, why not be honest enough to admit it? Then we can all go home."

Lashmar straightened up. "I am informed," he said, "that the remark was made to the head of your Security Service in this country, Mr. Yule."

"Then the matter can easily be settled, sir," said a voice from the back of the Court, "since I am present and quite prepared to give evidence. That is, if you think it necessary."

All heads turned. Fischer Yule had risen to his feet and was standing on the left of the front row of spectators. Unquestionably an impressive figure, thought Roger.

The Magistrate said, "Are you the Mr. Yule referred to by Counsel?"

"I am, sir."

"I see. Well, in the ordinary way I am averse to impromptu testimony. But since it seems to me to be of considerable importance to clear this matter up, I have no objection. Subject to the views of Counsel."

"I'm quite agreeable," said Bull.

"I also," said Lashmar, but he didn't sound as happy about it as Bull.

Yule strode forward, took the oath in a practised way and turned to face Lashmar who said, "I need not go back over the last part of my cross-examination. You heard the comment which I suggested that the accused had made. It is suggested that he made it to you."

"The suggestion is incorrect."

"He made no such statement."

"He did not."

This seemed to be the end of the matter, but Lashmar signalled to him to remain. He said, "There was one final matter which I intended to raise with Mr. Mullen, but on reflection it seems to me to be a question of fact which this witness may be able to deal with." Yule bowed fractionally, to suggest that he was prepared to deal with any question of fact that might arise.

"You are probably aware that Section 4 of the Act states that if any question of entitlement to diplomatic immunity should arise a certificate issued under the authority of the Secretary of State is to be conclusive evidence of the matter. So far as you know, Mr. Yule, has any such application been made?"

"I can answer that question. An application has been made, but it has not yet been answered."

"That is unfortunate," said the Magistrate. "However, since it is now past one o'clock I intend to adjourn this hearing until three o'clock. That will give us all time to have something to eat and will give me time to consider the question which now falls to me to decide. The bail to which the accused has surrendered to Court is renewed until three o'clock."

The Police Sergeant, who had been waiting for his cue, bellowed out, "All rise." Those who were seated scrambled to their feet and Mr. Lauderdale disappeared through a door behind the Bench.

Roger said, "That gives him nice time to walk to the Garrick and consume whatever the state of his interior allows him to consume."

"I belong to a more modest club than the Garrick," said Bull. "But it serves reasonable food. See if you can find a taxi,

Roger. I'd like to get Mullen away as quietly as possible. He looks as though he could do with a drink."

Fortunately the crowd which had been milling round the door when they arrived had also decided that it was lunch-time and they were impeded only by a woman carrying a banner which said, 'Down with Apartheid' on one side and 'Support W.A.A.M.' on the other side. They side-stepped her and drove off.

When Mr. Lauderdale reappeared at three o'clock it was clear that an excellently cooked light lunch and sympathetic conversation with his friends had restored him to something approaching good-humour.

He said, "I must confess that I should have been happier" – sharp glances at Bull – "if, as I had hoped, the relevant certificate under Section 4 of the Act *had* been obtained – "

I bet you'd never heard of Section 4 until you were told about it this morning, thought Roger.

"However, if this much-delayed matter is to proceed, it seems that I shall have to come to a decision myself on the evidence which has been presented. Viewing the matter in a common-sense way I have concluded that Mullen is really in this country to carry out one assignment, the extradition of the man called Jack Katanga and therefore that he cannot be considered as a regular member of the Mission. It follows that he is not, in my view, entitled to the diplomatic privileges and exemptions which he seeks. Accordingly – Yes, Mr. Bull?"

"I'm afraid, sir, that I may have to delay this hearing still further. Though not, I trust, for very long. My instructions are that, in the event that you found against my client's con-tention, I was to submit the question on appeal to the Div-isional Court."

"When you say 'not too long' – "

"I have already been in touch with the Crown Office. I told them that I did not anticipate that the argument on this point, if it arose, would occupy more than a day and I have been provisionally offered Thursday, October 25th."

"In that case," said Mr. Lauderdale, with a rare flash of good-humour, "we must wait for ten days so that the Lord Chief Justice and his learned brethren may decide whether I have been talking nonsense or not."

"All rise," said the Sergeant.

10

"Worth a guinea a minute," said the crime reporter of the *Sentinel* to the News Editor. "I thought at one time that Mullen was going to give that la-di-da lawyer a good smack on the kisser."

"Dudley Lashmar?"

"That's the one. Very Eton and Oxbridge. I only wish he had hit him. Then there'd have been something we *could* report."

"A great pity, yes."

"Of course, I don't understand these technical jim-jams, but I did wonder. This ban on reporting. Surely it only covers the case itself. Well, in fact, we didn't get to the case at all."

"I can tell you this," said the News Editor. "We've got to watch our step bloody carefully. Did you know that the Director of Public Prosecutions *and* the Special Branch both had observers in Court?"

"I saw two official-looking bods alongside Yule. I did wonder who they were."

"A lot of people have got an eye on it. And I've had this direct from the boss. We're not to take any risk of being run for contempt of Court. The *News* got done twenty-five thousand pounds and it was a less important case than this might turn out to be."

"I suppose we can write up the protest outside the Court. There was a Waam woman who made a speech."

"Come again."

"Women's Anti-Apartheid Movement. A very powerful lobby."

"All right. Anything outside the building is O.K. But once

you get inside the Court, watch your step."

"It does seem a pity," said the reporter, who was good at his job and hated to see promising news being suppressed. "You realise the whole thing may now go cold until it gets to the Crown Court. *If* it ever does."

"There are one or two ways," said the News Editor thoughtfully, "in which the pot could be kept on the boil – "

"And I am not particularly fond of committing perjury," said Yule.

"Of course not," said Mullen. "Naturally. But it killed the matter dead, didn't it?"

"I see that you don't appreciate the significance of what happened. Will you kindly devote some thought to it. The Crown lawyer put to you, word for word, a statement which you made to me, in this office, some days ago. Lewis Silverborn was the only other person present."

"You don't think that he – "

"That he repeated it to his legal opponents. That is the last thing I would believe. He is a professional and very little given, I should judge, to talking out of turn."

"Well, then – "

"What you said must have been overheard. And since the door was shut, I am forced to arrive at a disagreeable conclusion. I am afraid we have underestimated the opposition. That is why I waited until after the office was shut before talking to you about it."

"You mean we've been bugged."

"That's the only solution that fits the facts, isn't it?"

"I suppose so, but who – ?"

"Our friends from Mornington Square, no doubt. But it's not a question of who. It's a question of how." He cast a speculative glance around his tidy office. "A matter for experts. There's a young man in the Scientific Officers' Department at High Holborn. Before he came here he was attached to one of your sections in Pretoria, I believe. Hartfeldt, or some such name."

"Hartmann, I think you mean. Yes. He did investigation work at one time."

"He can do some more investigation work now."

Young Mr. Hartmann appeared on the following evening after the office had been shut. He brought a colleague with him. Working together, in two hours they took the room to pieces.

The filing cabinets were moved into the centre of the room and their contents were tipped out. Then the desk was treated in the same way. Once they were empty they could be minutely inspected, with an eye to any space in them that was unaccounted for. Two of the floorboards were taken up and the space under the boards was examined with a torch. The wooden wainscoting was prized away in sections and the walls were tapped. The chairs were turned over and their padding was probed with needles. The window-frames were iron and offered little scope for concealment, but the mirror which hung between them, the pictures on the walls and all the objects which had stood on Yule's desk, including the two telephones, were subjected to careful examination.

At the end of two hours Hartmann said, "Either something very elaborate has been done – like burying a transmitter in the wall and plastering it over – or you're clean."

"I don't think anyone would have had time to do anything like that. Even if they got in at night, they'd have to have finished before we opened up again. If you say we're clean, then I can only say I'm sorry to have troubled you."

"No trouble," said the young man. "I used to do a lot of this work back home. Glad of a chance to keep my hand in."

Yule looked at his watch and decided that, if he hurried, he could get to his club in time for dinner. As he was making for the door, Hartmann pointed to the bowler-hat which hung on the far end one of a line of pegs and said, "Not taking your hat with you?"

"That hat!" said Yule. "I bought it when I first came because I was told that it was correct wear for a gentleman in the City. First time I wore it I decided I looked absurd and I've never worn it since."

"Interesting," said Hartmann. He removed the hat gently from its peg. The transmitter was taped inside it.

When Hartmann and his friend had gone Mullen said, very red in the face, "This is an outrage. We must find out who put it there."

"Yes," said Yule. He was holding the little box in his hand, examining it curiously.

"It's going to be a bit difficult, isn't it? You aren't as careful about security here as we are back home. What about that girl who came last week to disinfect the telephones? She was left alone in the room. Only for a minute or two, but quite long enough."

"You're not thinking straight," said Yule. "The person who selected that hat as a hiding-place must have known I never used it."

"In that case – "

"Which means that the only really likely people are my secretary and the three girls next door. They knew about the hat *and* they're in and out of this room all day. Possibly someone from the second floor, but much less likely. If one of them wants to see me he has to come through my secretary's room and if I wasn't here she wouldn't, normally, let them in."

"It's still a wide field."

"I can think of a way of shortening it," said Yule. He was taping the box back into the hat. "First, we'll have to set the scene. I'll get Silverborn – I think we must trust him – to station himself at eleven o'clock at a point in the passage upstairs where he can see into the different offices, or at least move into them quickly. You, I suggest, will be standing between Mrs. Portland's room and the typists' room, with both doors open."

"And you?"

"I shall be in here, preparing a surprise for my staff."

"I hope you know what you're doing."

"It's very simple. They're going to have a race. And I'm going to be the starter." He was smiling as he said this, but not very pleasantly.

Next morning, at one minute before eleven, Yule took down the bowler-hat and placed it on the desk with the open side towards him. Then he took out a small pistol of the sort used for starting races, presented it close to the black box, said "One two three, go" and pulled the trigger.

The report was loud enough to reach the upper floor and Mr. Silverborn had to reassure the work-force and prevent them from coming down to catch the presumed assassin. Mrs. Portland rushed into Yule's office in horror and was relieved to see him standing by his desk, smiling. He pocketed the pistol and joined Mullen in the secretaries' room.

Here all attention was focused on Rosemary, who was slumped, face forward, on her desk, moaning. Mullen stalked over, seized her by the shoulders and shook her. Something tinkled down onto the floor. Mullen picked up the small golden receiver, stowed it away in his pocket and said, "Now we know, don't we? You filthy little spy. If you'd tried a trick like that in our country, you'd have been stripped and whipped."

Rosemary stared at him dazedly.

"Do you hear me, filthy bitch?"

She could see his lips moving, but could hear nothing. Her silence seemed to enrage him. He hit her, a swinging blow, on the side of her face. The ring he was wearing opened a long cut in her cheek.

"I think that's enough," said Yule. "Another effort by our Mornington Square friends, I imagine." And to the girls, "When she comes to her senses, you might tell her that we'll post her papers on to her."

"When she comes to her senses," said Mullen, who still seemed to be beside himself. "Surely you're not letting her stay another minute in this building. Throw the slut out into the street."

Kathleen, who was not lacking in courage, said, "I expect she'd be glad to get away. I know I should." She and Mavis helped Rosemary into her coat and down towards the street door, with an arm round her on each side.

The commissionaire said, "What's going on? I heard a shot."

"It was Mr. Yule," said Kathleen. "One of his jokes. Do you think you could whistle up a taxi?"

The fresh air seemed to have revived Rosemary. She said, "No. Please don't bother, I'm quite all right now."

"Are you sure?"

"Quite sure."

Mavis had brought down her handbag. She used a tissue out of it to dab away the blood from the long cut on her cheek.

"What's it all about?" said the commissionaire.

"Like I told you," said Kathleen, "Mr. Yule's been playing games. And they're not the sort of games that appeal to me, as I'll tell him when I hand in *my* notice."

"I don't expect I shall be staying, either," said Mavis. "Not with that Mullen horror hanging round."

Once she was outside and walking Rosemary felt better. The bomb which had gone off inside her head had blacked her out and deafened her. The thudding had slowed down and she could hear outside sounds again. Her one idea was to get home.

The mid-morning traffic on the underground had sunk to a trickle. Rosemary sank back thankfully into her seat in the half empty carriage. Getting out at the Angel station proved curiously difficult. There were moments when her legs did not seem to belong to her.

"Nearly home now," she said to herself as she set off down Goswell Road. One difficulty was that the pavement was soft. It seemed to be several inches deep in sand, so that she was forced to drag each foot out before she could replant it.

By this time she was not thinking very clearly, but clearly enough to realise that this was nonsense. As she turned into the long straight road which led past the reservoir she was saying, out loud, "This is nonsense. They don't sprinkle deep sand on London pavements."

When she was halfway down the road she noticed that the brick wall on her right, which skirted the reservoir grounds, was moving. First it was a very slight movement, as if the bricks were shaking themselves. Then it became more definite and more menacing. The wall was leaning forward. She saw that it was going to fall on top of her and crush her and that she must get out before it did so. That meant running, which was difficult, because the sand was so deep. The best thing to do was to lie down, quite flat.

A head looked over the wall. It belonged to a boy with red hair. He had pulled himself onto the top of the wall and was preparing to lower himself over it when he saw Rosemary. A shrill whistle, delivered through a gap in his front teeth, brought up two more heads, one blond, one mouse-coloured.

The heads belonged to three boys from the Finsbury Secondary School. They were there at that hour in the morning because the staff at their school had staged a lightning strike. This had enabled the boys to carry out, in daylight, a project over which they would have hesitated later in the day. They had decided to explore the wasteland round the reservoir.

They had pitched their base camp – a blanket over sticks – under the wall and had spent a gruesome, but happy, two hours searching for dead and dismembered bodies. When their stomachs told them it was lunch-time they had returned to camp.

They stared down at Rosemary. Dead, possibly. But not dismembered. Maybe not even dead. They saw one of her legs move. The red head, who was leader of the group, said, "Perhaps she's fainted." The blond boy said, "If she just lies there, she might die of cold. That's what happens when you've had a shock, I was told."

"Get the blanket," said the red head. The tent was dismantled and the blanket was dropped to the pavement. The boys followed it and were getting it tucked round Rosemary when a battered Morris four-door saloon drew up and a young man jumped out. He said, "Hallo, hallo. Killed someone, have you, Ginger? And trying to hide the body."

"Nothing like that, Mr. Tamplin," said the red head, who seemed to know the young man. "We found her here. Put our blanket over her."

"Shock," said the blond boy. "Keep her warm."

"Very sensible," said Fred Tamplin. "First thing to do is find out where she lives. Probably somewhere near here."

He had opened Rosemary's bag and found a City Northern Institute student's card in the name of Rosemary Herbert, address 10 Mornington Square.

"Good," he said. "That's just round the corner. Give us a hand and we'll take her there in the car."

Rosemary was deposited, by four pairs of hands, on the back seat of the car. Ginger, who felt her to be his personal property, got in beside her, the other two boys squashed into the front seat and the rescue party moved off.

The door of the Orange Consortium was opened by Boyo Sesolo. When he saw who it was they had in the car he opened the car door, picked Rosemary out, still wrapped in the blanket, and carried her into the house. Her weight was nothing to his great arms.

By now Fred Tamplin's professional curiosity was beginning to stir. He was the male half of the reporting staff on the *Highside Times and Journal*. With a feeling that a story of some sort was in the offing, he followed Sesolo into the house.

Sesolo started up the stairs, stopping for a moment to bellow something that sounded like 'Colin' or, perhaps, 'Captain'. A voice from higher up shouted, "What is it?" and footsteps came clattering down.

Sesolo jerked his head and said, "This gent brought her. I'll put her on her bed, shall I?"

"Would you do that? Then ring the Whittington Hospital. Ask for emergency and see if they can send a doctor."

Tamplin said, "Actually it was these boys found her. She was lying on the pavement. I happened to be along with my car."

"It was extremely kind of you. My daughter's been a bit under the weather lately. I expect they sent her home from work."

"More sensible if they'd sent her in a taxi. Would you mind very much if I waited until the doctor had seen her? I'd like to be certain she's all right."

Hartshorn looked faintly surprised, but said, "Of course. Why don't you wait in here?"

He opened the door of a small anteroom. It led to the main office from which Tamplin could hear the sound of more than one typewriter being bashed.

"Don't let me keep you," said Tamplin. "You'll want to be with your daughter when she surfaces."

When he was alone he sat for some time trying to make out, from the contents of the room, just exactly what the business of the Orange Consortium might be. He heard what he took to be the doctor arriving and running upstairs. There were four filing cabinets, but these told him nothing since the cards in the shelf slots were simply lettered A–B, C–E and so on. He transferred his attention to the bookshelf in the corner. It contained few books, but a stack of periodicals mostly dealing with South African matters. There were also a number of reports and blue books. One, which he extracted, was titled 'HMSO 134/00019/86 – Report of the Commission set up under the Commonwealth Relations Office as authorised by motion of the House of Commons tabled 13 February 1986'. Tamplin had taken this out to find out exactly what the Commonwealth Relations Office had got worried about in February 1986 when he heard the sound of someone coming downstairs and pushed the book back.

98

He thought it was the doctor, but the steps were much more deliberate. When the door opened and the newcomer appeared it turned out to be an elderly coloured gentleman, with a short grizzled beard and gold spectacles. He had apparently come to collect the cloak and wide-awake hat which were hanging behind the door. He said, "If you are waiting for Mr. Mkeba, I must apologise for keeping you. He is quite free now."

Tamplin had a reporter's memory for faces and names. He said, "Surely you are Professor Leon Macheli. Only the other day I was reading an account of the talk you gave at the London School of Economics and there was a photograph of you in the *Sentinel*."

"I'd no idea I was so famous."

"Your talk seems to have been well received."

"Yes, indeed. The young people showed great interest in what I was able to tell them about conditions in South Africa."

"It's a topic of interest to everyone today. Won't you sit down for a moment? That is, if you're not pressed for time."

"I'm not pressed for anything these days," said the Professor with a gentle smile. "Except, if I might be quite frank with you, for money."

"You're not the only one," said Tamplin. "I don't want to seem inquisitive, but are the people here able to help you?"

"Indeed, they are most generous. I hardly know what my wife and I would do without them. Am I right in thinking that it was you who picked up that poor girl?"

"I and my allies," said Tamplin. He could see the three boys perched on the railing that ran round Mornington Square. "I don't think it was anything more than a faint. The doctor will tell us when he comes down. And I imagine they've sent for her husband."

"Her husband?"

"Rosemary Herbert's husband."

"I'm afraid you've got that quite wrong. The girl upstairs, the one you so kindly picked up, is Rosemary Hartshorn. She's Captain Hartshorn's child. His only one and unmarried, as far as I know."

"Stupid of me. I must have got the name wrong. But tell me, Professor, why are you hiding your light under a bushel?"

"My light – ?"

"You're a well-known man. In your own line, one of the top men."

"It's good of you to say so."

"I'd like to say more and I'd like to say it in print." Tamplin produced his card. "We're not a national newspaper, but we're the one that most people read in this part of London. We've not got so many celebrities living among us that we can disregard one when he does arrive. If you could spare me the time, I'd like to do a piece about your work."

"Well, really," said the Professor, clearly delighted. "I should surmise that you are much busier than I am. But if you would really like to come and have a talk I can show you some papers and photographs which your readers might find interesting."

"I've got one or two things on my plate at the moment, but I should be free of them after the weekend."

Also, though he did not mention this, he disliked working on Saturday since he turned out for the extra 'A' Team of the South-West London Rugby Football Club.

"Should we say Monday morning, then?"

"Eleven o'clock. Right. Excellent. And that sounds like the doctor coming down. Now we'll find out what's what."

The doctor was a plump and cheerful young man more interested, at that stage in his career, in fast cars than in medicine. Also he knew Tamplin well, having fought out many bouts with him on the dart-board in the saloon bar of the Dick Whittington.

He said, "Surprise, surprise. So you were the hero of this episode."

"Nothing very heroic. How is the girl?"

"Fine. She'll do all right now." The doctor seemed to imply that the sight of his cheerful face had effected a medical miracle. "She talks about some sort of explosion inside her head. Could be imagination. Psychosomatic. There's a lot of it about."

Tamplin saw the doctor to his car, said to the boys, "It's all right. I haven't forgotten you," and went back to the house. The Professor, as he was leaving, said, "I'm afraid I haven't a card of my own. But I've written down my address and telephone number."

"Splendid," said Tamplin. "Until eleven o'clock Monday,

then." He watched the Professor drift off and made his way into the house, where he stood for a moment listening.

Every journalistic instinct that he possessed told him that there was something odd about the Orange Consortium, something that would repay investigation. He was convinced by now that it had no connection with the import or export of fruit. The place gave him the impression of an army head-quarters with staff officers in residence. The burly character who had carried off Rosemary had emerged from a door on the first-floor landing. A count of windows had shown four storeys above the ground-floor office, which suggested accommodation for five or six residents. A busy headquarters, he thought. A cosy little self-contained unit. What sort of mischief were they up to? And what about the girl whose name was Hartshorn, but called herself Herbert? He had a shrewd idea of how she had acquired her monumental head-ache and if he was right it raised a number of further ques-tions; questions which, he realised, no one in that building was going to answer.

He made his way back into the small outer office and took down the blue book which he had started to look at. The commission, which the Commonwealth Relations Office had set up in conjunction with the Treasury, had been formed to deal with the financial and political crisis which had been created by the unwillingness of foreign banks in 1985 to roll over outstanding credits to South Africa. Tamplin had only time to glance at the index and read a couple of pages when, thinking he heard someone coming, he replaced the book hastily and moved over to the window.

Two young men were coming up the front steps, students he guessed from the provocatively untidy way in which they were dressed. The larger of the two, who had a mop of fair hair, was limping.

They did not pause at the front door, but came straight in and climbed the stairs. He heard them knock on the door on the first landing and a murmur of voices. Friends, it seemed, of the large character who had taken charge of Rosemary. He was returning to the bookcase when a clatter of descending footsteps announced a new arrival – this time it was the Captain.

"Well," he said, "you'll be glad to hear that my daughter is

101

back on her feet again." He had left the door open and the suggestion that it was time for Tamplin to go was clear, if unspoken.

"I am indeed glad to hear it," said Tamplin. "And my only reason for staying so long is that I'm holding what you might call a proxy for the boys. The fact is, they want their blanket back."

"Good heavens! Of course. I'd forgotten. They shall have it."

When the Captain reappeared with the blanket he produced three pound coins. He said, "Would you, as their representative, give one to each of the boys, together with my thanks."

"I'll do that," said Tamplin.

The boys seemed more relieved at getting the blanket back – it had been 'borrowed' by Ginger from his parents' bedroom – than they were excited by the money. However, they cheered up when Tamplin suggested a visit to one of the teashops in Goswell Road. An explorer's lunch of sandwiches had left a void which needed filling. Fortified by buns, the boys were very willing to speculate about the Orange Consortium, but were a bit short on facts.

The blond boy, who was the only one who lived in the immediate neighbourhood, agreed that it was an odd set-up because, although he had seen a lot of people going in and out ('blacks and whites') there had been no sign of the vans and lorries which should have indicated a trade in fruit. He said that he'd heard that they'd once had a visit from the police.

This sounded more promising, but it seemed that it had only been connected with complaints by the neighbours about late-night parties. "It's that big buster," said the blond boy. "He's a weight-lifter, or sumpun. He's got a lot of big tough friends."

It was time to get back to work. Tamplin left behind enough money to pay the bill and to cover a further round of buns and departed amid expressions of gratitude.

11

The offices of the *Highside Times and Journal* were a modest set of rooms in the Pentonville Road. Gilbert Glaister, who was both editor and part proprietor of the paper, listened patiently to what Fred Tamplin had to say. He was patient because he realised that Fred was really a cut above them and would leave them, sooner or later, for one of the national papers.

Tamplin said, "I think I know what happened to Miss Hartshorn/Herbert. In my last job one of our youngsters was doing a bit of industrial espionage on the side. He got caught the same way. It made him deaf for a week."

"Who do you imagine that girl was spying on?"

"If I'm right about what the Orange crowd are up to, it was probably one of the official or semi-official South African outfits."

"It's odd you should say that," said Mr. Glaister, turning over the papers on his untidy desk. "I've got something here Bonnie put in — " Bonnie Parker was the female half of his reporting staff. "Yes. Here it is. She looked in at the Mullen hearing at Bow Street. I couldn't use it, because of the reporting ban, but it seems that Crown Counsel really rocked Mullen by putting to him something he was supposed to have said to Yule — he's Head of Security. Yule denied it, so it didn't come to anything, but Bonnie got the impression that Yule was lying and it *had* been said."

"It adds up," said Tamplin. "All the same, it seems a bit offside. I mean, it's the sort of thing the defence might do, using a spy to worm out awkward stuff, in an effort to help their client, but surely not the prosecution. Not the Crown. They're meant to play straight down the middle."

The two men looked at each other. Both had glimpsed the possibilities, the dangerous and exciting possibilities behind the story that chance had tossed to them. Finally Mr. Glaister said, "You commented just now that it 'all added up'. What I'm wondering is just what it does add up to. Is it the beginning of an official drive to crucify Mullen – howled on by the popular press? That must be what the *Sentinel* thinks. They've floated out a decoy duck and I'd guess the hidden guns are all ready to open fire."

He pushed across a copy of that day's issue of the *Sentinel*. "It's in the correspondence column. I've never seen anything more deliberately provocative in my life."

To the Editor:

Dear Sir,

I happened to be in Court at Bow Street on Monday when Karl Mullen, a South African diplomat, was being charged with some offence. I cannot be more precise about it, since the details were never explained to us.

I am not a lawyer, but I am a close follower of legal cases and it seemed perfectly clear to me that Mr. Mullen should not have been in Court at all. The Ambassador had stated that he was a member of his staff and that being so, by all existing rules and understandings, he was exempt from legal process in our Courts. I do not pretend that I am enamoured of this principle. It is irritating when a hundred minor functionaries park in prohibited spots and escape paying a fine. But the principle has long been established on grounds of international amity and reciprocal treatment and if ever there was a case in which it should have been respected, this surely was one such. Mr. Mullen is a man of standing in his own country and is here on an important mission. This seemed to provoke the Crown Counsel who indulged in one of the most spiteful and inconsequent cross-examinations that I have ever listened to. But this was not what I found most objectionable.

No, sir. What alarmed and upset me was the attitude of the presiding Magistrate. He should, above all things be, and be seen to be, impartial. He may not approve, personally, of the policies of the present South African government, but this does not in any way excuse his conduct. He had demonstrated his bias on a previous

104

occasion by criticising South African justice. Now he showed his feelings even more clearly by constantly interrupting what the accused was trying to say, by adopting a hectoring tone towards him and by addressing him, without courtesy, as 'Mullen', as though he had been proved to be a common sneak thief.

No doubt the Divisional Court will put him right on the law. The press, I think, should correct his manners.

I am, sir, yours faithfully,
Lover of Justice
(Name and address supplied)

"Sailing pretty close to the wind," said Tamplin.

"I don't think they can do him for contempt. He takes care to mention that he is not discussing the rights and wrongs of the case. No. It's quite clear what the *Sentinel* is up to. As soon as that letter is read, you can bet your boots they'll have forty or fifty answers to it. All of them anti-Mullen. Some will be from people who don't like to see our legal system criticised. Some from anti-apartheid fanatics and a few from people who were actually in Court and will know – from what Bonnie has told me – that in fact the Magistrate behaved well, under considerable provocation."

"And once the hunt is up, the other papers will follow."

"I'd guess so."

"And us?"

"Playing tail-end Charlie to the big boys isn't going to get us anywhere. That's clear. What we have to do is get some facts. If the facts turn out to be in Mullen's favour, we publish them."

"Lovely," said Tamplin. "We can be on the unpopular side for once."

"I don't object to being unpopular," said Mr. Glaister. "I only object to bankruptcy. By which I mean, carry on, but watch your step."

"Discretion shall be my watchword."

"Where were you planning to start?"

"I've got a date with Professor Leon Macheli on Monday. Incidentally, he'd be worth writing up on his own accord. I understand he really is a top expert on the structure of crystals. He published a book last year called *A Study of Cleavages*."

"It must have had a terrific sale," said Glaister.

When Fred Tamplin left the headquarters of the Orange Consortium and drove off with the three boys he was under observation from the window of the top-storey flat. Rosemary was lying back in a chair by the fire, recovered from her experiences except for an occasional 'ping' inside her head, as though someone was touching off a bicycle bell. Andrew Mkeba was watching her anxiously. He seemed to feel more responsibility than Rosemary's father for what had happened.

The Captain was looking out of the window. He said, "There he goes. A real sticker, that young man."

"Who? The one who brought Rosemary back?"

"Curious about us, too. He spent part of his time in our outer office reading one of the blue books. How do I know? Because he put it back in the wrong place and upside down."

"He probably read it to pass the time."

"Maybe. You can never tell with these newspaper men."

"He was – ?"

"That's right. A reporter on the local rag. It's on his car."

Rosemary, who had been listening to this, sat up and said, "Do you mean he's going to make a story out of it."

"I hope not. But I did overhear the doctor talking to him. A bit indiscreet for a medico, I thought. No sign of outside damage, he said, but an explosion inside the head. Well, that's not a newspaper story by itself. But it would become one if they could link it back to Yule's office."

"All I want to know," said Mkeba explosively, "is what we're going to do to that bastard. He hit her, didn't he? Cut her cheek. In the presence of two witnesses. That's assault. Maybe grievous bodily harm. We should report him to the police. Prefer charges."

"There are two very good reasons," said the Captain calmly, "for doing nothing of the sort. The first is that it would give the press a straight lead back to Axe Lane. Which, as you'd have heard, if you'd been listening to me, is just the thing we *don't* want. The second reason is even more important. When we got Rosemary her job we had to fake up a P45 form in the name of Rosemary Herbert. Details of last job, name of employer, date of leaving and so on. That's so that they could get her tax code right. Well, I needed help for that and got an old

106

friend of mine in the City to co-operate. If we now have to reveal that Miss Herbert is really Miss Hartshorn and had never been employed by this other firm – and if we started proceedings that would almost certainly come out – then my obliging friend would get into trouble. Serious trouble."

"We mustn't do that," said Rosemary. "I mean, I wasn't really hurt."

Mkeba was still out for blood. Someone's blood. He said, "I'll tip off Boyo. If that reporter comes sniffing round here he'll get something to remember us by."

"No," said Hartshorn. "I don't think I'd do that, Andrew. It's only a side issue. Let's keep our guns pointed at the target we really want to hit. Mr. Karl Mullen."

"What I'd really like to do," said Mkeba, "is give him a touch of his own pencil drill."

On Saturday morning, over breakfast in his digs, Fred Tamplin studied the correspondence columns of the *Sentinel*. He saw exactly what his editor had meant. A comment at the head of the column said, 'We have received forty-eight letters in reply to the one we published on Wednesday from a Lover of Justice. Forty-seven of them were hostile to the opinions he expressed. We have, of course, been careful to exclude from publication any which expressed views on the actual case, or those which were extreme in their wording, but the following will give our readers a sample of public opinion on this interesting case.'

If the half-dozen letters which followed were among the most reasonable, thought Tamplin, the others must have been fairly hot.

To the Editor:

Dear Sir,

My friends sometimes accuse me of being a chauvinist. This odd French word has had many different translations. To me it means, quite simply, that I put my own country first. The writer of the letter which you saw fit to publish last Wednesday apparently puts his own country last. And not only last, but behind a country like South Africa which has affronted every canon of civilised conduct. The latest sample of its citizenry, a man called Mullen, stands charged with the offence of shop-lifting. It seems that, rather than face this charge squarely, he is now trying to hide behind the doctrine of diplomatic privilege – a privilege developed in an age when one could, at least, rely on diplomats being gentlemen of honour, sent here by countries which respected the rule of law –

Dear Sir,

    I wonder how a Lover of Justice (self-styled) had the effrontery to write to you in the terms that he did and how you dared to publish his letter. Surely the appropriate comment was the one made by the magistrate when the matter first came before him. 'Put your own house in order before you criticise others' –

Dear Sir,

    As it happens I was in Court when the loud-mouthed bully now charged with a criminal offence was at Bow Street. In my view, far from treating him without respect, the magistrate would have been fully justified in finding the accused guilty of gross contempt of court –

Dear Sir,

    I also am a lover of justice so let me give some advice to Lover of Justice whose fatuous letter you published on Wednesday and to Karl Mullen, an unwelcome visitor to these shores –

Dear Sir,

    As an old Eighth Army man who remembers the surrender of Tobruk –

Truly, thought Fred Tamplin, they have let down their nets and have trawled up some fine fish.

He did not suppose that the correspondence, if he happened to read it, would prick Mullen's thick skin, but he had a feeling that if the matter came before a jury, it might be difficult to empanel twelve disinterested citizens. He wondered whether, in subsequent issues, the Sentinel might restore the balance by publishing a few letters on the other side. He guessed not.

The hunt was up and the hounds were beginning to cry.

12

"I'm not sure," said Professor Macheli, "how much you know about crystallography."

"Practically nothing," said Tamplin, "but don't let that worry you. I'm a great picker of other people's brains. So fire ahead."

"You must understand that my speciality is physical crystallography. That is to say, the study of the physical features of the crystalline form and their optical properties. These, as perhaps you know, can be uniaxial or biaxial. Take, for instance, a cubic octahedron – "

Fred listened patiently, understanding about one word in six. This did not bother him, nor did it distract him from observing the clean but shabby sitting-room and the signs which his experienced eye quickly noted of poverty near to, but not yet on the wrong side of, the subsistence line. He thought that the Professor was a nice, simple old man, and he decided that, without diverting from his main objective, he would do anything to help him that he could.

When the Professor had finished with the oblique rhomboidal prism and the double six-sided pyramid, and had paused for breath, he said, "Is it right that you've written a book on the subject of cleavages?"

A twinkle appeared in the Professor's eye. He said, "My – er – daughter Anna has explained to me that the word cleavage has a possible secondary meaning. I was not, of course, aware of that. Yes, I have written such a book. It was intended for popular consumption and I was therefore forced to simplify the subject."

"Just what I had in mind. Do you think you could write,

say, four or five thousand words on your subject – what you might call an introduction to crystallography for the layman? I'm sure we'd be happy to publish it in our weekend magazine section, with some of those really beautiful coloured photographs you've shown me. Our rate for such an article is around five pence a word."

"Well – " said the Professor, doing some rapid mental arithmetic, "I'm sure that would be very gratifying."

"I'd do a short piece, introducing you to our readers. If I'm to do that, I'd have to know a little about your past. When you came here and why. That sort of thing."

"When is easy. I came here about three years ago. Why is more difficult. I think the simplest way of putting it is that I was scared. South African forces have made so many incursions lately into neighbouring territories that they no longer feature as leading stories in the press of this country."

"I remember one. A surprise attack into Botswana, which ended in a lot of deaths – including a six-year-old girl. That's the sort of thing which does get reported here."

"The Lesotho raid was about six months after that one. We were living in Maseru at the time. That's on the western border. In fact, it's the only big town in Lesotho – I'll show you on the map – and you can see that it's the terminus of the railway which runs in from South African territory. From Johannesburg in the north and Kimberley in the west."

Tamplin examined the map. Lesotho, of which he had never heard before that morning, seemed to be very small and full of mountains. He said, "You're right. Maseru is the front door into the country."

"The back door out of it, too, I'm afraid. I mean that it's a convenient way for anyone from Mozambique or Zimbabwe who wants to get into South Africa without calling attention to themselves. We knew that there were a number of ANC supporters lying up, waiting for a chance to slip across. I suppose the South Africans knew it too. Anyway they descended on us one night, with tanks and armoured cars, and destroyed a number of houses – and people. None of them were anything to do with the ANC. There were no apologies. In fact, their State Security Council published a statement saying that they would probably repeat the dose. That's when I decided to leave."

111

"Don't blame you."

"It took a little time to arrange, but I had been a student at the Physics Department of London University and they supported my application. I was put in touch with the Orange Consortium. They arranged this house for me and got me some lecturing work. Things became a lot easier when my – when Anna got a job."

Tamplin said, with a smile, "I can't help noticing, Professor, that every time you mention Anna it seems to cause you some difficulty. I'm unable to make out whether she's your daughter, your granddaughter or your god-daughter."

"To be frank with you," said the Professor, "she isn't any of the three. She's an orphan, who came to work for us when she was about twelve. That was – let me see – it must have been six years ago. My wife and I have both become very fond of her and she pleaded not to be left behind, so in the end – I tell you this in strict confidence – I included her in my application as my daughter."

"Not a very serious offence and in anything I write, if she features at all, it shall be as your daughter. Her job you mentioned – "

"That was rather a coincidence. It turned out to be working for the author of that book everyone's talking about – "

"Jack Katanga?"

"Yes. It seems he moved house and could no longer employ the woman, a Mrs. Queen, who used to look after him – "

Tamplin was not really listening. He was trying to absorb the astonishing piece of information which had been dropped into his lap. He was uncertain what it meant, but sure that it meant something.

He said, "Katanga is one of the most interesting men to have come here from your country lately. I shall want to have a word with him. I wonder if you could give me his address."

"Certainly. It's called the Homestead, in West Mead Close, on the west side of Putney Heath – "

Having got the information he was angling for, Tamplin was now anxious to get away, but not wishing to forfeit the Professor's good opinion of him he sat on patiently for a further twenty minutes. When crystallography surfaced again he felt that it was time to apply the closure. He said. "I'll leave you to get on with that piece you're going to write for me. If you remember to keep it fairly simple, I'm sure it'll be what we want. Tell your wife I was sorry to miss her."

He had parked his car some yards down the road, opposite a tobacconist's shop. The words *Highside Times and Journal* were painted on the panel of the car door on the passenger's side. This had often proved useful. More than one promising story had started from people stopping him in the streets and talking to him.

The proprietor of the shop, who had been standing in the doorway, now came out and said, "You a reporter?"

"I am," said Tamplin. "Why?"

"Want a story?"

"Clean or dirty?"

The tobacconist sniggered and said, "I mean a real story. A news story."

"You can try me. But keep it short."

"I saw you coming out of that house. I can tell you something very interesting about the people who live there."

"Carry on."

"How much?"

"How much what?"

"What I mean is, how much will you pay me for this story?"

"You must be mistaking us for *The Times* or the *Telegraph*. We haven't got money to buy stories." So saying Tamplin opened the door of the car, but unhurriedly. He could see that the man was bursting to talk to him.

"Don't be like that," said Mr. Sundridge hastily. "I thought newspapers always paid for info. But I'll tell you what. If it turns out to be a story you can publish, will you mention my name? Jimmy Sundridge."

"Yes. I expect we could do that."

"Well, it happened the Saturday before last. Or rather, on Saturday *and* Sunday. They were here both days – "

When Mr. Sundridge had finished Tamplin said, "So who were these men? Did you get their names?"

"Not their names. But I know the firm they worked for. They showed me their card. City Detectives. It was an address in London Wall – "

"Do you think they were telling you the truth?"

"About the girl, you mean. And men-friends visiting her. No. I didn't really swallow that bit. I mean, why would men

113

come to the house where she's living with her father and mother? Both respectable people, I'd guess."

"Then what do you think they were doing?"

"I think they'd been following her, from wherever it was she'd come from. And then they followed her to see where she was going."

"Doesn't add up, really, does it? You say you've seen her before, coming here at lunch-time on Saturday and pushing off again on Sunday evening. Which means she's got a resident job somewhere and has the weekends off. Right?"

"I suppose that's right, yes."

"Then if they'd followed her from where she came from, why would they want to follow her back again to find out where it was?"

"When you put it like that, it does sound a bit odd," said Mr. Sundridge. He had a feeling that his story had fallen flat. "All I'm telling you is what happened, see."

"No one can do more than that," said Fred Tamplin blandly. "If it should come to anything I'll see you're not forgotten."

Chief Inspector Ancrum of West End Central Police Station studied, without pleasure, the document which had landed on his desk. Having read it through he handed it to his colleague, Inspector Brailey, and said, "What do you make of that?"

"Trouble," said the Inspector. "That's what it means. Trouble. Why can't these types stay at home? We don't want them here."

"Whether we want them or not," said Ancrum, "we've got 'em."

He quoted from the document in front of him.

"'It would seem that on the last occasion on which Karl Mullen appeared in Court at Bow Street in connection with a charge against him of shop-lifting there was a considerable public presence both inside and outside the Court.'"

"For 'public presence'," said Brailey, "substitute 'a shower of half-baked loonies'."

"'The appeal to the Divisional Court on the question of diplomatic privilege is now fixed for Thursday, October 25th. Either it will be successful or it will not.'"

"Amazing the way these Special Branch characters work

things out."

"'In either case, it will be remitted to the stipendiary, for the case to be dismissed, or for it to proceed. In both instances the reaction of the public is likely to be unfriendly to Mullen.'"

"'Unfriendly' means they'd like to castrate him."

"'It is therefore important that the police presence should be adequate.'"

"Adequate to restrain the public presence," said Brailey. "What a crowd they are. Why can't they look after these diplomats themselves? It's what they're paid to do."

"This Thursday," said Ancrum thoughtfully. "Better start looking at the leave rosters."

13

The following morning Fred Tamplin headed for Putney.

When he reached West Mead Road he drove past the turning to West Mead Close and parked his car some way along. The Close ran between the Convent of the Sacred Heart on one side and a plot of open ground on the other. There was only one house in it, a small two-storey building at the far end. A highly desirable location, he thought, for someone in search of privacy. He wondered by what string-pulling Katanga had secured it.

His glance had shown him a smart blue run-about parked outside the front gate. Jack Katanga's car, he supposed. He thought it would be worth waiting to see if Katanga emerged. The ostensible reason for his visit was to discuss Katanga's book, but he had a feeling that he would get more of the sort of information he really wanted if he could find Dorothy Katanga on her own.

Twenty minutes later his patience was rewarded. Katanga came out, jumped into the car and drove off. Tamplin gave him two minutes to get clear, then walked back to the Homestead and rang the bell.

The door was opened by an attractive black girl. She kept one foot behind the half-opened door and said, "Yes?"

"I'd like a word with Mr. Katanga."

"He's out."

"Then perhaps with Mrs. Katanga. I'm from the *Highside Times*." He pushed a card through the opening. The girl took it and retreated, leaving the door on the chain. He heard a murmur of voices, then she reappeared, removed the chain and said, "You can come in."

116

He followed her down the short hall into the room at the back, which was full of sunshine, with a bow window overlooking a neat garden. Dorothy Katanga was sitting in a chair under the window, with an embroidery frame in her lap. His files had told him something of her history. The mission-reared little girl, who had defied her father and married at eighteen, was still there, somewhere, but hidden by the passage of time and the disciplines of experience. Tamplin had spent much of his professional life studying faces. He examined her with interest. Her eyes were grey; neither the slate-grey of morning nor the velvet-grey of evening, but an indefinite midday-grey. There was determination in the lines of the chin, contradicted by a charming dimple in the middle of it. Not an easy woman to assess.

He noticed that the girl, who must be Anna Macheli, had settled down in a chair beside the kitchen door.

Taking out his notebook he embarked on a few of the routine questions he had prepared. Had it been difficult to get out of Mozambique? Yes, very difficult. When they got here, had they been helped over immigration formalities and over finding somewhere to live? The Orange Consortium had been most helpful. So who were they? They were an organisation opposed to the policies of the South African government, which assisted people who had escaped from it; they seemed to have quite a lot of money and were generous with it.

Had she any relations in England? Only her father. He had a living in Norfolk.

His earlier questions had been dealt with confidently. They were questions she had been asked and had answered many times before. When he mentioned her father he had felt, for the first time, that he might be trespassing. He concluded that he would get franker answers if they were alone. He swung round on Anna and said, "Talking of fathers, I had a very interesting discussion with your – er – father yesterday."

The inference, if a little pointed, hit home all right. Anna looked uncomfortable. Dorothy Katanga noticed it and seemed surprised. So, thought Tamplin, she doesn't know about that little deception. Interesting.

Seeing that Anna was upset, Dorothy said, "Do you think you could get us all a cup of coffee, love?" Anna whisked off into the kitchen and shut the door behind her.

117

"A nice girl," said Tamplin. "You were lucky. Home helps are difficult to get these days. How did you get onto her?"

"Someone sent us a note, out of the blue, giving details about her and mentioning the sort of salary she would expect – which was far from excessive. We snapped her up as quickly as possible. And now I hardly know what we should do without her. When we were in Hammersmith we had a woman – a Mrs. Queen. That was convenient, because she lived right next door. But Anna's people are the other side of London."

"Then I imagine you have to be reasonable about time off."

"We allow her from after breakfast on Saturday to Sunday supper-time. That means she only works a five-day week, but we pay her for seven."

"A generous arrangement. On the other hand, I suppose it's nice for you to have your husband to yourself for two days in the week."

Dorothy looked up sharply and then said, "Yes, of course."

"And I imagine your father comes to visit you sometimes."

"My father? No. He would not come here. He would not be welcome if he did."

A flush had come into her face, colouring her high cheek-bones with a crimson slash.

"Do I gather, then, that your father doesn't approve of your husband?"

"He hates him. You look surprised. Of course he hates him. He was immensely kind to Jack as a boy. He had him into his house. He gave him hours of instruction. And then – how did he show his gratitude? By stealing his daughter and – I am giving you his view – by dishonouring him."

"Not a very Christian view, surely."

"I suppose he's a Christian. But if he prays at all, he is praying that Jack will be sent back to Mozambique."

"Even though he would be going to his death."

"Because he would be."

The flushed patches had faded from her face leaving her very pale.

"Well," said Tamplin lightly, "it looks as though Mullen has got one supporter in this country at least."

Conscious that she had said more than she meant to, Dorothy added, "I must ask you not to print anything about that."

"I'll respect your confidence," said Tamplin with a smile. "But perhaps I might advise you to be a little more careful when dealing with representatives of the popular press."

As Anna arrived with the coffee, the doorbell sounded. Dorothy, who had just picked up her cup, started and slopped some of the coffee into the saucer.

"It's a woman," said Anna. "I saw her coming up the path. Don't worry. She don't look like a reporter."

"Then show her in. And fetch another cup."

The woman who came in certainly bore no resemblance to any reporter Tamplin had ever met. She looked, he thought, like a crow. Wrong. Not a crow. When you took in her glossy black coat with its discreet white frontal, her sharp nose and her beady black eyes, you realised that she was a magpie; an inquisitive, bouncing magpie with its eyes wide open for treasure.

"Why," said Dorothy, "if it isn't Mrs. Queen! How sweet of you to come all that way to pay us a visit."

"Not such a great way, my dear. Over Hammersmith Bridge, a bus down the Fulham Palace Road, a bus up Putney Hill and there I was. Almost, as you might say, on your doorstep."

In fact, nearly a mile to go, thought Tamplin, but a mile would mean nothing to those stout little legs. The accent puzzled him. Not cockney, certainly. Original West Country, perhaps, overlaid with big city sophistication. Devonshire cream in an East London supermarket.

"And how is everything back in Hammersmith?"

"We've missed you, love, that's a fact. The man who's got your house, he's a clurk. He's got five squalling kids and a wife who squalls louder'n them. Oh, thank you, me dear. I always think a cup of coffee's welcome at this time in the morning. I hope you look after the family as well as what I did."

"I hope I do," said Anna and bolted back into the kitchen.

"That's a pretty child," said Mrs. Queen. "Got a good figure, too." She sounded like a Roman matron examining an item from the slave market. "It must be a great comfort to your husband having her here, I'm sure."

Dorothy's head jerked up. Before she could speak, Mrs. Queen added smoothly, "Look how nice she keeps the house. I'm sure she's a better polisher than what I was." She swung

119

round to bring Tamplin under her guns. "The gentlemen of the press are here, I see."

His car had been fully twenty yards up the road, but those button eyes wouldn't have missed it.

"I suppose you're here about that book Mr. Katanga's written. Soon as I heard about it I went to our library and put my name down for it, but they told me it'd be months before I got it, it's that popular."

Dorothy said, "Perhaps my husband would lend you a copy."

"Do you think he would?" The idea pleased Mrs. Queen. "We didn't always hit it off. Not altogether. I had to stand up for myself, you know. But after a round or two we came to respect each other." Switch to Tamplin. "I couldn't altogether blame them for leaving Hammersmith. It was the neighbours. A nasty narrow-minded crowd, I called them. Their tongues longer than their noses." Back to Dorothy. "But I'll say this for you, dear. You've fallen on your feet and no mistake. You couldn't hardly have found a more sheltered love-nest."

There was a hint of malevolence in the way Mrs. Queen enunciated the words 'love-nest'. Tamplin thought, if I knew what was really going on inside that bird-brain of yours I might have a chance of understanding these people.

One thing was clear. He had caught Dorothy looking down at her watch more than once. So, she was hoping that Mrs. Queen would have finished her coffee and hopped away before her husband came back. Mrs. Queen did not seem to share her apprehension. She had settled herself comfortably in her chair. If the master of the house returned she was more than ready for him.

All the time that she was speaking her head had been swivelling round as she appraised the contents of the room. Now she switched back to Dorothy. "Your husband must be doing well, with his books and his articles, love. And now he's got himself involved in this shop-lifting business and that horrible policeman from South Africa. We're all following it in the papers. As good as a serial on the television. You can't tell what's going to happen next." Back to Tamplin. "It's all publicity, isn't it, sir?"

He said, "You hear people say, sometimes, that all publicity is good publicity even when it's bad. Actually, I don't believe that's true."

"Well, you should know. You're in the game, aren't you? Isn't that his car? I hope it is. I'd like to see the great man again."

It's what you came down here for, thought Tamplin. This could be interesting.

When Katanga strode into the room he upset most of Tamplin's preconceptions. He was a very good-looking man. As a boy, before life and responsibility had thickened him, he must have been stunning. The gossip columns had skirted delicately over his ancestry, but all of them had mentioned the Swedish blood. There was assurance in his face and bearing, but no arrogance, and there were lines round his eyes and mouth which might have been lines of humour, but could equally have been lines of cynicism. Mrs. Queen had called him the great man. He was not great yet and, hopefully, had enough humility to know it. But the promise of greatness was there all right.

"Well, if it isn't my Queenie," he said, "This is a surprise."

"A nice surprise, I hope, sir."

"Of course. What else could it be? Your brains are matched only by your unchanging beauty."

"Soft soap."

Ranging rounds, thought Tamplin. If battle were to be joined, it would not be one-sided. As a boy on a farm, he had seen magpies mobbing an eagle-owl.

"Would you like a cup of coffee?" said Dorothy hastily.

"Coffee?" said Mrs. Queen. "Half past twelve isn't coffee time, is it? Not unless I'm losing my memory. A glass of whisky before dinner and another one, or maybe two, before supper. That was the regular drill, wasn't it?"

"You've an excellent memory," said Katanga. "But there's one thing I must correct you about. Now that we've moved up in the world, we call what we eat in the middle of the day lunch, not dinner."

"Oh dear, oh dear. You'll have to forgive my vulgar ways," said Mrs. Queen, with a touch of pink in her cheeks.

Katanga had extracted a bottle of Haig from the corner cupboard. Now he paused in front of the sideboard to select one of the glasses on it. There was a larger one, Tamplin saw, half hidden behind a pile of books; not a drinking glass, more

121

an open-mouthed glass pipkin of the sort chemists use for mixing their brews.

"Careful to pick the right glass," chirruped Mrs. Queen. "We don't want another accident, do we?"

If she hadn't been piqued she wouldn't have said that, thought Tamplin. Katanga swung round. "And just what exactly do you mean by that?"

"Nothing, sir. Nothing at all. What should I mean?"

"I'll get you some ice from the fridge," said Dorothy, half-way out of her chair.

"Stay where you are," said Katanga. He turned about and made for the kitchen. Dorothy gave a small sigh.

The kitchen was only divided from the living-room by a partition and they could hear Katanga talking to Anna. He had evidently recovered his temper – if, indeed, he had lost it – and Anna was laughing at something he was saying.

By the time he came back with the drink, Mrs. Queen had, at last, concluded that she had outstayed her welcome. She had extracted herself from her chair and recovered her umbrella which, like so many Londoners, she carried more as a walking-stick and a weapon than as shelter from the rain.

"Are you off?" said Katanga, just politely enough. "Could I give you a lift home, perhaps?"

"In that nice new car of yours?" said Mrs. Queen. "That would be a treat. I hope you don't have the same trouble starting it as you did with the old one."

The silence which followed this innocent remark was crackling with undischarged electricity. Tamplin realised that the principals were so intent on their private fight that they had almost forgotten he was there. He decided, reluctantly, to break it up. Climbing to his feet, he said, "No need to drag Mr. Katanga away from his lunch. I can easily run you home myself."

"Two gentlemen competing to do me favours," simpered Mrs. Queen. "I'll entrust myself to the gentleman from the press, if it isn't taking him too far out of his way."

"Hammersmith is on my way."

"Then I have great pleasure in accepting."

Whether it was a pleasure for her or not, one thing was clear to Tamplin. The thought of him having the chance of a private talk with Mrs. Queen was no pleasure to either of the

Katangas. *Very* interesting.

As they were bowling north up Putney Park Lane, Tamplin said, "As it happens, I know the Castelnau area well. When I first came to London I lived just south of Hammersmith Bridge, in Riverview Gardens."

"To think of that. Not a long way from my little house. The world's a small place, isn't it? Do I gather that you've moved off now?"

"I had to move away when I got my job on the *Highside Times*. But I didn't lose touch. I'd started playing rugby for South-West London. They use the Mill Lodge ground. So, most Saturdays, there I am, back again."

"Rugby?" said Mrs. Queen. "That's the game with the funny-shaped ball, isn't it? I saw on television that girls were playing it now. I fancy I might have enjoyed that."

Just the right shape for a front row forward, thought Tamplin. They proceeded in silence for a minute. Mrs. Queen, he knew, had something to say and sooner or later she was going to say it.

It came as they slowed to cross the Upper Richmond Road. "Tell me, Mr. Tamplin, does your paper pay money for information?"

"Occasionally. Very small sums. We usually call them expenses. It makes our informants feel more comfortable about it."

"Small sums," said Mrs. Queen thoughtfully. "Even when the information is so important that it might make a lot of difference?"

"The trouble is that we're not a very important paper. Not one of the big league."

"But if you was to get hold of a story the others hadn't got, that might give you a lift into the big league."

"True," said Tamplin. He was aware that he was dealing with a much tougher character than the newsagent, Sundridge. Whatever this lady had for sale he would not get it for blarney. He said, "What sort of sum had you in mind?"

"Should we say five hundred pounds? Half of it down and the other half when you've used the information."

The promptness with which Mrs. Queen rattled this off made it clear to Tamplin that the project had been taking shape in her mind for some time. When he said nothing she reverted to her wheedling tone. "Jackie Katanga's an important man, isn't he?"

"He's a witness in a criminal case which wouldn't ordinarily take up more than half a dozen lines in any paper."

"Come along, sir, come along. Don't talk about lines. I can read between lines. Maybe the shop-lifting isn't all that important, but being in the case is making his name known, isn't it? He's going places, isn't he?"

"You could be right and when he gets there maybe we'll come back and see what it is you've got for sale."

"And maybe by that time," said Mrs. Queen tartly, "you'll find you're not at the head of the queue. It's Boswell Road we want. First on the right."

They had crossed Hammersmith Bridge by now and were in Barnes Avenue. Up to this point he had not needed directions. It was familiar territory. Barnes Avenue led to the home ground of the South-West London Club and they were, at that very moment, passing the Secretary's flat which he had so often attended on selection nights.

"Turn right at that telephone box. That's the one. My little home-from-home is number 9. I share it with my married sister and her husband. *Their* children are all grown-up, thank the Lord. Are you married, Mr. Tamplin?"

"Not yet."

"You're lucky. It's usually a mistake."

"Was yours?"

"Since you ask," said Mrs. Queen, "I'll be frank with you. My husband is what you might call a figment. I felt it due to my age and position that people should start addressing me as a married woman, that's all it was. Here we are and thanks for the lift. I've a feeling we shall be seeing more of each other. Goodbye to you."

Tamplin watched as she hopped nimbly up the front steps. Numbers 7 and 9 Boswell Road, though not semi-detached, were so squashed together that they might, without loss of dignity, have edged up a yard closer and completed the attachment. When the Katangas had lived in No. 7 they and the Queen household must have been very much in each other's laps.

As Mrs. Queen went in and slammed the front door behind her, Tamplin moved forward slowly. Boswell Road was a one-

124

way street with cars parked nose to tail along the nearside. At the far end he had a choice. He could turn right and re-cross Hammersmith Bridge, heading back to *Highside* and an overdue lunch. Or he could turn left and park in a spot wellknown to him between his own club ground and the playing fields of St. Paul's School.

At the moment he felt that a short interval for thought was more important than food, so he turned left. As he did so a battered grey BMW Alpina pulled out of the line of cars opposite Mrs. Queen's front gate. When it reached the end of Boswell Road it, also, turned to the left.

The place that Tamplin had chosen was well suited to reflection. Both playing fields were empty and the earlyafternoon sun was slanting across the grass and silvering the ruffled waters of the Thames which formed a backdrop to the scene. Now a few boys in football clothes were coming out of the school block and were heading for where he sat, passing a ball between themselves or kicking it ahead and chasing it.

He ignored them and concentrated on his problem.

There were still too many pieces missing for him to be able to put together a coherent picture; but if the enquiry which he had asked Bonnie Parker to make turned out as he anticipated he would unquestionably have enough information to interest the lawyers for the defence. They were the people who were going to fight the next round. Armed with his information, they could at least fight with their eyes open.

If he decided to help them.

One of the boys had kicked the ball a long way ahead and another boy was running after it. He pulled off the difficult catch a few yards away from where the car was parked. Tamplin said, "Well played," and the boy smiled before turning to kick the ball back.

As Tamplin started his car and headed back towards the road, the BMW Alpina drew across the opening, blocking it.

The man who got out was young, fair-haired and heavily built. He walked with a limp. The last time Tamplin had seen him he had been coming up the steps of the Orange Consortium.

He hobbled up and leaned in at the nearside window of the car. He said, "Reporter?" managing to make it sound insulting.

125

Tamplin said, "Reporter's old hat. I prefer to call myself a newspaper man."

"Don't mind what you call yourself, chum. But a word in season. We saw you dropping Mrs. Queen at her house."

'We' apparently included the other young man, who was in the driving seat of the BMW.

"I congratulate you," said Tamplin, "on the excellence of your eyesight. I did indeed drop Mrs. Queen at her house and I fail to see what the hell it's got to do with you."

"You could find out. If you bothered the old girl again."

"Just move your car. And stop talking like a B-movie heavy."

The young man looked at him thoughtfully for a long moment, as though memorising his face. Then he signalled to the driver, who cleared the entrance.

"I'm obliged to you," said Tamplin. "No. I didn't mean for moving your car. I meant for helping me to make up my mind."

14

When Tamplin got back to the *Highside Times* he found the reporters' room empty. Bonnie Parker had left a note on his table. She had done the job which he had suggested.

Introducing herself as an old school-friend of Rosemary Herbert she had extracted from the Secretary of the City Northern Institute the two addresses which they had on record. One was 10 Mornington Square, N1. The second, and more interesting one, was 10 Axe Lane, EC2.

"We like to have a record of both the home and the office address," explained the Secretary, who was a girl of around Bonnie's age and inclined to be friendly. "Axe Lane's in the City. I imagine that would be the office one, wouldn't you?"

Bonnie had agreed that this was likely and had proceeded to Axe Lane. There was no indication of the business carried on at No. 10, but Bonnie, who did not believe in hanging about, had marched in and tackled the commissionaire, this time in the character of a girl looking for a job.

The commissionaire had told her who the owners of the premises were and had added that, seeing as how they'd lost two of their three girls recently, they'd probably be glad to take her on. When she asked what sort of person the head-man was the commissionaire had been discreet, but unenthusiastic.

At the foot of her note Bonnie had written, 'I expect the girl you're interested in was one of the two who left Axe Lane last week.'

Tamplin added the note to his file and turned up the *Sentinel*'s account of the hearing at Bow Street. This gave him the name of the solicitor who had been acting for Mullen and he walked across to the public library in Liverpool Road to examine the Law List. There were three Shermans in it, but only one in London. A member of Bantings, the well-known Lincoln's Inn firm, but not, it seemed, a partner. So much the better. More approachable.

He dialled Bantings number and after the usual rigmarole of telephonist and secretary, was put through to Roger Sherman. He had considered, very carefully, what he was going to say and hoped that he struck the right note.

After giving his name and his office address, but without mentioning that it was a newspaper, he said, "Quite by chance, I've come across some information connected with the Mullen shop-lifting case. I feel you should have it, but I'd prefer to give it to you personally."

After a fairly long pause, Sherman said, "That's very good of you. I shall be tied up for the rest of the afternoon. Could you possibly drop in this evening at my flat?"

"Willingly," said Tamplin and meant it. An interview away from the formal atmosphere of the office would be preferable.

When he arrived at Osnaburgh Terrace the only member of the Sherman family present was sixteen-year-old Michael. He had a plummy mouth which, when he opened it, showed a gap in his front teeth.

"It was dead stupid," he explained, speaking with some difficulty. "If it had been a school match it wouldn't have mattered so much, but it was just a pick-up game."

"How did it happen?"

"Someone trod on my face. I've been allowed home because I've got a date with our own dentist first thing tomorrow. Really, I'm a bit young for false teeth, wouldn't you say?"

He sounded so aggrieved that Tamplin couldn't help laughing. He said, "They'll make a beautiful job of it. Soon you won't know they're there. Actually I believe I saw you kicking about before the game."

"Was that you in the car? We all thought it must be a talent scout from the Harlequins."

"Sorry. Nothing so grand. I play for one of the South-West London teams, on the ground next to yours."

"Are you coming to talk to dad about rugger, or about law?"

"Law."

128

"About this shop-lifting case?"

"Yes."

"I hope you're on his side, then."

"Strictly speaking, I'm not on anyone's side. But I've picked up a piece of information that might be useful to him."

"I'm glad about that. Some people seem to think dad shouldn't have taken on the case. I don't think that at all." He added, speaking as seriously as the state of his face allowed, "It doesn't matter if someone's unpopular. That shouldn't prevent him from getting a fair deal."

"Life would be a lot simpler if everyone thought that."

"Don't they?" said Michael. He sounded genuinely surprised. "I should have thought it was obvious. That sounds like dad."

Tamplin's first feeling on seeing Sherman was one of relief. He had had little experience of solicitors and none at all of the exotic type who operated from Lincoln's Inn. He had pictured them as serious, rather elderly men wearing glasses and conversing in learned and measured periods. This sample looked like a soldier and spoke like a man who, when aroused, would have relied more on four-letter words than on polysyllables.

"I hope my son has been entertaining you," he said. "But I see he's forgotten to offer you a drink. What's your tipple?"

"Beer, if available."

"Splendid. Two bottles, Mike. And two glasses."

When these hospitable preliminaries had been concluded and Michael had resisted a half-hearted attempt to eject him, Tamplin said, "When I confess that I'm a newspaper man, I hope you're not going to sling me out."

"Bantings may be old-fashioned," said Sherman, "but our intelligence department is second-to-none. We had already located you. The *Highside Times and Journal*, if I'm not mistaken?"

"Correct. A small outfit, but progressive. The point is that my side-kick, Miss Parker, was in Court and was intrigued when the prosecution seemed able to quote something which Mullen had said, in private, to his chief."

"Which his chief denied."

"Indeed. But Mullen had already fluffed so much that I doubt if anyone believed either of them."

129

"I certainly didn't. I'm quite sure he said it. The only puzzle was how the Crown got to hear about it."

"That's one of the things I've come to tell you," said Tamplin. And did so.

"You mean that this Herbert – Hartshorn – girl had planted a bug and they blew it and her up?"

"I'm sure that's right. A colleague of mine had the same trick played on him. He was indulging in a piece of industrial espionage. In that case they used a high-powered Guy Fawkes cracker. Which was poetic justice, since the firm he was spying on was one which manufactured fireworks. He was stone-deaf for a week."

"That certainly explains how they got the information," said Sherman slowly. "But it doesn't explain how they contrived to feed it to the opposition."

"I don't know exactly how they did that, but I've a fair idea of the way they'd have set about it. Have you really got any idea of the sort of organisation you're up against? This self-styled Orange Consortium."

"No. But I'm learning."

"The thing you have to remember is that a lot of people would approve of what they're doing. Up to now they've concentrated on the fight against apartheid. What is not quite so creditable is the way they did it. I can give you a personal example. I'm a supporter of our local volley-ball team. We had reached the final in the London Cup. Three of our best players happened to be South African students. We'd kept this fact under wraps, but somehow it got out. As the game was starting a task-force organised by the Orange Consortium rushed the hall. In the ensuing free-for-all one of the South African students had his arm broken and whilst he was being looked after other people were busy spreading fuel oil on the pitch. The game, of course, was abandoned."

"And the people responsible got it in the neck, I hope."

"I wish they had. In fact, nothing happened to them at all."

"That doesn't sound possible."

"But it's a fact. The volley-ball people went after the ones they took to be the ring-leaders. They didn't know their names, but they identified them to the police fairly closely. One of them had red hair and another had a broken nose and so on. The police did quite a thorough investigation – one of

130

them had been playing in our team and they were angry about it. They organised an identity parade and three youths were pointed out to them and charged. All of them had respectable family backgrounds and by the time they came to court they all had the most comprehensive alibis. The magistrate decided it was a case of mistaken identity and that was that."

"And the alibis were organised – don't tell me – by one of the firms in the City that specialise in that sort of thing."

Michael said, in a voice choked by outrage and a split lip. "Then it's true. Firms like that really do exist."

His father said, "They exist all right, Michael. In the year you were born – I remember the date from that – the Commissioner of the Metropolitan Police, Robert Mark, gave the Dimbleby Lecture on the BBC. All the previous lectures had been by important people, so they attracted a very large audience. This one was a bombshell. Because Mark stated, as a matter of cold fact and without any qualification, that there were half a dozen firms of solicitors, known to the police, who fabricated evidence."

Tamplin said, "And I suppose the legal unions started screaming."

"It was before I came into the law, but a friend of mine went, on the morning after the lecture, to have lunch at the Law Society. I don't know whether the unions were screaming or not, but he told me that he sensed no feeling of hysterical outrage in *that* dining-room. He remembered one man saying, 'Well, we all know the names of four of the firms the Commissioner was talking about. I wonder which the other two are?'"

Tamplin laughed, but Michael was not amused. He started to say something, fielded a look from his father and choked it off.

"With lawyers like that on your side," Sherman agreed, "I suppose it wouldn't be difficult to filter information through to the opposition."

"Two other points," said Tamplin, "which might or might not interest you. First, let me tell you about Anna."

When he had finished, Sherman said, "I can see that having Anna under their thumb would feed South African intelligence a lot of information about the Katanga household. But

131

it isn't Katanga who's on trial."

"I agree. Then let us turn to another less attractive and even more confusing member of the female sex. One Mrs. Queen."

Again, Sherman heard him out in silence. When Tamplin had finished, he said, "I'm sure that what you're telling me is important, but I can't quite see how anything this good woman can have found out could affect Mullen's defence."

Michael said, "Katanga's an important prosecution witness, isn't he?"

"Certainly. In fact, without his evidence there wouldn't be a case at all."

"Then suppose Mrs. Queen knew that he'd been concerned in another case – here or in South Africa – and had been found to have given perjured evidence. That would blow him out of court, wouldn't it?"

"It's possible."

"Well, you said that Mullen had his government's money behind him. Surely *they* could afford five hundred pounds to find out what this woman knows."

"No doubt. But I couldn't involve my client in that sort of expenditure off my own bat. It would have to be a partnership decision."

"But surely, if you explained how important it was."

Sherman sighed. He said, "I suppose I might be able to persuade them. But Bantings is an old-fashioned firm. We handle a lot of civil litigation, which is comparatively gentlemanly. We aren't experienced in criminal work and all the infighting that's involved in it. I'm sorry, but there it is."

That same evening, and not much more than a mile away, the same problem was being discussed in the smaller saloon bar of the Dick Whittington public house. This had become the recognised meeting place of Sesolo's private army. Half a dozen of its regular members were there.

"Have you got any idea, Boyo," said Norman Hicks, owner of the BMW Alpina, "why the boss wants us to keep an eye on that old bag in Boswell Road?"

"No idea, Norm."

"It's not as if she was worth looking at. Now when we were put on to watching that little black packet at Katanga's house,

132

that was no hardship."

"Wheels within wheels," said Boyo.

"Must be something going on. Otherwise, why was the press snooping round her this morning?"

"I'll tell you what I think," said Jepson. The others suspended their drinking to listen. He was clearly the leader. "I don't think it's anything to do with Katanga at all. I think that old buzzard has picked up something about *Mullen*. Something that would do him no good at all if it came out. And she's waiting to sell it to the highest bidder."

"That's an idea, Ronnie," said Boyo. He did not have many ideas himself, but was prepared to give credit to those who did. "Let's order another round."

There was no dissent to this proposal.

Had Mrs. Queen known that two different sets of men were discussing her, she would, no doubt, have been much gratified by this evidence of her popularity and importance.

15

"We had every hope," said Leopold de Morgan, "that the Foreign Office would give us a certificate under Section 4 which would have settled the question of your immunity once and for all."

"And they've refused?" said Mullen. "I find that difficult to believe."

"No. They have not refused. They have now given their certificate. They have decided that you are *not* in this country as a diplomatic agent."

"Clearly a political decision," said Yule. "I suppose one should have guessed that they would spare no effort to be uncooperative."

"Not uncooperative," said Mullen. "Hostile."

De Morgan looked at the three men on the other side of his big, bare mahogany table. Yule and Mullen were angry. Roger Sherman looked worried. He said, "I suppose there's no way of reversing their decision."

"None at all. Section 4 says that their decision shall be conclusive in all proceedings."

"Then we have no choice. We must fight the shop-lifting charge in the Magistrates' Court."

"Not necessarily." De Morgan looked at Martin Bull who was sitting beside him. "We have discussed this development and I am indebted to my junior who has perceived what may be an alternative solution. I'll ask him to tell you about it."

"It's in the Consular Relations Act, 1968," said Bull. "It's a less comprehensive protection, but it's worth trying. We shall argue that even if Mr. Mullen is not a diplomatic agent — which we have to accept, although we think it's an unreason-

134

able decision – it can still be argued that he is a consular officer. And there's one thing to be said for it. It's a matter for legal decision. The Foreign Office can't interfere with it."

"I'm relieved to hear it," said Yule. "I will not conceal from you that I regard your Foreign Office as prejudiced and unreasonable. Now explain the drawbacks which, I am sure, exist."

"*If* we establish that your premises, in Axe Lane, are part of your consular organisation – which should not be difficult – *and* that you, Mr. Mullen, are attached there – "

"Which I am."

"Then it will be hard for the Crown to argue that you are not a consular officer. However – "

Yule said, "I felt sure there was a 'however' in it somewhere."

"However," continued Roger patiently, "consular officers are only immune from proceedings – I'll give you the exact words of the Act – 'in respect of acts performed in the exercise of consular functions'."

There was quite a long silence while Yule and Mullen thought this one out. Yule said, "If I say that I despatched Mr. Mullen to that bookshop to obtain copies of Katanga's book, is that not the performance by him of a consular function?"

"An affidavit on those lines would be most helpful. I will leave it to you and Mr. Sherman to work out the wording."

When the South Africans and their solicitor had left, Bull said, "Do you really think we've got a chance, sir? The Court's not going to like our changing horses in mid-stream."

Leopold de Morgan, who had lit his favourite pipe and was now lying back in his chair emitting a cloud of tobacco smoke, said, "I thought we might have had an outside chance when I heard that Ackworth was going to head the Court."

Martin wondered why his task would have been made any easier if he had to argue in front of Lord Ackworth, one of the most formidable Lord Chief Justices of the century. He was about to say this when de Morgan added, expelling another puff of smoke, "Because I'm told that young Lashmar cornered Ackworth in his Club the other day and spent half an hour proving to him that the sun went round the earth."

"That should be helpful," agreed Martin.

"It would have been extremely helpful. Almost, you might say, decisive, if Lashmar had been going to handle the appeal."

"You mean – ?"

"I mean that the Attorney General doesn't appear to have quite such a high opinion of young Mr. Lashmar as Lashmar has of himself."

"Then they're going to use someone else?"

"So Messenger tells me."

Mr. Messenger was their senior clerk.

"Did he tell you who's tipped for the job?"

"He thinks it will be Eileen Wyvil."

Martin whistled. He said, "That's a different proposition, isn't it?"

When she had first arrived, the schoolboy humour of the Junior Bar had translated 'Wyvil' into 'Weevil'. But as she progressed upwards, attaining the position of Attorney General's devil and Treasury Counsel, this disrespectful nickname had fallen out of use. To her friends in Chambers, like fat Sue Studd, she had become 'Steeple', a reference both to her height of five feet eleven inches and to her celebrated ancestor, Bishop Wyvil, who had built the world-famous spire of Salisbury Cathedral.

"She's clever," agreed de Morgan. "And she does her homework. It's going to be a difficult case to argue anyway. You might not even have got home if they'd stuck to Lashmar."

"It's a pity they didn't. I've seen Steeple in action. She'll twist those old boys round her elegant little finger."

"So it seems," said Captain Hartshorn, "that the pencil story has leaked out."

"That's right," said Sesolo. "A man at the Whittington was talking about it last night."

"I'm sorry it should have broken."

"Why?" said Mkeba. "It's powerful medicine."

"Agreed. But like all medicinal draughts it's only really effective if it's administered at the right time."

"And you don't think this is the right time?"

"Almost, but not quite. Our legal friends tell us that this second attempt to wriggle out on diplomatic grounds is likely

136

to fail. That means that Mullen goes back to Court. He'll opt, no doubt, for the Crown Court and that means a jury of good men and true."

"And women."

"Certainly. We mustn't forget the women. Now if we could have arranged it so that the pencil story broke on the morning of the hearing, they'd all have been so revolted that they wouldn't have had to leave the box before finding Mullen guilty."

Rosemary had been urging her father for some time to let her find another job. "Anything," she said. "I don't care what it is. I just want to get out and do something." He had pointed out that this risked an enquiry into her P45 which could lead back to his friends in the City. Rosemary had agreed, reluctantly.

However, that morning a letter had arrived which contained a promise of action. She showed it to her father, who looked first at the signature and said, "Who's Kathleen?"

"She worked with me at Yule's office. She left a week after I did."

"And now she's got this job at the Newspaper Library at Colindale."

"Andrew told me you'd put a detective onto watching that solicitor – I forget his name – "

"Sherman."

"That's the one. He followed him to the library, didn't he? But he wasn't able to get in, so he never found out what Sherman was looking for. Would you like me to find out?"

The Captain looked at his daughter thoughtfully. So much had happened since then that he had almost forgotten why he had considered this particular piece of information important. However, it would get his daughter out of the flat.

He said, "How would you set about it?"

"If you look at the last page, she says that being the new girl she's naturally landed the dullest job. Checking the slips."

"Yes," said the Captain. He had skipped the last page. Now he read it more carefully.

It seemed that anyone requiring a newspaper had to sign a slip which identified the paper required and also gave the name and address of the enquirer.

He said, "I see. So your friend could find out which papers

137

Sherman had out and could produce them for you. I'll have to get hold of a library card from one of Sesolo's students. What won't be easy is spotting what Sherman was after, since you haven't any idea what he was looking for. It might have been nothing to do with the Mullen case at all."

"It's a long shot," agreed Rosemary. "But it'll be better than sitting round here all day twiddling my fingers."

"What a filthy idea," said Chief Inspector Ancrum. West End Central had got the pencil story twenty-four hours after it hit the Stock Exchange. He had been told it twice already. Neither of his informants had thought it funny.

Inspector Brailey said, "I mentioned it to a doctor friend of mine yesterday evening. He said that if you did something like that to someone and weren't very careful you'd be likely to kill him. Pain and shock."

"It isn't going to make our job any easier."

"You mean that we'll have to arrange to protect that bastard?"

"Fortunately, no. It's only because the shop-lifting occurred in our area and the case being heard at Bow Street, that we were landed with the job of seeing that he gets in and out of Court without being lynched."

"A quick lynching would solve all our difficulties."

"However," said Ancrum – being senior to Brailey he tended to take a more responsible view of the situation – "fortunately he lives in Axe Lane, which is in the City."

"So the City boys have got to look after him. That's the first bit of good news I've heard."

"Possibly. On the other hand it's one of the duties of Special Branch to guard eminent foreign visitors. Baron won't be happy about that."

"As long as it's someone else, not us," said Brailey.

"I hope you're fully prepared to do battle," said the Attorney General. He felt much happier now that he had Wyvil behind him.

She said, "The other side has put in a long list of authorities they intend to refer to. Some of them are American."

"Can they do that?"

"I haven't had time to read them all. But I'm not sure that,

138

on balance, they aren't more helpful to us than to them. If I decide that they are" – she showed her excellent teeth – "I shan't object to them being put in."

"I had a word with the P.M. in the House this morning. Make no mistake about it. This is a case he wants us to win."

"Is there a political angle to it?"

"There's a political angle to everything these days," said Sir Humphrey gloomily. "What he wants is quite clear. He wants the case remitted to Bow Street, Mullen to be found guilty, fined and kicked out of the country. If, by any chance, he escaped on a technicality, the press – or certain portions of it – will immediately imply that it was a put-up job to save the government from embarrassment with their friends in South Africa."

"I'll bear it in mind," said Wyvil. She did not sound worried.

That same afternoon, at about four o'clock, Mullen, who had been up to the West End to get his hair cut, turned into Axe Lane from the Gresham Street end. He had set out without raincoat or umbrella and had been caught by one of the short, but violent, showers which had been plaguing Londoners that autumn. The rain had stopped as suddenly as it had started and the sun was now reflected from wet pavements.

Bloody weather, bloody country, bloody people, thought Mullen. The desire to be out of it and back in South Africa had gone far beyond wishing and hoping. It was a passion.

As he rounded the corner he saw a crowd of young men approaching from the far end of the Lane. They seemed happy enough, God rot them, and were roaring with laughter at something said by a thickset character who was limping along with them.

As they came closer he saw that they all seemed to be equipped with new-looking, newly-sharpened pencils. Most of them had two or three sticking out of their top pockets. Clerks, he supposed, but he was puzzled to make out what they could be doing loafing about the streets in mid-afternoon. He was still puzzling about it when two of them grabbed him.

Mullen reacted instinctively. A scything blow felled one of his captors and as the other loosened his grip he shook him off and jumped for the nearest shelter. This was the entrance to one of the banks which flanked the South Africans' office. At that hour the heavy double doors were shut, but considered as a place of refuge it had advantages. It was too narrow for more than two men to come at him at a time and the jutting door handles behind his back offered him a useful pivot.

Holding one of them in his left hand, he swung out anti-clockwise at the first man who tried to rush him. Mullen was thickset and powerful and bad temper added weight to the blow which landed squarely in his opponent's stomach and sent him to the ground, crowing and retching. Quickly reversing his hands and swinging clockwise, he hit the one who was coming up on the other side, in the throat.

There were now twenty or thirty men in front of him, but none of them seemed anxious to try their luck. Their leader shouted, "Go for his legs." This was not a happy idea. Supported by the useful door handles, Mullen kicked the first one who dived for him full in the face.

As the opposition showed signs of demoralisation, Mullen decided to make for home. His own door was only ten yards away. He charged forward, bellowing like an enraged bull. He might have made it, too, and was nearly there when his foot slipped on the wet pavement. The next moment he was flat on his face with two or three men on top of him.

The thickset man who seemed to be the leader had stood back, so far, from the action. Now he edged his way forward and shouted, "Pull off the bugger's trousers. Then you can use your pencils. Stick 'em in anywhere you like."

To de-bag a man who had no thought of submitting was not a simple matter. And they were still rolling together on the ground when there was a shout of, "Police!" Alerted on the telephone by Yule, squads from Wood Street and Cloak Lane had arrived. A van load stopped at each end of the lane and the men jumped out. There were only eight in each party, but they knew their job. The front ones linked arms, the others formed a wedge behind them and they went in like a human tank. The outer fringes of the crowd offered little resistance, but when the police reached the heart of the disturbance they met opposition and half a dozen private fights developed.

By now the narrow lane was a scene of the wildest confusion, added to by the shouts of the spectators who leaned dangerously out from the windows on both sides of the street, cheering or hooting the police as their sympathies directed. An enterprising young man in the block at the far end, who had an excellent camera with a telescopic attachment took a number of pictures which he subsequently sold to the *Evening Standard*.

For some minutes the fight was a level one. Then a further reinforcement from Wood Street settled the matter.

Whilst this was going on, Mullen seemed to have been forgotten. Now he was back on his feet, with blood running down from a cut on his forehead, but still full of fight. He was feeling really happy for the first time since his arrival in England.

He forced his way back to the doorway of the Bank where three of his opponents were still being looked after by their friends. Mullen said to the Inspector who had come with him, "I identify these three as men who attacked me."

"Splendid," said the Inspector. "We'll take them back and charge them."

"There was one other. Seemed to be the leader. Limped a bit. I can't see him anywhere."

Ronnie Jepson, Norman Hicks and two of their principal aides had left the scene of the battle some minutes earlier. Their instructions had been that if they got into trouble they would find help in No. 15. This was one of the few doors giving onto the street which had not been barred as soon as the trouble started.

Ratter, who was waiting behind it, had it open in a flash and slammed it shut behind them. Then he led them up to the third floor. They met no one on the stairs. The occupants of the other offices where still craning out of their windows.

"I was told you boys might be paying us a visit," said Ratter. "Better keep your heads down until the street's clear."

Rosemary examined, with distaste, the thick folder which contained the twenty-six weekly numbers of the *Oxford News and Journal*, each of between forty-eight and fifty-two pages.

She had finished with the *University Gazette*, which had contained short lists of university and ecclesiastical appointments, and long lists of examination results, and with the *Oxfordshire and Buckinghamshire Recorder* which ignored the City and

141

concerned itself mainly with the difficulties and complaints of the farming community.

The *News and Journal* certainly promised to be more interesting. But there was an awful lot of it. Rosemary gritted her teeth and plunged in.

The battle of Axe Lane was given some coverage in the press. It was not a lead story, but most of the papers had it. The three students who had been charged had admitted that the general objective had been to de-bag Mullen. No mention was made of the idea of following this up by sticking sharpened pencils into private parts of his body.

The tone of the reports was that it was a reprehensible example of misplaced undergraduate humour, but that if people like Mullen came to this country they must expect to encounter expressions of popular dissent.

The Times reminded its readers that, in 1850, when an Austrian general with a talent for flogging women had visited London, the draymen of Barclays Brewery had chased him down Bankside and bombarded him with mud pies. The *Sentinel* which seemed to be heading the anti-Mullen crusade commented, in a second leader, that the scratches he had sustained in this romp (a carefully selected word) had to be multiplied a thousand times before one could begin to compare them with the damage which South African policemen and soldiers had inflicted on the townsfolk of Soweto.

On the following morning Max Freustadt summoned Mullen to King Charles II Street. When he came in Max noted that Mullen seemed to be in better spirits. There was a sparkle in his eye and an aggressive jut to his chin. Apparently his experience of combat had boosted his slipping morale. It was clear that if more fighting was called for he would go into it with all the vigour and lack of scruple that had raised him to his commanding position in the Pretoria hierarchy.

Just as well, thought Freustadt.

He said, "I gather that no one has much faith in your lawyer's last-ditch attempt to wriggle out of this shop-lifting case by a backdoor. It *could* succeed, but I wouldn't put money on it myself."

"So?" said Mullen.

"So we have to face facts. If you are found guilty and fined, or sent to prison – yes, that's possible in the current state of feeling – we all read about what happened yesterday – "

"So?" said Mullen again.

"If you go back to South Africa with any sort of penal sentence, even if it's only a fine, you're finished. I can't put it more clearly than this. Either you kill the case, or the case kills you."

"You've told me nothing that I didn't know already," said Mullen coldly. "Naturally I've been thinking about it and I realised, very early on, that Katanga mustn't give evidence. He is the only witness that matters. The charge of shop-lifting is far-fetched enough. Without him it falls flat on its face."

"And you think you can do something about it?"

"Yes, I do. I shall have to speak to my office in Pretoria and I shall need a line which is absolutely secure."

"I think I can manage that," said Freustadt thoughtfully.

On Tuesday, October 30th, the second day of the hearing of *Regina* v. *The Chief Metropolitan Magistrate ex-parte Mullen* was in full swing. It had originally been set down for October 25th and had been twice postponed owing to the difficulty of assembling three High Court judges.

For most of the first afternoon the Lord Chief Justice, flanked by Mr. Justice Lord and Mr. Justice Attenborough, had listened patiently, if unenthusiastically, to the attempts of Martin Bull to persuade them of something which they felt, in their heart of hearts, was a legal wangle.

Martin had done his work conscientiously and had scoured the authorities on both sides of the Atlantic for legal comment and judicial precedent. He had been particularly pleased with a paragraph in the American Law Institute Restatement of 1983 which started, 'It is increasingly accepted that immunities like those enjoyed by diplomatic agents are accorded to high officials of a foreign state *when on an official visit.*' He had emphasised the last five words.

"Even if, therefore, your Lordships conclude that Mr. Mullen was not himself a consular agent and are convinced by the arguments put forward in the Lower Court, to the effect that he was only in this country to carry out certain negotiations over the extradition of Katanga, is it not clear that he

143

must be accorded the same protection as a diplomatic agent? Surely it is not disputed that he is a high official and he was certainly here on official business – "

On de Morgan's advice he had deliberately drawn out the preliminaries so that he was able to make this his strongest point when they resumed on the second morning.

"They're old men," said de Morgan. "By the end of the day they're so tired that they hardly listen to what you're saying. All they want to do is get back to the Club for their evening gin. Save it for the morning. Then they may listen to you."

Then Eileen Wyvil, adjusting her wig with one finger in exactly the gesture of a lady bringing an Ascot hat into prominence, had taken the wind out of all their sails by stating, "I could have saved the Court a great deal of trouble if I had been allowed to make it clear that it is *not* disputed that Karl Mullen is a consular agent."

This broadside was homed accurately onto the Lord Chief Justice who responded with a gratified smile.

"I noted," continued Eileen, "with some surprise, that my learned friend had called in aid a document which, as you will see from the copy in front of you, is no more than a restatement of the law submitted, *for discussion*, to the members of the American Law Institute. However, since my learned friend has laid this document before you, perhaps I may be allowed to look a little further into the cases which it cites."

Martin Bull said, "Damn," under his breath. As soon as she mentioned cases he knew what was coming.

"The point at issue and the only point is whether the alleged offence took place when Karl Mullen was engaged on his consular duties. There would seem to be no decision in this country which helps us. However, American case-law does provide us with some assistance. I am at page 63, paragraph 264."

The three Lord Justices busily leafed through the pages of the document in front of them.

"You will see the reference there to the case of the United States and Velasco. The facts were as follows. It seems that the Argentine Consul General was attending a diplomatic drinks party when it suddenly occurred to him that he was overdue at a committee meeting at the Panamanian Embassy. Excusing himself hurriedly to his hosts, he sped from the building only to find that, although his official car was there, his official chauffeur was not. Luckily Louis Velasco, one of his consular aides, had come out with him and he offered to drive the car. No doubt the Consul instructed him to drive as fast as he could and although it appears that he jumped several lights and caused a number of innocent pedestrians to leap for safety, he did no actual damage until, arriving at the Panamanian Embassy, he could find no room in the limited space available to park his car. So he decided to make a space for himself. Which he did by the simple device of ramming a car in front of him and driving it across the pavement. At that moment the owner of the car arrived – as also did a policeman. In the proceedings, for what we should call criminal damage, which ensued, immunity as a consular agent was claimed for Velasco."

Eileen Wyvil paused while the judges scribbled vigorously.

"The point which the judge had to decide was precisely the same as we have here. Was Velasco driving the car *in his capacity as a consular agent*? In other words, was it a necessary part of his consular duty? The judge seemed to have had little difficulty in deciding that it was not. Would you ask yourselves, therefore, the same question? Was Karl Mullen fetching these books from Lampards Bookshop as a necessary part of his consular duty? Surely not. It was a chore which could have been carried out by any minor functionary or even entrusted to a messenger service. I do not think I need labour the point – "

The warm smile on the face of the Lord Chief Justice assured her that her point needed no labouring. Martin Bull gathered together his papers with the gesture of a poker player who has bid as high as he dared on a weak hand and throws in his cards.

The result of the Divisional Court hearing was featured briefly in the late edition of the evening papers and dealt with more fully in the morning papers on the following day.

In announcing the decision of the Court, which was unanimous, the Lord Chief Justice had said that none of them doubted that Karl Mullen was a high official in his own government and was in this country on official business. However, it was quite clear that he was not, in fact, acting in his consular capacity when he visited Lampards Bookshop, and that therefore the immunity from criminal process conferred by the Vienna Convention has no application in this case. He had added that this decision must not be considered to pre-empt in any way the outcome of the case now pending. That was something for the Lower Court to decide. The matter would be remitted to the Magistrate.

The writer of this account added that he understood that the case was likely to be before the Magistrate on the following Monday, November 5th.

"Make a note of that date in your diary," said Chief Inspector Ancrum to Inspector Brailey. "Cancel all leave."

Brailey said, "Damn." He had been hoping for some leave himself.

On the afternoon of that Thursday Rosemary paid what she hoped would be her last visit to the Newspaper Library at Colindale. It was already four o'clock and the library shut at six, but there were only half a dozen numbers of the *News and Journal* remaining to be dealt with. She had become heartily sick of her self-imposed task, but she had read the news of the Divisional Court decision. It seemed that, at last, after so many delays and difficulties, Mullen was going to face justice. The thought encouraged her to continue and conclude her work.

When she saw the report of Charles Mullen pleading guilty to the theft of a book at Oxford she could hardly believe her eyes. She had no doubt at all that this was what the solicitor had been looking for. And had found. The difference of Christian names meant nothing. People used different names at different points in their career.

She made a careful note of the date of the paper and the location of the paragraph and returned the book to the counter. Kathleen, who was waiting there, said, "Did you find what you wanted, then?"

"Yes, I did."

"And it's something about that pig?"

"It certainly is," said Rosemary and showed her the entry.

Kathleen said, "If it's the same man, it's going to cook his goose, isn't it? I hope they send him down for a good long stretch. That'll be something back for what he did to you."

146

Rosemary touched the scar on her face with one finger.

When she got home she found her father and Mkeba together. She said, "I've got a bit of news for you." She tried to hide her triumph under an assumption of indifference. "If, by any chance, when Karl Mullen was at Oxford he used to call himself Charles Mullen he's got a previous conviction for shop-lifting. What do you think of that?"

For the first time she noticed that both men were looking unhappy. She said, "What's up? Has something happened?"

Her father said, "I'm afraid the case against Mullen is no longer a runner. It was on the six o'clock news. Jack Katanga died this afternoon. Natural causes."

16

"You mustn't blame yourself," said Dr. Moy-Williams. "You did all that you could. No one could have done more."

He was a white-haired teddy bear, an old-fashioned practitioner who believed that more than half of a doctor's job was keeping his patients from worrying.

"You knew that this might happen at any time, without warning. Of course, I realise that it doesn't make it any easier for you – "

Dorothy said something which might have been 'yes' or 'no'. She had been crying in a helpless way, like a child, and she still spoke with difficulty, but the doctor could see that there was something important she wanted to add. In the end she got it out.

"Could we – do you think – could we put something over him?"

When the doctor arrived, Katanga had been on the floor. With Anna's help they had lifted him onto the sofa so that he could be examined.

"Of course, my dear. Stupid of me. Fetch a sheet, will you?" When Anna returned with one he spread it carefully over the body. "Now, my dear, I'm going to use your telephone, if I may. I'll get my secretary to come round herself and bring something that will help you. Just sit back and see if you can relax. Not easy, I know. But try."

Whilst they were waiting for his secretary the doctor drew his chair up to hers and said, "Would you see if you could answer a few questions? You'll find the effort will do you good."

"I'll try."

148

"Tell me then. When did you first notice that anything was wrong with your husband?"

For a moment he thought that she was not going to answer him. Then she seemed to pull herself together. She said, "We had some lunch ready, in the kitchen. He didn't seem to want anything. So he came back in here. When he had gone Anna and I started our own lunch. After about five minutes – "

"More like ten," said Anna.

"It might have been ten minutes, we heard him cry out. We both ran in. He was sitting in that chair and seemed to be gasping for breath. He'd had this difficulty in breathing before. At night sometimes it was quite bad. So I wasn't too much alarmed. After a bit he seemed to get better."

"Got much better," said Anna. "I thought maybe some black coffee would do him good. I went out to the kitchen to put on the kettle. Then I heard him cry out again. It was a sort of terrible choking cry. When I ran in, he was on the floor."

It seemed to the doctor that Anna was deriving a not unpleasurable excitement from the drama of the moment. Dorothy had her eyes shut. He said, "Yes, I quite understand. And then you telephoned for me."

At this point a ring at the doorbell announced the arrival of the doctor's secretary, a snub-nosed girl with very wide-awake eyes. The doctor poured out a generous dose from the bottle she had brought. The girl said, "I'd better be getting back. There are two or three people waiting."

"Doctor Blain will have to take my afternoon surgery. Tell him about this – " He waved a hand at the shrouded sofa. "I can't see anyone else today."

The girl hardly waited for him to finish before she was out of the door. She had a cousin in the BBC and she was aware that Katanga was news.

"Before I give you this," said the doctor, "there's just one more question. It's something you're sure to be asked. Your husband used that – that instrument – to clear his throat. How often did he do this?"

"It used to be every three or four days. Lately it has been every day."

"I see. Yes. He complained of a sore throat. That was about a fortnight ago, when I came to see him. And you say that since then he has used it every day. Do you happen to know if he had done so today?"

When Dorothy hesitated Anna said, "Yes. He used it today."

"You're sure?"

"Certain sure." She pointed to the glass container on the sideboard, with the bougie standing up in it. "He kept that pushed away, behind those books. Now, you see, it's been pulled out. He would do that when he used it."

"Thank you. I just wanted to be clear about that. Now, my dear. Drink this. It will give you a good night's sleep. That's right. Down it goes. Anna and I can help you up to bed."

"No help needed," said Anna. "I can manage."

When they had gone, the doctor stood quite still for a moment. Then he moved across and examined, without touching it, the glass container on the sideboard. It was half full of olive oil. This had been his own suggestion. He thought it would ease the bougie down. Swallowing it and bringing it up cannot have been agreeable, but no worse, he supposed, than self-injection by a diabetic.

Upstairs the two women heard the front door close and the doctor's car starting and driving away.

Dorothy undressed and got into bed. When Anna said "Is there anything I can get you?" she shook her head. Her eyes were now wide open, as though she was fighting against the sedative she had been given, afraid perhaps of what images sleep might bring. Anna tip-toed out.

After some minutes, when she could fight no more, Dorothy's eyes closed and silence descended on the house, shrouding and covering it like the sheet over the body in the room below.

At nine o'clock on the following morning, as Dr. Moy-Williams approached the Homestead he noticed that the police, who must have listened to the six o'clock news the night before, had posted a man at the entrance to West Mead Close, a sensible precaution, he thought, to keep off unwanted sightseers. He found Dorothy sitting up in bed and saw that she had eaten most of the breakfast that Anna had brought up for her. A night's sleep had drawn its merciful curtain between past and present. He was glad of this. There were a number of things that had to be attended to.

He said, "I hope you won't think that I'm taking too much on myself, but I've had a word with Cyril Larch – I expect you've seen his shop in the High Street – Larch and Parsons, Funeral Directors – "

"And he'll be able to take charge of – of everything?"

"Certainly. That's his job. He's a very experienced man. He's coming round here at half past nine. There's no need for you to come down."

"But I will," said Dorothy. "I'll feel better when I'm up."

"You'll find him very helpful. And I had a word with the rector last night. He was most sympathetic and although your husband was – well, I suppose we should say, an alien – he's sure that he will be able to find a site for his interment. Now, I'll leave you to get dressed."

From her bedroom window Dorothy could see Mr. Larch's car, a dark-blue saloon with an extended hatchback. By the time she got down, her husband's body had been carried out and the car had gone and Anna had swept and tidied the room.

Dr. Moy-Williams said, "Now, we've got some formalities to attend to. I had to inform the Coroner. No need to get upset. Don't, please, start thinking in terms of inquests and post-mortems. No, no. As soon as I handed him a copy of my death certificate, he agreed that there was no reason for the interment to be postponed. It could take place as soon as Mr. Larch and the vicar were ready – "

The front doorbell rang and Anna appeared. She said, "Will I tell them to go away?"

"Well," said the doctor reasonably, "that rather depends who it is, doesn't it? If it's just a snooper the constable would have stopped him. Better go and see."

Anna departed reluctantly. When she came back she was followed by a man with a thin outcrop of sandy hair around an island of pink baldness. His most noticeable features were the prominence of his nose and the size of the horn-rimmed glasses which straddled it. The doctor, who evidently knew him, said, "Hallo, Arthur. You're early on the job." And Dorothy, more coldly, "Good morning, Mr. Pauling." There was a distinct question mark at the end of her words.

"Indeed, you must be surprised to see me," agreed Mr. Pauling. "Normally a solicitor, in circumstances like this, is only too happy to leave affairs in the hands – the very capable hands – of the doctor and the undertaker." He added, with a smile, "I expect you have read in books about the family solicitor arriving within a few hours of his client's decease and reading the will to the assembled family. I can only say that, in forty years of practice, I have never known this to happen. No. Normally the solicitor's part comes later. In this case, however, I had to say my piece before – well, before any irrevocable steps were taken. *Was* that Mr. Larch's car I passed at the end of the road?"

"I imagine so," said the doctor. "Why?"

"Allow me, then, to read you part of the will. It's the opening clause, so it's clearly a point that Mr. Katanga desired to emphasise. It says, 'I instruct my solicitor, in priority to all other matters, that on death my body be cremated.'"

There was silence in the room. It only lasted for a few seconds, but it seemed to stretch long fingers into the future.

Dr. Moy-Williams said, "I see. This may, of course, affect my certificate."

Mr. Pauling nodded. "You will have to bring in a second doctor. Not one of your partners."

"That makes it a bit difficult. I and my partners look after all the people in this area. I don't really know – "

"Then perhaps I can make a suggestion. Dr. Thom, who is a consultant at Hammersmith Hospital."

"Ian Thom. Well, yes – I suppose – "

"You sound doubtful. I can assure you that he's an able man. He gave evidence for a client of mine in a manslaughter case last years and did it very competently."

Dr. Moy-Williams's hesitation was not based on any doubt as to Dr. Thom's ability. The fact was that Thom did a lot of work for the police and it seemed somehow unsuitable to bring him into a family matter. He realised that he was being unnecessarily sensitive. He said, "So be it. As you know him personally, perhaps you'd be kind enough to give him a ring and tell him what we want."

"Certainly. And meanwhile we'd better give Mr. Larch a call as well and tell him about this development."

Dorothy said, "Doctor. Please."

The two professional men swung round at the interruption –

"Please, could you stay with me when Dr. Thom comes?"

"Of course, my dear," said Dr. Moy-Williams. It seemed to him that he might be a very necessary shield between Dorothy and the brusqueness of a police surgeon.

As soon as the solicitor had departed to use the telephone, Dorothy grabbed him by the arm and said, "What – what does it mean? Why should he have put that in his will? Why should he want another doctor?"

"I'm afraid, my dear, that you've jumped to the wrong conclusion. I would doubt very much whether he knew the rule about a certificate leading to cremation having to be signed by two doctors. Nor do I think he was questioning my – ah – competence."

"Then why?"

"It's a fact that people do insert a clause in their wills with the understandable object of making certain that they are dead before they are buried. Sometimes it takes the form of the provision of a small sum of money to a surgeon to open their veins. Or to ascertain by some recognised method that life has indeed departed."

"I see," said Dorothy faintly. "You must think I'm stupid, but I couldn't help wondering – "

She was cut short by the return of Mr. Pauling, who said, "That's all right, then. I was lucky enough to catch Thom before he left the hospital. He's coming straight round here." He looked at his watch. "Ten thirty. I'm already late for an appointment so I'm afraid I'll have to leave you to it."

He did not add that, speaking on the telephone, Dr. Thom had given him his professional opinion of Dr. Moy-Williams. It had been a terse thumb-nail sketch. Clearly there was every possibility of ructions and he considered, as a prudent solicitor, that he would be wise to steer clear of them.

When Dr. Thom arrived he wasted no time. He said, "As you know, doctor, I have two jobs imposed on me by the regulations. The first is to discuss the whole matter with you. The other is to speak to the nurse who was in charge of the patient at the end. It might be sensible, in this case, to carry out the second function first."

"As you wish," said Moy-Williams. "No outside nurse was involved, but the deceased's wife acted in that capacity – under my superintendence – and was with him during the onset of the last attack."

"Thank you. Then, if there is somewhere we could be private."

Dorothy said, "There's a room my husband used as an office." She indicated a door at the foot of the staircase. "It's very small, I'm afraid. Just room for a table and two chairs."

"Two chairs will be all we want," said Dr. Thom pointedly.

"Then you don't wish me to be present?"

"I always find, doctor, that in these cases it is better for me to form my own opinion, quite independently. In here, you mean? Yes, that will do excellently." He followed Dorothy in and he closed the door behind him.

In the sitting-room Dr. Moy-Williams listened, with growing impatience, to the murmur of voices. Most of it seemed to be Dorothy, who was speaking with increasing fluency, her voice rippling along like a shallow stream, breaking against an occasional boulder in the form of a question from Dr. Thom.

There was no conceivable pretext for him to intervene. Thom was not bullying her. But he was certainly leading her on. They had been together for more than half an hour. What could they be finding to talk about?

When the door opened at last Thom came out and crossed the hall towards the living-room. Dorothy did not come with him. She started slowly up the stairs.

Thom said, "I'm afraid I trespassed on your department. She's had such a trying two days that I suggested that she should go up and lie down for a wee while."

"The more rest she gets the better," said Moy-Williams shortly. He did not add, though tempted to do so, that the most trying part of the morning must have been her recent session with Thom. "I imagine," he added, "that you'd like now to discuss the medical aspects of the case with me."

"Yes," said Thom. He had wandered across and was looking out of the window at the smooth lawn and weedless paths. "Certainly. We shall have to discuss that. I have already been able to obtain some useful information from Mrs. Katanga. Did you know that she was a trained nurse?"

"No. I didn't."

"She had to do a lot of that sort of work in her father's mission station in Africa. However, I did not feel able to put to her the one question which will certainly have to be

154

answered."

"What do you mean?"

"You know what I mean as well as I do," said Thom, swinging round and looking the other in the face.

There was a long moment of complete silence. Then Moy-Williams said, "Explain please." But he said it in a tone of voice which suggested that he guessed what was coming.

"The object of using that bougie was *not*, of course, to clear the oesophagus. It was to keep the scar which had developed there soft. If it was not treated regularly it would harden and shrink and might cause total atresia of the gullet."

"Which is, of course, why I recommended that particular treatment."

"Certainly. But can you explain why, when this treatment was used yesterday, *it had exactly the opposite effect*? The bougie, far from softening the scar, would appear to have burst it open."

"Not necessarily. It is quite possible that the oedema which had been forming in the gullet had spread to such an extent that it caused a corresponding blockage in the windpipe. That would account for the spasmodic difficulty in breathing."

"But surely, the process you are describing is quite a slow one. This was quick – and fatal."

"I can see," said Moy-Williams coldly, "that you have a solution to propound. Might I hear it?"

"The only answer that makes any sense to me is that there was some other substance *on the bougie*. Something added, perhaps to the olive oil in the jar. Something strong enough to break down the scar altogether and precipitate oedema into the windpipe."

For a moment Moy-Williams seemed to find difficulty in speaking. Then he said, in a voice which anger and disbelief had reduced almost to inaudibility, "No doubt, since you are producing such ingenious theories, you would like to go a little further and suggest what member of this household could have done such a thing. You have a restricted choice. Mrs. Katanga or the girl, Anna. Or perhaps you would like to add me to the list."

It was Thom's turn to look surprised. He said, "I thought you had questioned Mrs. Katanga about the events of yesterday."

155

"Certainly. She told me that the first sign of trouble was when her husband refused his lunch – "

"But nothing about the earlier part of the morning."

"I saw no reason – "

"So you were not aware that Karl Mullen – you know who I am talking about?"

"Of course."

"You were not aware that he telephoned at about ten o'clock and that Anna told him that Katanga was out, at a meeting with his publishers and his wife was out shopping? She told him that both of them were expected back at about midday. Mullen thanked her and rang off. *But it seems that he took care to arrive in very good time.* In fact, he was here before half past eleven. Anna let him in. Having done so, she naturally retired to the kitchen."

"Leaving Mullen alone in this room."

It was clear from the tone of voice in which Moy-Williams said this that he was being driven from the defensive. It was not yet a medical alliance, but it was approaching it.

"Exactly. And I hope that answers your question."

"It is suggestive, though not, I think, conclusive. I have been following the Mullen case in the papers – in so far as they were allowed to report anything – and it seems clear that Mullen had pressing reason to – well – to hope that Katanga would not be in a position to give evidence against him."

"If you mean," said Thom, with youthful brutality, "that he had every reason to finish him off, why not say so?"

"Possibly because I am an older man than you," said Moy-Williams. "And therefore slower to jump to conclusions. Tell me, if you happen to know. What excuse, if any, did Mullen give for calling?"

"Yes, as it happens, I do know that. But let me continue with what Mrs. Katanga told me. Her husband got back to the house ahead of her and by the time she arrived he was already in deep discussion with Mullen in here. So she joined Anna in the kitchen. As you may have noticed there is only the thinnest of partitions between kitchen and living-room. The two women were able to hear almost everything that was said. After a few insincere civilities Mullen came straight to the point. Katanga's mother and his two sisters had been arrested and were being held by the police in Pretoria on charges of

156

suspected terrorist activity. Evidence had been found. Here, it seems, Katanga interrupted to say 'or planted'. Mullen brushed this aside. He said the evidence would no doubt be supported by statements made, eventually, by the women. The way in which he said this admitted of no doubt as to what was in store for them."

"Unless Katanga did what he was told."

"Exactly."

"And what did Katanga do?"

"He told Mullen to go to hell. Mullen said, 'On your head be it', or words to that effect. As it was clear that the meeting was breaking up, Anna went out to open the front door. The two men left the room together. When they were out in the hall Mrs. Katanga couldn't hear clearly what they said, though Anna, no doubt, could. Anyway, they went down the front path, still arguing. Anna watched them from the front door. She saw them stop, once or twice, to continue their argument – 'both very angry', she said. Finally Mullen got into his car and drove off. Katanga came back. Anna shut the door and went into the kitchen."

Dr. Moy-Williams was not a man whose mind moved very quickly, or very clearly. He was trying to grasp the implications of what he had been told and was finding it difficult. One step at a time was enough for him.

He said, "How do you suppose that a man in Mullen's position would get hold of poison?"

"Unfortunately there are poisons which are only too easy to get hold of. I was admiring the garden and the way the paths had been cleared. No one nowadays bothers about weeding by hand. They just go to a gardening shop and ask for the latest weedkiller. They used to be nicotine-based. Now they're even more deadly. Paradol is one I use myself. It's based on paraquat. A touch of anything of that sort on the bougie would break down the scar at once and a mass of oedema would penetrate the windpipe with immediately fatal results."

"Yes," said Moy-Williams. He said it reluctantly. The things that were being discussed were still possibilities, not probabilities. None the less, if matters did develop in the way Thom was suggesting, everything they now did and said would come under the microscope of the law. Action might be fatal. Inaction might be even more so. He said, "So what do

157

you suggest?"

It was an armistice proposal.

"On the assumption that your certificate may have to be amended, we must put the coroner in the picture. We shall have to agree to an autopsy. The best person to carry it out would be my old chief at Guy's, Dr. Summerson. If he's available, he'd do it at once."

"We must tell Mr. Larch to suspend any preparation of the body and ask him to transfer it to the mortuary. I'd better do that. He's more likely to accept instructions from me."

"Right. You do that first. I'll tackle the coroner and Summerson."

In the kitchen Anna had her ear unashamedly pressed to the door. She did not grasp everything that had been said. She spoke English better than she understood it and some of the technical terms had gone over her head. But she had heard enough to make her both excited and worried.

She heard the doctors go out into the hall and the sound of dialling; then one of them, the fat doctor she thought, saying, "Mr. Larch? Moy-Williams here. Look, there have been developments – "

17

Dr. Summerson was one of the honorary Home Office path-
ologists who shared the work-load that had killed Sir Bernard
Spilsbury forty years before. He was reputed to be the most
meticulous and the most cold-blooded of the three. He picked
up the telephone.

The number that he dialled was unlisted. It bypassed both
operator and receptionist and took him straight to the desk
of Trevor Underhill, Deputy Director of Public Prosecutions.
Both men were aware of the explosive potentiality of the
names Mullen and Katanga and it took Dr. Summerson very
few minutes to explain what had happened and his own
involvement in it.

He said, "I'm not throwing any stones at the family doctor,
an old buffer called Moy-Williams. His professional qualifica-
tions aren't staggering, but knowing what he did about the
earlier accident it was quite a reasonable conclusion to come to
– that cumulative oedema in the gullet might have exerted
pressure on the windpipe. What he had overlooked was some
severe blistering at the back of the mouth and tongue and in
the oesophagus."

"Perhaps he didn't look for it."

"Maybe not. But remember that until he heard about
Mullen inviting himself round there on Thursday morning he
had no grounds for suspicion."

Underhill grinned. One doctor sticking up for another. He
said, "Point taken. What next?"

"I've made sections of the oesophagus, the larynx, the trachea and the stomach. I gather that speed is important in this
case."

"No question about that."

"I did think of carrying out the analysis in my own laboratory at the hospital. Or of bringing in the Metropolitan Police Laboratory. But I rejected both ideas. Though the Police Laboratory will strenuously deny this, we're neither of us as well equipped as the Home Office Central Research Establishment at Aldermaston. I propose to send them the sections, along with the glass jar of olive oil and the bougie."

"Fingerprints?" said Underhill.

"I tested them myself."

"The jar and the bougie?"

"Yes. Several sets muddled and overlapping on the bougie. One plain set on the jar. They all looked to me to be from the same hand. The Police Laboratory will tell us when they see my photographs."

"Will sending the stuff to Aldermaston involve delay?"

"No. I shall take it up by car myself. I know Gadney, the doctor in charge, very well. He'll co-operate. In fact, I'm sure he'll work all night if necessary. You shall have a preliminary report by tomorrow midday at the latest."

"Very well." Underhill consulted his diary. "I'll fix up an appointment with the Director for three o'clock."

"You haven't forgotten that tomorrow's Saturday."

"In view of the background to this case," said Underhill drily, "I think that even Saturday golf will have to take second place."

The Coroner's Officer at Putney who was in charge of the Putney Mortuary was an ex-policeman. His service, only recently concluded, had been with the Roehampton sub-station of the Putney Division. This meant that he still felt some loyalty to his previous superior, Inspector Blanchard. Accordingly, as soon as Dr. Summerson had left the mortuary building it seemed natural for him to telephone the Inspector and bring him up to date. It was Blanchard who had posted a man in West Mead Close. He was aware that the ground he was treading on was sown with mines.

He said, "I don't suppose Summerson said anything to you?"

"He didn't say anything, sir. You wouldn't expect it with a cold fish like that. But he took away a lot of bits and pieces, including a glass jar with a sort of implement in it. And I heard him telephoning Aldermaston to expect him. I couldn't help thinking, what's the hurry?"

"The less you think about it the better, my son," said Blanchard. But after he had rung off he did some thinking himself.

If death had *not* been from natural causes, if poison had been involved – and the likelihoood of this seemed to be growing – then there were two possibilities. Death might, of course, have been the result of an accident. Was there not some history of a previous accident? On the other hand it might have been caused deliberately. In either case, ought not the house to be searched as soon as possible? As against this sensible course of action stood the objection that he would not get a search warrant in time to be of any use to him. But there might be a way round that.

One thing which influenced his thinking was the fact that in that district dustbins were emptied on Monday mornings.

Dr. Summerson looked with envy at the gleaming array of apparatus on the bench. He remembered the primitive quartz spectrographs of his own early years. These had been followed by the first gas chromatographs, which had been considered the most useful weapon in the investigative armoury, and now even these were yielding place to the ion-ray chromatograph which could, used with patience and a modicum of luck, isolate the smallest constituents in any sample.

"I wouldn't do it for anyone but you," growled Dr. Gadney, who still looked like the formidable rugby player he had once been.

"Very kind of you to say so," said Summerson, who had known him long enough not to be alarmed by him.

"But if I'm going to lose a night's sleep, you're going to sit up with me."

"I wouldn't dream of doing anything else," said Summerson.

"I hope you won't think I'm butting in," said Inspector Blanchard.

He was a good-looking man, still on the right side of thirty, assets which he had found useful before when dealing with

161

female witnesses.

"When I heard about your husband's death I took the liberty, as you'll have seen, of posting one of my men at the end of the lane."

"It was very thoughtful of you," said Dorothy.

"And you must forgive me for calling on you at this un-Christian hour – " It was still short of nine o'clock.

"That's quite all right," said Dorothy. "What can I do for you?"

"I'll tell you. It occurred to me that it was possible – just possible – that your husband's death might have been the result of an accident."

"Yes," said Dorothy faintly. Her mind was still running on what Anna had overheard and had poured out to her the night before.

"And that being so, I thought it would be sensible to have a quick look round to see if any bottles or tins had been left lying about. I could only do so, you understand, if you agreed – "

"Well, yes. I suppose there'd be no objection to that – "

"Right," said Blanchard. "Leave it to us." He signalled to the Detective Sergeant who had been standing in the doorway. Two other men were visible behind him.

The quick look round seemed to involve a lot of opening of cupboard doors, upstairs as well as downstairs, and the clanging of dustbin lids. Anna had come in from the kitchen and was saying, "You ought to stop them. They've got no right – " when Dr. Moy-Williams arrived.

He said, "What on earth are those men doing ferreting round your dustbins?" And to Inspector Blanchard, who came in from the kitchen at this moment, "What the devil do you think you're doing? Have you got a search warrant?"

"No, but I've got Mrs Katanga's permission – "

She said faintly, "When he talked about a quick look round I'd no idea – "

"Of course you hadn't. The whole thing's a try-on. Get out of here at once and take your men with you."

Blanchard looked at Dorothy, who said, "Yes. Please go."

"You understand that, I hope," said the doctor. "Any consent which was given has been revoked. And don't think that's an end of the matter. I'm going to have a word with the As-

sistant Commissioner – I happen to know him personally –
and we'll see what *he* has got to say about it."

"Right," said the Director of Public Prosecutions. He was a
grey badger of a man, worn old and dry by the responsibilities
of his post. "Oh, before I start, I'm not sure if you know Chief
Superintendent Baron, doctor."

Dr. Summerson indicated, with a smile, that he did know
the head of the Special Branch.

"In view of the decision of the Divisional Court that Mullen
is to be considered a consular agent, I felt that the matter
came within the remit of his Branch."

Baron signified his agreement, unenthusiastically.

"We can regard the doctor who originally examined
Katanga with some sympathy – "

"Well-meaning, but old-fashioned," said Summerson. "In
the circumstances it was natural that he gave the certificate
which he did."

"Ye-e-s," said the Director. "And but for the requirements
of the Cremation Act Katanga would, by now, have been a
handful of ashes. However, in this instance it worked to our
advantage. Public opinion, and the press, have been diverted
by the immediate announcement that death was from natural
causes. As long as that verdict is unquestioned, it gives us a
breathing-space."

"But not a very long one," said Baron. "The shop-lifting
charge comes up at Bow Street on Monday and as things
stand now, it's almost bound to be dismissed. Once that happens, Mullen will be out of the country within twenty-four
hours."

"Or less," said Underhill.

"I think we could give ourselves a little more time than
that," said the Director. "Lashmar will have to be instructed to
apply for a short adjournment so as to consider the position
brought about by Katanga's death. If necessary the Attorney
General could make the application in person. I had a word
with the Home Secretary just before you came in. He fully
appreciates the difficulty of the position."

Baron looked even less happy. Now it only needed the
Prime Minister to step in, which he was quite capable of
doing.

163

"Then let us see where we stand. First we have Dr. Thom's account of the events of Thursday morning. And now the report – which they emphasise is only a preliminary report – from Aldermaston. Could we have your views on that, doctor?"

"It establishes," said Summerson slowly, "with reasonable certainty, the presence of paraquat in the mixture in the jar and on the bougie. Also what may be chlordane."

"Both of which are found in the weedkiller which is marketed as Paradol."

"Yes. But before they can speak with certainty there are a number of elimination tests to be made. However, they are working hard and should be in a position to let us have a further report quite soon."

"Which means?"

"The elimination tests are delicate. They can't be rushed. A week at the earliest. Probably more."

The Director thought about this. A legal time-limit *and* a medical time-limit. It was not a happy position for a man who liked to proceed with deliberation and had to be reasonably certain before he moved.

Finally he said, "On the assumption that we can get at least a week's adjournment of the shop-lifting case, we will reconvene this meeting on Wednesday. One other thing meanwhile. We shall have to call off the local police. I've had the Assistant Commissioner on the telephone. It seems they pushed in, without a warrant, and searched the house. If you're going to handle the case, you'll need rather more experienced help than that."

"I shall need all the help I can get," said Baron. "Special Branch isn't equipped to carry out criminal investigations."

"Right. I thought about giving it to C.1. But there's maybe a better alternative. West End Central have been looking after the original case. They know the background and the people involved."

"Ancrum and Brailey. Yes. Both very experienced. I'd be happy to work with them."

"Their first and most important job will be to find out if Mullen had access to weedkiller. It's not the sort of thing he'd find lying about in his office. If he wanted it he must have bought it somewhere."

"I'll get them going on it," said Baron.

At the Homestead Dr. Moy-Williams had his moment of triumph. He said, "I thought the A.C. would scare off those cowboys. You won't have any more trouble with *them*. I promise you."

Afterwards, when he had Anna alone, he said, "I know you get weekends off, but I think, on this occasion, it would be helpful if you stayed in the house. Particularly tonight and early tomorrow. Those are the bad times for delayed shock."

"With Mrs. Katanga I have already spoken. She insists that I go home Sunday. She says that the Professor will be worrying."

"Couldn't you give him a ring? He'd understand the position."

"No doubt he would understand. But we have no telephone."

"Isn't there someone who could pass a message?"

"There is a young man from the local newspaper. It is, I think, the *Highside Times*. He is called Fred. He has been helpful to us."

"I'll give the paper a ring and see what can be done. And please remember. If you worry, Mrs. Katanga will worry. So keep quite calm."

"I try to be calm," said Anna.

She was scared and worried, and as dangerous as compacted cordite.

18

Professor Macheli was rarely upset, and more by the minor rubs than by the major crises of life. But on this occasion he felt that he had reason to be disgruntled.

On the previous afternoon, as he and his wife were beginning to wonder what had happened to Anna, Fred Tamplin had appeared. He had explained that some sort of storm had blown up in the Katanga household and that Anna was staying to help cope with it, but hoped to be with them on Sunday. He had brought some good news, too. The *Highside Times* was pleased with the summary of the Professor's article and much approved of the photographs he intended to use. He had brought an advance of a hundred pounds and knowing that the Professor might have difficulty with a cheque he had brought it in cash.

The Professor had at once despatched his wife to the shops. Her instructions were to purchase the material for a stupendous Sunday lunch. Since he knew that Anna was fond of chops, chops should be bought in quantities and a creamy confection to follow.

Never had a celebration fallen more flat.

Anna, arriving on Sunday morning, had shown no interest in the food, or in the windfall which had paid for it. From the moment of her arrival she had hardly opened her mouth, sitting glumly through lunch, condemning it to a series of miserable silences. She had turned aside, with a terseness that was almost brutal, any questions as to what had happened to keep her in Putney. As soon as the meal was over she had scuttled upstairs to her own room.

"If she was a few years younger," said Mrs. Macheli, a

tougher person than her husband, "I should have given that young miss a good spanking."

The Professor was not so sure. He knew Anna well enough to be certain that something had happened to upset her badly. In all the years that she had been with them she had never carried on in that way before. Sometimes when people behaved like that it was better to leave them alone. But he was shrewd enough to realise that such conduct could also be a cry for help.

By teatime he could stand it no longer. He tip-toed upstairs and listened outside Anna's door. What he could hear increased his discomfort. The door was unlocked. He opened it and looked in. Anna was huddled on her bed, crying in a desperate, gulping way. He did not speak. He walked across, sat down beside her and put one arm round her shoulders. She did not repulse him and they sat like that for some minutes whilst her sobbing died down.

Then he said, "If you want to – but only if you want to – tell me what has happened to upset you."

Anna said, and the relief in her voice was clear, "Yes. I will tell you everything."

At a few minutes before midnight Mrs. Macheli rolled over in bed and said to her husband, "Why are you not sleeping?"

"Because I am thinking."

"Thinking about what that girl told you?"

"Yes."

"It worries you?"

"It not only worries me, it presents me with a very difficult problem."

"Difficult problems are better solved after a night's sleep," said his wife, and set him a good example by rolling over and going to sleep herself. But the Professor lay awake for a long time, looking at the reflection on the ceiling from the street lamps in the road outside.

Once she had made up her mind to talk, Anna had kept nothing back. She had not only told him of the clouds of suspicion that were gathering round the death of Katanga. She had gone back further than that and had told him about the hold which the South Africans had obtained over her and of the visits she had been forced to pay to Fischer Yule's office

167

every Saturday morning to report.

"I sometimes thought," she said, "that I would rather go to prison than obey their orders. Then I thought that you, too, would be punished. I had to do as they said."

"You're a good girl," Professor Macheli had said, patting her on the shoulder. "But I do not think you should worry too much. What we did was not a grave matter. Certainly not one for which you or I would be imprisoned."

The first part of what she told him had interested him, the second part had infuriated him. The anger was still with him. What Yule had done was typical of all that was bestial in the South African government. To make little Anna spy and sneak on her employer. To torment her with threats until she bowed to their demands. He would have liked to relieve his feelings by getting out of bed and pacing up and down, but that would have disturbed his wife. Besides, there was a more practical step that he could take, and he would take it that coming morning.

On this thought, he finally succeeded in getting to sleep.

On the Monday afternoon the Orange Consortium was in session. Captain Hartshorn was in the chair. Raymond Masangi was absent on duty, at Bow Street, but Andrew Mkeba, Govan Kabaka and Boyo Sesolo were there. All of them were excited.

"I saw that old Professor character arriving," said Sesolo. "I imagine all this stuff you've given us came from him."

Hartshorn said, "Actually, it came, originally, from his daughter Anna. You've read the report from City Detectives."

"Cute little girl," said Mkeba, "with a foot in both camps."

"From what we've learnt now," said Hartshorn, "it seems that she was more a victim than a plotter. Yule had found out about the irregularity in her position and was squeezing her."

It did not occur to any of them to express surprise or disgust. The tactics of the South African authorities were familiar to them.

"I suppose we can assume that she is speaking the truth now," said Kabaka.

"Yes, Govan. I think so. The Professor, who knows her very well, had no doubt about it."

"Then it is, indeed, good news."

"Lovely," rumbled Sesolo.

"As far as it goes," said Hartshorn, "it is excellent news. The authorities clearly have it in mind that Jack Katanga was murdered. And the only conceivable murderer is Mullen. He was there, he had constructed an opportunity to administer poison and had the strongest possible reason for doing so. But is that enough to force them to act? I wish I could say 'yes', but I have some doubts at the back of my mind."

"If he used poison," said Mkeba, "is there any idea what it was?"

"From what Anna overheard the idea seems to be centring on some form of weedkiller. Paradol was mentioned. This would certainly be logical. He could go into a big garden shop and buy weedkiller without attracting any attention at all."

At this point the telephone on Hartshorn's desk sounded off. He picked up the receiver and listened for nearly two minutes without interrupting. Then he said, "Thank you. That's very clear," and replaced the receiver.

"That was Raymond. He was in court this morning when the prosecution applied for a stay of action to let them consider the situation. The Magistrate was most unwilling to grant it. He said that the case had dragged on long enough and it was his duty to see that it was settled as soon as possible. Now that the Divisional Court, in their joint wisdom, had remitted the matter to him, he said he saw no reason to hang about. It needed a very forceful application by the Attorney General in person to get him to change his mind. He granted a stay of one week and he made it clear that that was as far as he was prepared to go. One week," said Captain Hartshorn thoughtfully.

How, and when, did the possibility that Katanga had been murdered, become public property? So far as the media were concerned the story, briefly noted, was that he had finally succumbed to an affliction which had troubled him for some years. A handful of people outside the Katanga and Macheli households knew of the suspicious circumstances, but they were professional people, trained to keep their mouths shut. The Orange Consortium might have spread the news, but Captain Hartshorn had said 'no'. Fate had dealt him a good hand and he was determined to play it carefully. But by whatever crack or cranny the rumour emerged, once it was out it spread with the force and fury of fire through tinder-dry scrub.

It reached Pretoria on Monday and produced a reaction which startled even the phlegmatic Dieter Langenhoven. He was in conference with Max Freustadt and there were two radio-telegrams on the desk in front of him. The longer one was in the normal consular code and had been deciphered by the staff. The shorter one was in a private cypher, the only book of which lived in Langenhoven's safe.

"It appears," he said, picking up the longer telegram, "that our masters are displeased with us. We have been showing a lack of drive and initiative in our support of Mullen and we seem signally to have failed to realise the disastrous propaganda effect of a successful prosecution."

"Do they say what they want us to do?" said Freustadt. "Or is it all piss and wind?"

"Let me see. We should feel ourselves entitled to spend money on this object without any limit – "

"On what?"

"They are a little shy of practical suggestions, but they do say that since the prosecution is making use of private detectives, we should not hesitate to employ the best available detectives ourselves."

"To detect what?"

"That they do not specify. I shall entrust this part of the operation to Yule. He is more accustomed to such manoeuvres than I am. I have, however, one suggestion to make. Some of this money which has been placed so freely at our disposal should be passed across – a handsome interim payment – to Mullen's solicitors. Solicitors always work harder with money in their pockets."

When the arrangements for this payment had been made and Freustadt had left him, Langenhoven re-read the shorter telegram, which he had decoded himself. Its contents appeared to worry him a lot more than the windy exhortations in the longer one. It premised certain things which might never happen. Which were perhaps unlikely to happen. But if they did he was directed, in clear terms which admitted of no argument, to take certain steps; steps which, if they became known, or were even suspected, would certainly lead to his recall.

He noted that the message had a small red star at the beginning and another at the end of the text. This meant that the sender had not retained a copy. The one in his hands was unique.

He placed it on top of the code book in his private safe and locked the safe.

Captain Hartshorn had fixed his appointment with Roland Auchstraw for seven o'clock on that Tuesday evening. He drove himself down, through the early-November dusk. Leaving his car in Finsbury Circus he crossed London Wall and approached Basinghall Street from the far end.

When he arrived, Auchstraw was alone, his table was clear and his filing cabinets were locked. His greeting was as genial as ever. He poured out a generous glass of the malt whisky which he knew was the Captain's favourite drink and a smaller one for himself. But behind the façade there was a perceptible tension, as though both men knew that the matters on which they were engaged were approaching a crisis.

"When I was at home yesterday evening," said the solicitor, "I walked up with my family onto the Heath. There were a lot of bonfires."

"Of course! Guy Fawkes night."

"Right. Except that it wasn't Guy Fawkes on the bonfires. On a lot of them it was Karl Mullen."

Hartshorn smiled, but Auchstraw was not looking amused. He said, "I don't like getting involved in affairs when there's too much public interest washing round them. In one scandal lately – I needn't mention the names – it was put to me by third parties that I might take a hand. I turned it down and I'm glad that I did so. If my name had appeared I'd have been very unpopular."

Hartshorn said, with a smile, "You needn't let that worry you. In this case, I can promise you, you'll be on the popular side."

"If that's the way it is – tell me what you want me to do."

"The first thing is quite easy. I want you to extend the watch on Fischer Yule's office. It must be continuous through the twenty-four hours. I've checked that the lighting in Axe Lane stays on all night, so it shouldn't be difficult."

171

"Not difficult, but expensive. Two men can't do it. We'd need four – maybe a fifth."

"Expense need not be considered."

"Is that so?" Mr Auchstraw sounded happier. "Is there anything in particular they'll be looking for?"

"We want a record kept of the names and details of everyone who visits Mullen. His flat's on the top floor of the office and the only way in or out is by the door in Axe Lane. If the person who turns up is a stranger, they must try to identify them."

"It'd be a help if you could give us some idea what sort of person to expect."

"It could be a private detective. I heard from Captain Smedley, who's an old friend of mind. A bod from the South African government wanted to hire his agency. He turned it down, but there are plenty of other people he can go to."

"Indeed," said Auchstraw. "Private investigation seems to be one of our growth industries. Did you say there was another matter you wished me to attend to?"

"The second matter is rather more difficult." The Captain paused to look round the office. "Do you, by any chance, make a tape-recording of things that are said to you here?"

"My dear Hartshorn," Auchstraw sounded genuinely pained. "An old client like yourself. A trusted friend. Certainly not."

"Very well, then. I'll explain what we want. The precise details I shall have to leave to you."

He spoke for ten minutes. The only sign of emotion that Mr. Auchstraw displayed was to take off his glasses, polish them carefully, and replace them.

Then he said, "I shall need two thousand pounds in used notes."

19

"Now," said the Director, "let us see what we've got pinned down."

This was a favourite expression of his. He liked evidence to be fastened firmly, with a drawing pin in each corner, a precaution against the winds of chance and the wiles of the opposition.

On this occasion, as well as the Deputy Director and the Head of the Special Branch, Chief Inspector Ancrum was there from West End Central. He had brought with him his number two, Detective Inspector Brailey, who was keeping himself modestly in the background. Dr. Summerson was not there. The matter had passed out of the hands of the scientists and into those of the police.

The Director said, "The second report from Aldermaston confirms, beyond question, that a mixture containing paraquat had been added to the olive oil in the jar. Possibly chlordane as well. That's not certain, but it's not important since paraquat by itself would have done the job."

"If that's right," said Underhill, "does it suggest any particular weedkiller?"

"Paradol contains both those elements. It's a garden weed-killer much used for clearing paths. Sold, so the producers tell us, in at least five hundred shops and stores in Greater London."

"And another five hundred outside it, no doubt," said Ancrum gloomily.

"Possibly. The tins are rectangular, with a rather eye-catching red and gold label. Not the sort of thing which could be easily overlooked."

Inspector Brailey said, diffidently, "I had a word with Blanchard about that."

"I take it," said the Director, "that you are referring to the officer who made that most irregular search of the premises." The suggestion of a smile which accompanied this seemed to suggest that he did not consider it a very flagrant breach of the rules.

Brailey said, "It was irregular, sir. But I saw no reason why we shouldn't use his report. I have it here. It's quite clear that there was no tin or bottle of any sort of weedkiller in the house. He had time to do quite a thorough job before that old medical pussy turned up. I don't think he'd have missed it if it had been there. He knows his job."

"Interesting," said the Director. "In fact, very interesting." He had in front of him a sheet of paper on which he had written the words, 'Motive', 'Opportunity' and 'Means'. He said, "We need not waste much time over motive. You all know the bookshop story. Statements were taken from the manager, Mr. Snow, from his assistant, Miss Widdicombe, and from that private detective, Harold Ratter. They were never used, because the case was never heard, but they'll all be available to give evidence. When we come to opportunity, we note that Mullen was alone in that room for quite half an hour."

Underhill said, "Significant, also, that he had manufactured the opportunity by telephoning to find out when Katanga was expected back and by arriving early."

"The point had not escaped me," said the Director. "It is when we come to means that the position is less satisfactory. So far we have no evidence that Mullen had, or could have obtained, paraquat in any form."

He looked at the four men round the table. The decision was the Director's and his alone.

He said, "Until we have made every effort to close that gap in the evidence, I don't feel justified in authorising a charge of murder against Mullen."

In the silence which followed the three policemen looked at Underhill. He was the only person who could voice their objections effectively. He said, "We all appreciate your reluctance, sir. But it has to be borne in mind that if no charge is brought Mullen will be out of the country by Monday evening."

"And it's Wednesday today. That means that in the next four days you will all have to work very hard. There are two questions to be answered. Where the paraquat came from and what happened to it. That suggests a division of work. West End Central can have any help from other divisions and districts that they want. Every shop in and around London which sells weedkiller must be visited. The officers will have a photograph of Mullen with them. Next, the question of the container." He turned to Brailey. "Do I understand that you know Inspector Blanchard?"

"Yes, sir. Quite well."

"Then have a word with him and tell him that his technical breaches of the rules will be forgiven if he shows suitable energy and initiative now. He is to get a team of his men to examine the area round the Katanga house. The gutters and drains in the streets and the whole area of Putney Common. They will be looking for any can or bottle which might have contained weedkiller. And they have four days to find it. Progress reports by six o'clock every evening, please."

On that same afternoon an indignation meeting was being held in Gilbert Glaister's office at the *Highside Times and Journal*. His faithful staff, Fred Tamplin and Bonnie Parker, were in attendance.

Tamplin said, "I was beginning to think that we had an exclusive angle on the bookshop case. Now, if what everyone is saying is true, it's turned into a murder story. If that's right, it will be wide open."

"But *is* something that everyone is saying necessarily true?" said Glaister.

"I've had it from three people. I don't know where they got it from, but they're all singing the same tune. Some sort of poison was put in that throat-clearing apparatus – incidentally, I saw the jar when I was down there on Friday."

Bonnie said, "I guess the rumour was started by one of those people in Mornington Square. That big Boyo could never keep his mouth shut."

"Whoever started it," said Tamplin, "once a charge has been made everyone will put their top crime reporters onto it and we shall be tail-end Charlie."

175

"Maybe," said Miss Parker, "but not many of them will be on Mullen's side. Which, I assume, we still are."

She looked at Glaister who nodded. He said, "Certainly. And I've thought of a step which might, in certain contingencies, keep our name in the public eye."

The Reverend Simon Ramsay was sitting in his study, a large room in a house of large rooms. The Rectory at Ucklebury Cross had been built in the reign of Queen Anne. A Victorian incumbent with private means and fourteen children had added two wings to it. Simon Ramsay inhabited it in solitary splendour. He did not object to solitude. Much of his life had been spent in wild places and he was used to looking after himself.

His parishioners, on the whole, approved of him. He would not, perhaps, have been a success in the Home Counties, but he seemed to fit into this northern tip of East Anglia, which is one of the most remote and primitive corners of England. They knew, of course, of his connection with Dorothy Katanga and they sympathised with his feelings about mixed marriages. Marriages in that part of the world were more often incestuous than mixed.

Ramsay had in front of him the local newspaper which had copied from the London press the early stories of Katanga's death. It produced in him a reaction which would have been understood perfectly by his flock.

His loathing of Katanga was deep and personal. He would say, like the song in *As You Like It*, 'Freeze, freeze, thou bitter sky, That dost not bite so nigh As benefits forgot.' He had done everything for Jack Katanga and had been rewarded by a slap in the face. He was glad Katanga was dead, certainly; what displeased him was the manner of his death. 'Peacefully at his home', one of the papers had said. It was a lot more than he deserved. Or, looked at in another way, much less.

Earlier he had followed, keenly, reports of the efforts that the South African government were making to extradite Katanga and bring him back to trial and, no doubt, to death on the scaffold. 'Peacefully at his home'! He was not used to questioning the ways of God, but he did feel that, on this occasion, the Almighty had slipped up.

He folded the newspaper, extracted a pad of paper from

176

the drawer and started to make notes for his next Sunday's sermon. Romans 12:19 – 'Vengeance *is* mine; I will repay, saith the Lord.'

Yes. But what if the repayment was inadequate? That demanded thought.

"I take it you realise," said Detective Constable Corp to his friend Detective Constable Fagg, "that Putney Common is just about a mile square."

"Much as that, is it?" said Fagg.

"And do you know how many square yards there are in a square mile?"

"You're the brain-box round here, you tell me."

"Three million, ninety-seven thousand six hundred."

"And that's what we've got to search?"

"Right."

"Just the two of us?"

"Just us two. And that's not all. There's nearly half a mile of drains and gutters as well."

"Cheer up," said Fagg. "Soon be Christmas."

The news came to the Director at five o'clock on Friday evening. Underhill brought it in person. It was too important for the telephone.

"It's just come in," he said. "From the Superintendent at Wood Street. A man called Luck turned up this afternoon and made a statement. He's the owner of a small shop in Pipe Street called The General Stores. He says that a man he had identified as Mullen from his photograph in the papers, bought a tin of Paradol from him on Wednesday, October 31st."

Underhill knew the Director too well to expect him to leap out of his chair with a glad cry of 'Eureka'. He was pleased, certainly, but cautious.

He said, "October 31st. A significant date. The day after the Divisional Court rejected Mullen's plea of immunity."

"Exactly."

"I imagine we shall get this in writing."

"It's on its way over. A signed statement."

"General Stores? It sounds an odd sort of place to be selling weedkiller."

"I thought so, too. But apparently there are one or two shops like it in the City. They cater mainly for bachelor businessmen who have to do their shopping in the lunch interval. They sell everything from toothpaste and bacon to tobacco and washing-up liquid."

"I see. And had this shop been visited by the team from West End Central?"

"Apparently not, sir. It wasn't on their first list. No doubt they would have tried it when they had drawn blank at the more likely places."

"So it would seem to have been, in both senses of the word," the Director smiled faintly, "a matter of luck."

"Good luck," said Underhill.

"Yes. Well, we deserve a little occasionally. We get plenty of the other sort. I'll see the statement as soon as it arrives. If it seems definite and trustworthy, I'll authorise Baron to go ahead. It's in my mind that Mullen's flat is in the City."

"It's above part of Yule's security outfit. A couple of rooms above the office."

"Then Baron will have to take a member of the City Police with him to make the arrest and charge. And since it's now been decided – correct me if I'm wrong – that Yule's offices are consular premises, he'll have to watch his step."

"I can assure you," said Underhill, "that everyone concerned has studied the Consular Relations Act with the greatest possible care."

"I'm happy to hear you say so," said the Director. "With de Morgan on the other side we can't afford to make mistakes."

At eleven o'clock on the following morning Chief Superintendent Baron called at No. 10 Axe Lane. The commissionaire greeted him without enthusiasm. In spite of being paid time-and-a-half he objected to working on a Saturday morning. He agreed that Mr. Yule was in. Mr. Mullen had gone out.

Both these facts had already been reported to Baron by his own men. He showed no impatience, but asked if the commissionaire knew when Mr. Mullen was expected back.

The commissionaire did not know. And added that it was no part of his job to question the comings and goings of the tenants.

"Understood," said Baron. "Perhaps you could give Mr. Yule a ring and tell him I'm here. I think he may be expecting me. It's a first-floor office, isn't it? Thank you. I won't bother about the lift."

As he turned to go he said, as though it was the most ordinary matter in the world, "When I'm gone, you will lock the front door and keep it locked until I return."

"I'll do nothing of the bloody sort," said the commissionaire. "Who do you think you are?"

Baron showed him who he was and the commissionaire, shaken, did as he was told and stood staring as the trim figure disappeared up the stairs.

Yule was expecting the visit. He had heard rumours about Katanga's death, but had discounted them. He imagined that this policeman was coming to discuss the dropping of the shop-lifting charge. And in fact this seemed to be one of the matters he had come to discuss.

He had seated himself in a chair which commanded a view of Axe Lane. After some preliminary politenesses he agreed with Yule that the death of Katanga had radically altered the position. He had been the only witness who had seen Mullen handle the book.

"Alleged that he had seen."

Baron accepted the correction.

A statement in the form of a proof of evidence had been taken from Katanga, but they had been advised that, now that Katanga was dead, the prosecution would not wish to rely on it.

"Of course they wouldn't," said Yule. "Seeing he couldn't be cross-examined on it. I imagine we shall hear on Monday that the charge has been dropped."

"That is correct."

"A charge, if I may say so, which should never have been brought."

The Chief Superintendent had turned his head to look out of the window, but apart from that movement was entirely still. In his youth he had hunted big game in Africa and his companions had often noted this total immobility in the few moments before he pulled the trigger.

Mullen had come in sight, approaching from the far end of Axe Lane. Two men who had been waiting in the doorway of

179

the block opposite strolled across to meet him. Some words were spoken. There was a moment when the three men stood looking at each other. Mullen had made a move towards the front door of the block, but one of the men had reached it before he did. He said something. Mullen tried the handle and finding the door locked, fell back. After a further short exchange the three men moved off. Mullen in the middle, the men on either side.

Yule, who had come across to see what his visitor was finding so interesting, said, "What the hell's going on? Who are those men?"

"I don't know their names," said Baron. "But my guess would be that they are a detective inspector and a detective sergeant from the Wood Street Station."

"So what are they doing?"

"They are taking Mullen into custody. When the Court sits on Monday he will be charged with the murder of Jack Katanga. I'll leave you now. You'll have much to do."

After he had gone Yule returned to his chair and sat for five minutes. No one looking at him would have suspected that he was worried or upset. The disturbance was internal and was soon under control.

As Baron had said, there was much to do.

He made three telephone calls. One to Lewis Silverborn, whom he found in his garden at home, one to Max Freustadt, who was in his office in King Charles II Street and a final one, after some thought, to a private number in Pretoria.

20

It is quite possible that the news would not have broken until the Court proceedings on Monday, and since these proceedings should not have occupied more than a few minutes it might have been late on Monday before the press machine got into gear.

The fact that everything happened so much sooner was due to stout Harold Ratter. From his vantage point in Axe Lane he had observed and understood what was happening to Mullen. Moreover he had recognised one of the City detectives as an old friend. Catching him as he came off duty he had, over a drink, extracted all that he needed to know.

"Had to pick him up in the street," explained his friend. "Some bloody stupid rule about not going into consular premises. Can't think why we wrap these buggers up in cotton-wool, can you?"

Ratter agreed that it was stupid. "Wouldn't worry about that sort of thing in South Africa, would they?"

Somewhat to his friend's surprise he refused the offer of a second drink. There was a news agency with which he had dealt in the past and which paid for inside information. And this particular item was not only valuable, but, as he appreciated, the fresher it was the more he could get for it.

Accordingly the arrest of Karl Mullen on a charge of murdering Jack Katanga became headline news in all the leading Sunday papers. It was not much more than the headlines because only the bare fact was, as yet, known. But it was pregnant with possibilities.

The News Editor of the *Sentinel* convened a meeting of his principal assistants at midday on Sunday. He said, "We shall

181

have to be careful about the contempt of court angle with this new case, but as soon as the shop-lifting charge is thrown out – which it will be, I understand, tomorrow morning – we can say what we like about that. The political and diplomatic angles – "

"And all Mullen's efforts to wriggle out under diplomatic cover," suggested his number two, who had been infuriated by the existing gag.

"All that, yes. And when we're talking about the book – a bestseller now, I reckon – you can work in the whole Katanga story. So there's a lot of lines to be hunted. Mrs. Katanga should have something to say. And we've been having a flow of stuff from some bods in North London who call themselves the Orange Consortium. Get after them. And the lawyers – "

On that Sunday morning three households were particularly interested in the news.

Mr. Banting's partner, John Benson, read it over the breakfast table in his Roehampton house. He said to his wife, "Now that it's stopped being a rumour and become a hard fact we can get our teeth into it."

"I believe you're starting to enjoy it," said his wife.

"I don't know about enjoying it. We can do some real work on it now."

"Talking about real work," said his wife, "I was walking with the children on Putney Heath yesterday and found two policemen having a quiet smoke behind the old bomb-shelter. When I asked them what they were doing they said, without batting an eyelid, that they were searching the Heath. If that was the way they were doing their job I don't imagine they're going to find whatever it is they're meant to be looking for."

"Searching the Heath, were they?" said Benson thoughtfully. "Interesting. I'd like to know what they *were* looking for."

"Would it help you if you found out?"

"It would depend what it turned out to be. If it was a tin of weedkiller it might be very interesting indeed."

"Then why not let me have a look for it."

"You?"

"Perhaps you've forgotten," said his wife coldly, "that I am District Commissioner of the Scouts *and* the Guides. I could put two hundred boys and girls onto the Heath. We'd dress it up, of course, as nature study or a treasure hunt. Something like that."

Benson thought about it. He said, "It's an idea. But just at the moment, I think not. We'll let the regular machinery of the law turn over for a bit before we bring in the irregulars."

In the Sherman household the news meant that Roger was on the telephone for most of the morning. First he spoke to Mr. Banting, who had missed the news and was pleased and a little shocked by it. Bantings had never handled a murder case in the whole of its decorous existence. "I'm sure," he said, "that I can leave it to John Benson and you with every confidence."

Next he tracked down Martin Bull, who was on the golf-course, and de Morgan who was at his weekend cottage in Sussex. Both agreed to make themselves available for a consultation at half past eight the next day. When he bespoke his breakfast for seven o'clock his wife said, "What's the hurry?"

"Mullen will be brought up at the Mansion House at half past ten. It may only be formal, but we've got to be ready for it."

"Why the Mansion House?"

"Because," said Roger, "Mullen was arrested in the City. It's just possible that the prosecution may find themselves regretting that fact."

The Rectory at Ucklebury Cross got its newspapers at lunch-time. It had been the rector's intention to preach a sermon at evensong on the vanity of human wishes; a composition in a minor key, not so much protesting against fate as accepting the down-turns graciously. He had selected an appropriate text from the Book of Isaiah: 'I shall go softly all my years in the bitterness of my soul.'

Now his whole outlook was transformed. It seemed that it had not been an impersonal natural justice that had removed his enemy and allowed him to die peacefully in his bed. Not so. He had been murdered in cold-blood and what made this ending particularly sweet to Ramsay was that it seemed likely that he had brought it on himself.

He turned for his text to Ecclesiastes. 'He that diggeth a pit shall fall into it; and whoso breaketh an hedge, a serpent shall bite him.' For Ramsay, Mullen had taken on the role of the angel with the fiery sword, the minister of ultimate justice.

183

Finding it impossible to bring him back to his own country to a felon's death, he had struck down Katanga where he stood.

His parishioners were astonished at their rector's exultation. "Looks like he's backed a long odds winner," said the rector's warden, himself a keen betting man.

On Monday morning, the car which brought Mullen from the police station to the Mansion House had started through back streets and it was only when it emerged into the open space in front of the Royal Exchange that he glimpsed the head of the crowd. They had been turned down Walbrook by the police. None of them had, now, any hope of getting into court, but it seemed that they were prepared to put up with hours of discomfort merely to catch a glimpse of the man all the papers were talking about.

There were a few scattered shouts and boos, but no real hostile demonstration as he was hurried up the steep front steps and into the building.

Once he was inside Mullen, who had started out in a sour temper from his night in the cell, found himself subtly flattered and mollified by the dignity of his surroundings: the white panelled walls, the enormous central light, the tall windows, the stamped leather chairs and benches. So different from the sordid functionalism of Bow Street.

To the blue-uniformed attendant who had shown him where to stand he said, "This is more like my idea of a court."

"It is, in fact, a court," said the attendant politely, "but it is not our custom to refer to it as such. We prefer to call it the Justice Room. And as you can see from the mace having been placed under the sword" – he indicated the dais with three chairs on it – "that indicates that the Lord Mayor will be sitting."

"You mean he's going to take the case himself?"

"Certainly, sir. He makes a point of sitting whenever an exceptional matter is involved."

Mullen grunted. This, too, seemed to accord with his importance and dignity. The place was packed. The gallery had seats for fifteen. Thirty members of the public had been squeezed in before the closure was applied. The press were even less fortunate. There was hardly any room for them at all.

184

Looking down from the dock Mullen could see Martin Bull and behind him Roger Sherman. Roger had already spent half an hour with him at Wood Street and had explained to him the decision which had been reached at his early morning discussion with Counsel, a decision with which he was in full agreement.

"All rise," said the clerk as the Lord Mayor appeared and took his place, flanked by his two senior aldermen. As soon as he was seated, Dudley Lashmar got up. He said, "I appear for the Crown, sir. My learned friend, Mr. Bull, appears for the defence."

(The Attorney General's opinion of Lashmar had not improved, but as Eileen Wyvil had said, "It's only a formality. Let him do it. Even Dudley can't make a mess of it.")

The Lord Mayor identified the two Counsel, nodded towards them and said, "Yes, Mr. Lashmar."

"The accused is charged with the murder of Jack Katanga on November 1st by the administration of weedkiller containing paraquat and other noxious substances. I have only one application to make at the moment. That is to ask for an adjournment."

"I assume that the defence concurs."

Martin Bull said, "If you please, my Lord Mayor. It was, of course, anticipated that such an application would be made and the defence has no objection to it. However, there is one further matter."

"Yes, Mr. Bull."

"At the moment when the accused was arrested he was on bail for a previous offence. A charge which is, I understand, to be dropped. My application is for an extension of bail to this charge – "

Lashmar was already on his feet.

"I hardly think my learned friend can be serious. Surely he is able to distinguish between a charge of shop-lifting and a charge of murder."

Noting that Bull had not resumed his seat the Lord Mayor said, "I deprecate Counsel interrupting each other as though they were squabbling round the dinner-table. Yes, Mr. Bull."

"I was about to explain, my Lord, that although the present charge is a serious one there are, I would submit, special circumstances which ought to be taken note of. The first is

185

that, as a member of the South African military police, the accused is being subjected by the press to a campaign of vilification. If he is to defend himself properly it is essential that he should be at liberty – subject to the usual restraints which you will no doubt impose. Secondly I should say that his own government has so much confidence in him that it has expressed, through its Ambassador, its willingness to stand surety on his behalf for five hundred thousand pounds; or for more, should more be thought appropriate."

Lashmar, who had resumed his seat unwillingly, was up again almost before Bull had finished speaking. He said, "I totally fail to see what the attitude of the newspapers towards the accused has to do with the grant of bail. His advisers will have full access to him to help him prepare his defence. Nor am I impressed by the sum of money which the South African government is prepared to put down in order to rescue him."

"I'm afraid I don't understand that, Mr. Lashmar," said the Lord Mayor. "Are you implying that the South African government would put down this money to secure Mr. Mullen's temporary liberty and would then connive at his removal from this country?"

Exactly what you were implying, thought Roger. Interesting to see how you play that one.

Lashmar, already irritated, elected to say, in his most schoolmasterly tone, "I'm sorry that you should read anything so improbable into what I had hoped was a simple statement of fact. The object of sureties for bail is that people should be forced to pledge sums of money which they could not easily afford to lose. Surely it is obvious that five hundred thousand pounds or a million pounds means nothing to one of the wealthiest governments in the world."

He had succeeded in side-stepping the question, but at the cost of annoying the Lord Mayor, who did not appreciate being told that he had overlooked something obvious. At the same time he realised that he was being asked to take an unusual step. There was a pregnant silence while he considered the matter.

Then he said, "I am not, although Mr. Lashmar appears to think so, unaware of the facts behind this case. I also appreciate his argument – it might, I think, have been put forward with a little more respect to the Court – that the object of bail

186

is to ask for sums of money that the sureties concerned would be loath to lose. It appears that the accused is unpopular in this country. I propose, therefore, to adjourn this application for forty-eight hours. If, in that time, two members of the public are prepared to come forward and be bound in the sum of – shall we say five thousand pounds each – I shall feel inclined to grant bail, subject to conditions. The accused's passport will be impounded and he will be obliged to report to the police station at Wood Street every evening. If there is nothing more, Mr. Bull – "

Martin bowed respectfully. Lashmar gave a petulant jerk of his head and the next accused, a motorist who had foolishly parked his car in the forecourt of the Guildhall, forced his way into the Court. Most of the people who were there seemed anxious only to get out.

The Attorney General said, "What the hell did that blazing ass have to go and put the Lord Mayor's back up for?"

"I think," said Eileen Wyvil, "that the real mistake was having him arrested by the City Police. If the application had been heard at Bow Street, the idea of bail would have been thrown out straightaway."

"Would it be any use if you turned up on Wednesday and tried to soothe the old boy down?"

"I'll try if you want me to. But I don't think it'll do much good. I gather he's an obstinate man."

"He's not a lawyer, for God's sake. He's a successful fish-monger. It's high time that Court was abolished. It's an anachronism."

"Of course, there *are* still the two private sureties to find. There won't be any rush for that job."

"A couple of cranks will turn up."

"Ready to put down five thousand pounds each?"

"Well, perhaps not."

On the Tuesday afternoon a middle-aged lady, in well-cut tweeds and wearing the sort of hat which must have graced many a village fête, called in at The General Stores in Pipe Street. She seemed to be interested in garden appliances. Mr. Luck, who was alone at the time, was forced to rummage in his back room for rakes, trowels and spades. Finally she

187

selected an electric hedge trimmer. The little shop was so
badly lit that she had to take it out into the street to examine it
properly. Mr. Luck followed her and was framed in the
doorway for some seconds. Whilst this was going on a man
standing back from an open window in the building opposite
took two quick photographs. The lighting was not ideal, but it
was an excellent camera and he thought that they would be
what was wanted.

"I understand, Mr. Bull," said the Lord Mayor, "that two
members of the public have come forward in support of an
application by the accused for bail."

"That is so, my Lord."

"And both of them have deposited the required security
with the Court."

"That is correct."

"And they are both here?"

"They are here and ready to answer any questions you may
have for them. Mr. Glaister, will you stand up?"

"Full name and address, please."

"Gilbert Charles Glaister of 14 Mountview Court, Highgate."

"Now, Mr. Glaister. The first question is this. Have you any
connection with the accused?"

"No connection at all, sir."

"Then your reason for taking this step?"

"I am the editor and proprietor of the *Highside Times and
Journal*." He said this slowly so that the reporters could get it
down correctly. "Like all newspaper men I have been following both this case and the previous charge against Mullen very
closely. I do not wish to make accusations of prejudice, but it
seems to me that public opinion was being heavily weighted
against the accused. That being so, he ought to have *every*
facility to defend himself."

"And in your view," said the Lord Mayor, "the accused
would be better able to conduct his defence if he were given
his liberty. A somewhat restricted liberty, I should add."

"That is correct, sir."

"Thank you. You may sit down. Next, Mr. Bull – "

The Reverend Simon Ramsay was already on his feet. An
arresting figure, dressed from head to foot in black, topped

by a mop of snowy-white hair. When he had given his name and his address the Lord Mayor put the same question to him. Simon Ramsay said, "I have no connection with the accused and have never met him before."

Eileen Wyvil looked up from her notes with a frown.

"And your reasons for taking this step?"

"They are the same as those very adequately expressed to you by Mr. Glaister."

"Very well, then — " said the Lord Mayor and then noticed that Eileen Wyvil was on her feet.

"Before you finally decide on this matter," she said, in the voice which one of her colleagues had described as being equal parts of honey and vinegar, "might I, on behalf of the Crown, ask this surety to clarify one point?"

"Only if you think it is relevant."

"It arises directly from his reply that he had no connection with the accused. Which may, literally, be true. I would like to change the question somewhat and ask him whether he had any connection with the man Karl Mullen is accused of murdering."

"Yes. He may answer that."

Ramsay said, placidly, "He was my son-in-law."

"And in spite of this fact, you are prepared to assist Mullen."

"I did not allow it to weigh with me in any way in my desire to see that justice was done."

Eileen Wyvil said, "Thank you." And to the Lord Mayor, "I felt that the position should be made clear."

The Lord Mayor said, "The object of questioning sureties for bail is to make certain that they have no ulterior motive for assisting the accused. In this case, it seems to me that the opposite is the case. In spite of feelings which might have been supposed to lead him in a contrary direction, the Reverend Simon Ramsay has put the interests of justice above other more personal considerations. Very well, subject to the conditions which I mentioned on Monday, I am prepared to grant bail in this case."

Roger had a taxi standing by in Mansion House Lane and as soon as the necessary formalities had been completed he installed Mullen in it and they were driven back to Dr. Johnson's Buildings. Martin Bull, who had gone ahead, was waiting for them in de Morgan's room.

"No trouble, I hope," said de Morgan.

"Some mindless yapping from the crowd," said Mullen. The dignity of the Court and the success of the bail application had gone far to restore his self-possession.

"Yes. I suppose we must expect exhibitions of that sort. Let me update you. An inquest on Katanga has taken place and, as expected, has been adjourned. The next step will be committal proceedings. The prosecution will produce its witnesses, who can be examined and cross-examined in the usual way. It will then be for the Magistrate to decide whether a prima facie case has been established, so that the matter can go forward to the Central Criminal Court at the Old Bailey. You understand me, Mr. Mullen?"

"Sounds to me like taking two bites at the same cherry."

"In a way. But it has advantages for us. We can see the whole case we have to meet. Also, recently, a useful alternative procedure has been introduced. Instead of appearing in person, the witnesses' statements are served on us in written form. I propose, on your behalf, to agree to that."

"We're in your hands," grunted Mullen. It was clear that he was in some awe of the ex-Attorney General.

"Very well. Let us look now at our side of the case. First, I'd like you to tell us how and why you went to see Katanga on that Thursday morning."

This dive into the heart of the matter produced a visible tension in Mullen. After a pause he said, "I had heard some news from Pretoria which I felt it was my duty to pass on to Katanga."

"Yes?"

"I was informed that his mother and his two sisters had been taken into custody and that charges were pending."

"Charges of what?"

"Of conspiring against the State."

"And you felt that he could help them?"

"He could certainly have helped them. For instance, if he had been prepared to drop the absurd and unfounded evidence which he seemed prepared to give against me, that would naturally have been accepted as willingness to co-operate with our government."

De Morgan considered this statement carefully. The choplogic in it was clear to all of them, but instead of pursuing it he said, "Let me go back a little. Exactly how did you set up this meeting?"

"By telephone. From Yule's office. Before going all the way to Putney, I naturally needed to be certain that Katanga would be there."

"Of course. And you were told – ?"

"That the Katangas were both out. He had some business to transact with his publishers – about a second or third edition of his precious book, no doubt – and that he would be back at some time between eleven thirty and twelve."

"And his wife?"

"I had no interest in her movements. But I think that the girl – Anna – did tell me that she was out shopping and would be back at about the same time."

"Between eleven thirty and twelve."

"Yes."

"You are sure about that?"

"I'm sure that's what she said about Katanga. I think she said it about his wife. I didn't listen carefully to that. I had nothing to discuss with her."

"Nothing?"

Mullen looked up sharply. He said, "What are you getting at?"

"Surely your news concerned her mother-in-law and two sisters-in-law."

"Oh, that! I wouldn't discuss that sort of thing with a woman."

De Morgan thought about this for a moment. He was visualising what Mullen said as answers to questions in cross-examination. None of it made him very happy. He said, "And you're quite firm on the time of Katanga's return?"

"Do you want me to say it again?"

"I'm pressing you because you are certain to be pressed on it by the Attorney General. You realise, I hope, that the half-hour between eleven thirty and twelve is the most important thirty minutes in the whole case."

Mullen said nothing. Roger thought, He's not a fool. Surely he can see it.

De Morgan said, "I am assuming, of course, that it *was* the only time you were alone in the room. When your discussion

191

finished, did you go out ahead of Katanga, or did he lead the way to the front door?"

"We went out together. Why does it matter? What's it all about?"

Instead of answering him, de Morgan extracted one of the documents from the folder in front of him. He said, "We have had a word with our own medical adviser. Dr. Thoroughgood of the London Laboratory. We cannot put him fully in the picture until we see their medical evidence, but it is already clear that the suggestion will be that someone had been able to add an irritant liquid to the olive oil in which the bougie was standing."

"Bougie?"

"You don't know, then, about Katanga's previous accident and the treatment he was having? There was a lot about it in one of the Sunday papers."

"Sunday papers were not delivered to my cell at Wood Street."

"No. Of course not. I'd better explain then."

When he had finished, Mullen said, slowly, "Now that you mention it I did see a sort of glass jar on the sideboard. That's the one I'm meant to have tampered with, is it?"

"Yes. And now I hope you understand the importance of that half-hour. And of the evidence which Anna will give."

"She can't give any evidence about it. She wasn't in the room."

"She was next door. And, as we have now discovered, the partition between the kitchen and the living-room is so thin that it constitutes no real obstacle."

"However thin it was, she couldn't see through it."

"No," said de Morgan softly. "But she could use her ears."

The silence which followed seemed to Roger to take a long stride into the future. It was Mullen who broke it. He said, in a stifled voice, "And just what is she supposed to have heard?"

"Let me give you two alternatives. Neither of them may be true, but you will be able to judge, between them, the possible parameters of her evidence. She might say that during that half-hour she heard nothing apart from an occasional creak from the chair you were sitting in and perhaps an occasional rustle from the paper which you picked up from the table beside you and were passing the time by reading. Or she

192

might say something quite different. She might say, for instance, that you were pacing up and down. That at one point, hearing a particular board squeak, she knew that you had come to a halt in front of the sideboard. That she heard what sounded like a clink of glass and she wondered what you could have been up to. And that you returned hurriedly to your chair when you heard Katanga put his key into the front door."

"You're making it up."

"Of course I'm making things up," said de Morgan sharply. "Until we hear exactly what this witness tells the Court we can only guess what she will say."

"Yes," said Mullen. He seemed to have recovered his poise. "And since we're both playing guessing games, perhaps I could give you my own guess. Her story will be a lot closer to your first version than to your second."

"I'm sure we all share your confidence," said de Morgan.

As Mullen was leaving, de Morgan signalled to Roger to stay behind. When they were alone he said, "I couldn't help wondering why our client was so confident that this girl Anna would be on his side. Taking account of her nationality and background one would have supposed that she'd be only too glad to see him go down."

"I think I can explain that," said Roger. "We've had a lot of help from a young reporter on the *Highside Times and Journal* – "

When he had finished, de Morgan said, "Not easy for the girl. One sees that." With the end of the formal part of the conference he had got his favourite pipe going. "Glad you were able to put us in the picture, Mr. Sherman. Because" – puff – "it's pretty clear" – puff – "that this girl is going to need *very* careful handling."

21

On Thursday the *Sentinel* published, on its leader page, an article, under a one-word headline in its blackest print:

AGAIN?

It began without preamble.

In March 1984, four South Africans (Air Force Colonel Hendrik Botha and three businessmen, Stephanus de Jager, William Meteler Kamp and Jacobus La Grange) were arrested by British Customs and charged with illicit arms dealing. The charge was not disputed. It was shown that, in the six years between 1978 and 1984, they had channelled millions of pounds worth of high technology air force equipment from America and Europe to South Africa. The four men were first remanded in custody by the Coventry magistrates and in April were granted bail. To secure this, the First Secretary at the South African Embassy offered surety in the sum of £200,000. The men's passports were confiscated and they were ordered to report daily to the police.

When, six weeks later, the magistrates refused to relax these bail conditions, an application was made to Mr. Justice Leonard, in Chambers. In a ruling which was described at the time as unusual (one can think of other descriptions) the four men were allowed to go back to South Africa, on condition that they returned for the hearing of their case. *They did not return.* The bail sum, which had been increased to £400,000, was forfeited.

At a press conference in South Africa Colonel Botha

spoke, with pride, of the way he and his colleagues had helped South Africa to develop many weapon systems. He pointed out that £400,000 was 'peanuts' compared with the money they had saved their country in weapon purchases.

Bearing all this in mind our readers will be interested to learn that yesterday, Colonel Karl Mullen appeared at the Mansion House on resumed committal proceedings. He stood charged with the murder of a citizen of Mozambique, Jack Katanga. An application was made on his behalf for bail. It was granted on condition that his passport was confiscated and he reported daily to the police. We cannot speak with absolute certainty, but as far as we have been able to discover this is the first occasion on which a person charged with the crime of murder has been granted bail. We can only hope that the outcome will not be as humiliating to this country as it was on the previous occasion.

The Comet was crisper. It headed its article 'A Champion Wriggler' and said:

Those who have followed the twists and turns of the bookshop case will remember Mullen's two attempts – both unsuccessful – to wriggle out under pleas of diplomatic privilege. Though those two tricks were trumped, fate has now handed him an untrumpable card. The chief witness for the prosecution has been removed. How? Mullen is charged with his murder. Coincidence?

"Have you noticed," said Eileen Wyvil, "what a curious cross-fertilisation of information there is in this case?"

The Attorney General said, "I'm not sure that I understand what you mean." Like most of the members of the Chambers he was in some awe of his devil.

"In most cases, until we get to court and hear what the other side has got to say, we have no idea of what's been going on behind the scenes. Sometimes not even then. In this case we are both being fed, all the time, with the choicest tit-bits. Ours come mainly from these people who call themselves the Orange Consortium. Naturally they're all out to help us. The defence, on the other hand, seem to be hand in glove with a north London newspaper who are equally well informed, but

195

are against us."

"And is all this information going to be of any use to us?"

"I'd go as far as to say that *any* information about this girl Anna is of paramount importance."

The Attorney General thought about it. He had not yet had time to study the case as closely as Eileen had, but he could see the force of this. "I suppose," he said, "that it really boils down . to a question of which side she intends to support."

"Exactly. And at the moment we know that she is being successfully pressurised to support the defence."

"You mean that business about irregularity in her residence permit?"

"A very minor irregularity, really. *De facto*, if not in law, she is Professor Macheli's adopted daughter."

"I suppose you might say so."

"So it occurred to me that we might be able to take steps to remove the pressure."

"Steps?"

"Let me explain what I had in mind."

The Attorney General listened attentively. Then he said, "You realise I shall have to speak to the Home Secretary?"

"In view of the anxiety of the government that nothing should go wrong in this matter, I fancy that you will find him a not unsympathetic listener."

After the excitement of the bail proceedings the tempo had slowed. Representatives of the press had tapped all promising sources. They had been headed off by the police from Dorothy and Anna, had received an interesting lecture on crystallography from Professor Macheli and a prepared statement, drafted by Govan Kabaka, on behalf of the Orange Consortium.

The committal proceedings, being documentary, had proved unexciting and were, in any event, under a total reporting embargo. The press were not discouraged. They could feel the ground swell of public opinion and knew that the breakers would come roaring in when the Old Bailey was reached.

Questioned about this in the House, the Attorney General had said that the Honourable Members would not expect him to go into details about a pending case, but he would assure

196

them that the Crown and the defence were equally determined to waste no time. He thought it likely that, if nothing
unforeseen transpired, the matter could be brought on before
the end of January.

Like the press the Honourable Members, it seemed, were
happy to wait. As for Mullen, he had become as resigned as a
man of his temper could be to his evening visits to Wood
Street Police Station. On a dark evening, with snow threaten-
ing, the Desk Sergeant had said, "Soon be Christmas, Mr.
Mullen." And it was, in fact, ten days before that great Christian festival that he received a summons to King Charles II
Street. It was the first word he had heard from there for
nearly a month.

He went unwillingly. He did not consider that the Consul
General and his aides had taken his plight seriously enough.
Fischer Yule had been a staunch supporter, and his lawyers
had pulled out all the stops, but what had the representatives
of his own government done, except point out unpleasant
facts to him, as brutally as possible?

On this occasion Dieter Langenhoven received him alone.
As soon as his visitor was seated he switched on the warning
light which indicated that he was not to be disturbed. The
tape-recorder by his desk had already been disconnected.

Without saying a word, he pushed across a copy of the
London Gazette for that week.

The page at which it was folded open was headed, 'The
Aliens Department of the Home Office' – 'The Home Secretary has had his attention drawn to ten cases of infringe-
ment by proposing immigrants of the Regulations made by
him under S.R. and O. 917 for 1985. Although offences, in
the cases subjoined, have been established they are all of a
comparatively minor and technical character. It has therefore
been decided that in order to relieve the pressure on the
Immigration Tribunal, in the subjoined cases no further steps
need to be taken. This is *not* to be construed as a concession
that, should further similar cases occur, they will be treated in
a like manner.'

A list followed. Judging by the names, three of the parties
concerned were Indian, two were Pakistani and five were
West Indian. Mullen skipped the list and looked quickly down
to the paragraph at the end, which had been side-lined in red.

'For parity of treatment, in three further cases to which the attention of the department has been drawn, but in which proceedings have not yet commenced, it has been decided that no further steps need be taken.'

The last of the three names was Professor Leon Macheli.

Mullen stared at the entry for a long moment whilst its implications came home to him. He had hardly realised before how confidently he was relying on the friendly testimony of Anna. Now, for the first time, the future outlined itself before his eyes in uncompromising colours; a bleak landscape of disaster and disgrace.

He was incapable of speech. It was Langenhoven who broke the silence. He said, "I see that you realise the implications of this. A notable piece of chicanery by the British government. It will turn this girl from a friendly, or maybe a neutral witness, into one who will lie her head off to send you down."

"Yes," said Mullen.

Footsteps across the floor. A creaking board in front of the sideboard. The tell-tale clink of glass. Suddenly, it was all horribly probable.

"However," said Langenhoven, "this is a game that two can play. You understand that we cannot allow you to appear before a British Court with a prejudiced jury, lying witnesses and a judge who has probably been instructed to secure your conviction. That cannot be allowed."

"No," said Mullen.

"So. You will be in your flat at half past six tomorrow evening. Yule will have ensured that by that time the office is empty and the commissionaire has left. There will be a visitor for you. A Mr. Brown. Yule will admit him, bring him up to you and leave you with him. He will give you certain instructions. You will follow them implicitly. You understand what I am saying?"

"Yes," said Mullen, thickly. He understood very well.

When Mr. Brown arrived, punctual to the minute, Mullen thought he had never seen anyone so nondescript. Normal height, normal build, unremarkable face, no outstanding characteristics.

He said, "You must understand that I have no official position with the Embassy. I am occasionally asked to help them. I am glad to do so. That is all."

His accent told Mullen nothing. It could have been of any class or any country. Maybe a South African, but long resident in England.

"I have a passport for you. You will note from it that your name is George Alexander. You work for a firm called Alpine Tours, who have an office in Pimlico and specialise in arranging skiing holidays. A ticket has been purchased for you – a return ticket, of course" – Mr. Brown smiled faintly – "and a place booked for you on the 8.15 flight tomorrow from Heathrow to Geneva. You will pick the ticket up at the Swissair desk, identifying yourself by this passport. Is that quite clear?"

Mullen had been examining the photograph on the passport. Mr. Brown said, "Yes. You will need to make a few, very simple, alterations to your personal appearance. Nothing elaborate. Passport photographs are rarely examined closely. Your beard will have to go. To cover any signs of its removal, you will wash your whole face over with a light-brown stain. I have the stuff here. And you will wear these heavy gold-rimmed spectacles which match those in the photograph. They will not interfere with your sight, the glass in them is plain. You have English money? Of course. And there are Swiss francs in this envelope. You will not need much. Arrangements have been made to look after you on arrival. Carry only this brief-case. Clothes? Your normal outfit, but I suggest that you wear this light overcoat. It will be cold enough in the early morning for it to appear a natural thing to do. Travel by underground. Use the Bank station rather than St. Paul's. It is more crowded. Allow yourself ample time to reach Heathrow by half past seven. Is there anything more?"

"No," said Mullen. He felt oddly breathless. "No, I think that covers everything."

The five men who operated the watch on Yule's office worked in six-hour shifts, an arrangement which allowed them one day off in four. Harold Ratter came on duty that morning at 2.0 a.m. He studied the reports of his two predecessors. Chris Woodray, taking the 2.0 p.m. to 8.0 p.m. shift, had finished his report with a note. 'A man, not previously identified, arrived at half past six. Could have been a salesman. Was

199

slung out pretty quick. Yule left ten minutes later.' The next man had simply noted, 'No comings and goings.' His own stint, he guessed, would not get lively before eight o'clock.

At a few minutes before seven he jerked upright in his chair. The front door had opened and someone had come out. Viewed from above, in the half-light, changes in facial appearance were unimportant. He knew, from his shape and his walk, that it was Mullen. No shadow of doubt about it. He had watched him, twenty times, coming and going. He noted the topcoat and the brief-case and jumped immediately to the right conclusion.

Before Mullen had reached the end of Axe Lane, he was speaking on the telephone.

It was the stout detective's final and decisive intervention in the Mullen case.

"It was cleverly done," said Chief Superintendent Baron. "And if you want my honest opinion, if we hadn't been tipped off, I think he'd have got away with it. Our men at the airport had photographs, but they'd never actually met Mullen. I think the slight changes in his appearance would have got him through all right."

"Thank God they didn't," said the Director. He knew that if Mullen had got to Switzerland the resultant gale would have blown anyone held responsible out into the street.

"We let him pick up his tickets and took him when he went through Customs. I thought, for a moment, he was going to try to bolt, but he must have realised that he hadn't a chance."

"So where is he now?"

"We're holding him in the Remand Wing at Brixton. He'll stay there until he goes to the Bailey. We shall have to mount a full-scale security operation for that move."

"You think he may try to escape?"

"No," said Baron. "To prevent him being lynched."

This was not an exaggeration. As soon as the news broke the press pulled out all their stops, the great organs blared and the chorus of public opinion was roaring behind them.

The *Sentinel* was openly triumphant. They republished the whole of their previous article, and finished with a comment that nearly got them into trouble. 'At his next Mansion House banquet we hope that one of the courses eaten by the Lord

Mayor will be humble pie.'

A few arrows were shot at the South African Embassy, but it was not the main target. It was assumed that a man in Mullen's position would hold a number of alternative passports and could have organised his own evasion. There was, of course, the question of the tickets, but the girl at the Swissair desk was unable to give any description of the man who had ordered and paid for them. She tried very hard, but "I didn't really notice him," was all she could say.

The popular press concentrated on the personal sureties. Nobody would have cared if the South African government had forfeited a million, or ten million, pounds, but they were outraged by the idea that two private citizens, who had come to Mullen's assistance, with no thought of gain, but from an abstract idea of justice, should have been threatened with the loss of their life's savings.

Newspapers are never notably keen to puff a rival, but the *Highside Times and Journal* was felt to be sufficiently small to be allowed a modest share of approval. Simon Ramsay became a national hero. Finding, as many people have done, that sitting on a pedestal is uncomfortable, after three tiresome days he took himself off into retreat with a body of Anglican Friars.

With the tit-bit of the trial ahead of them none of the papers felt like letting the matter go. Recalling a previous conversation, the News Editor of the *Sentinel* said to his number two, "We couldn't see that it would develop in just this way, but it's top class news now, no question. We'll still have to steer clear of the rights and wrongs of the case, but we can say what we like about Mullen's conduct."

"Lovely," said his number two. "I was thinking of something on the lines of 'a South African snake whose final wriggle has landed him with his head in a noose'."

The Orange Consortium were more interested in deeds than in words. Andrew Mkeba said to Boyo Sesolo, "When it reaches the Old Bailey, how many of your men do you think you can put on the streets?"

"Real fighters? People who mean business? Possibly two hundred. If this shit gets a life sentence they'll be there to cheer. If by any chance he shouldn't get all he deserves, then they could show their disapproval, couldn't they?"

"How exactly?"

"Leave it to me," said Boyo. "We'll think up something pretty dramatic."

22

On Monday, January 7th, after a shortened Christmas vacation, the Bar resumed business. The Courts had not yet reopened and this gave the Attorney General and his devil an opportunity for an in-depth study of the Mullen papers.

Two hours of this was more than enough for Eileen. Her brain worked faster than the Attorney General's. Restoring the witness statements and other documents to her own copy of the brief and re-swathing it in white tape, she said, "I hear that Mullen has been moved to the hospital wing at Brixton. The only visitor he's been allowed so far is the resident psychiatrist."

"I don't suppose he got much out of him."

"He got nothing. Except a few well-chosen insults and a lot of obscenity."

"He's his own worst enemy," said the Attorney General. He was still busy with his own papers, arranging and rearranging them. "I think we've put together a pretty solid case."

"The defence can peck at it," agreed Eileen, "but they won't pull it down."

"Nothing's certain in the law. And it's bad tactics to assume that you're in for an easy ride. De Morgan will make every possible point, but there's one thing he can't get over or round. His client tried to bolt. It would have been an admission of defeat in itself – but by trying to leave his sureties in the lurch he's lost any shred of sympathy from the jury." When Eileen said nothing, he added, "You agree with that, I'm sure."

She said, "Oddly enough, that's the only aspect of the case that worries me. Given a solid, intelligent, middle-of-the-road

jury who will listen to evidence and are capable of understanding it, we should get home every time. But I can't help
thinking of these two sureties."

"The newspaper man and the padre?"

"Right. No doubt the journalist did it for publicity and the
clergyman because he loathed Katanga, but does either
reason really add up to a chance of losing five thousand
pounds – a chance which nearly came off?"

"So?"

"In my book, they were fanatics. And this is the sort of case
that breeds fanatics. Get two or three on the jury and little
matters like proof and logic are going by the board."

The Attorney General said, "I see what you mean. I think
I'd better have a word with my clerk."

Mr. Messenger was the oldest, and richest, member of the
Chambers. Since there was no retiring age for barristers'
clerks it was felt to be on the cards that he would celebrate his
hundredth birthday in harness. No one would have dreamed
of suggesting his removal. He was far too valuable. He knew,
personally, everyone connected with the administration of the
law in London. Most of them he had first met as schoolboys. It
would have seemed perfectly natural – though he would
never have taken such a liberty – had he addressed the Lord
Chief Justice as 'Shrimp', his school nickname.

He listened carefully to what the Attorney General had to
say. He had a great respect for Sir Humphrey Belling, not
only as head of Chambers, but as a staunch upholder of the
right in law and politics.

He said, "I'll have a word with the clerk at the Bailey.
Youngish, of course" – Mr. Messenger meant that he was
under fifty – "but quite a sound man. The first thing is to
make certain that the panel for your Court is drawn from
Plumstead and Dulwich. *Not* from Lambeth and Hackney.
You might imagine that Lambeth would be reliable, with its
ecclesiastical connection, and so it was once, but I'm afraid it's
gone sadly downhill lately. Then you'll have them all vetted
by the C.R.O., the Special Branch and the Anti-terrorist
Squad."

"Of course."

"So far as the final selection goes – "

"I don't want any men with long hair or girls with short

204

hair. In fact, I'd be happier without any girls at all."

"But a few middle-aged women."

"Oh certainly. We don't want to be accused of sex discrimination."

"I think that sort of thing can best be attended to when the jury cards are handed out. If the clerk knows what you want, it's surprising how the cards seem to be arranged in the appropriate order."

"Do you think he will be helpful?"

"I had an idea about that, sir. The head-clerkship at the R.C.J. is falling vacant this summer. If I were to suggest to him that you would support his application – "

"It's not in my gift," said the Attorney General.

"No, sir. But a candidate with your support would be almost certain of the post."

The Attorney General saw the force of this. The head-clerkship at the Royal Courts of Justice was a plum. Its holder often finished up with a knighthood.

He said, "I have no objection, as long as the suggestion is not supposed to come from me."

"Certainly not," said Mr. Messenger. "That would be most improper."

"You look worried, Andrew," said Captain Hartshorn. "Why? Are you nervous because everything seems to be going too well?"

"Not really," said Mkeba. "Though it's the sort of situation that drives you to look round for snags. No. It's you I was worried about. Suppose you were run over by a bus."

"It might happen. Though I'm a very careful pedestrian."

"What I mean is, you keep too much to yourself."

"A weakness bred into sergeant-majors. They hear so many secrets, that they have to learn to keep their mouths buttoned. Were you thinking of anything in particular?"

"I was thinking of Mrs. Queen. Do you realise that you've never explained to anyone why you wanted her watched – or why you thought she was important?"

"No," said Hartshorn. "I haven't. All right. You've made your point. About the bus, I mean. So I'll tell you. But it's on the strict understanding that it goes no further."

"Of course."

"Very well. Mrs. Queen was first mentioned to me more than two years ago, when Katanga was still living in Hammersmith. We were, of course, in close touch with each other and when he came to see me one day he said that he regarded Mrs. Queen – his exact words – as a very dangerous woman. He was a bit shy of explaining exactly what he meant. All he would say was that she had been spreading stories about him. I gather he actually wanted some of Sesolo's troops to beat her up. Of course, I said 'No.'"

"Of course."

"It would have been stupid and worse than stupid. If an attack had been made on Mrs. Queen her stories would have become infinitely more damaging. No. What I did was to move him. I got hold of that house in Putney from one of our well-wishers and I thought that was the end of the matter. Then, when the bookshop incident occurred – and it became clear that Katanga was the one vital witness – I told them to keep an eye on him, but on no account to threaten Mrs. Queen."

"A watching brief."

"Exactly. However, when I was told about that journalist, Tamplin, going to see her, I did say that they could close up on her a bit. If she noticed what they were doing, it might make her think twice if she contemplated mischief."

"So the Queen is now in balk," said Mkeba, who appeared to be confusing chess and billiards.

"And will stay there until the trial's over," said Hartshorn firmly.

"We're set down," said de Morgan, "for Monday, January 14th. And, provisionally, we've been allotted the rest of the week, which is generous, as the Crown witness list is not a long one and ours is even shorter."

On this occasion John Benson was there with Roger. He said, "You must understand that, as a firm, we are somewhat inexperienced in this sort of thing. Don't misunderstand me. We've taken it on and we're fully behind you, from the senior partner down to the office boy, who has already lost a tooth in defence of our client. But when it comes to technicalities, we're totally in your hands. And Mr. Bull's hands, of course."

Martin smiled politely. De Morgan said, "Very well. There

are three matters we have to decide. The first is indeed a technical one. From the witnesses the Crown are calling it's clear that they are relying on the bookshop incident as proof of motive. It would be open to us to object. To say that they are attempting to bring in a previous conviction – and that, of course, is something that's never allowed."

Benson said, "Surely they'll maintain that it wasn't a conviction."

"Nevertheless we could criticise it as an attempt to smear Mullen by dragging in a previous charge. I don't think we should succeed in excluding it altogether and I'm inclined to think it would be better to save it, if I find it necessary to refer to it at all, for comment in my closing."

"Besides which," said Martin, "every member of the jury will know all about it anyway."

"Probably. The next point is whether we put Mullen in the box. If he runs true to form he will antagonise everyone – Bench, Bar and jury. As defender, I'd be much happier if the Criminal Evidence Act, 1898, had never got into the statute book. Nine prisoners in ten convict themselves out of their own mouths. On the other hand, it can be extremely dangerous *not* to call him. It makes the jury say to themselves, 'What's he got to hide?' It's particularly difficult in this case, but my feeling, at the moment, is to keep him out of the box."

"From the way he performed in the police court," said Roger, "I couldn't agree with you more."

"Which brings me to my last and most important point. The girl, Anna. The difficulty here is that we simply don't know what she's going to say. Her evidence on committal was cleverly kept down to the statement that she was in the next room during the vital half-hour. She does say that the partition between the two rooms was very thin, so that she knew that Mullen was there and could hear if he moved about. You can imagine the Attorney General picking up this point and saying, 'Do you think you could elaborate a little on that, Miss Macheli?'"

"And then she can say what she likes."

"Within reason."

Silence descended on the room. It was broken by Benson, who said, "You must excuse my ignorance of the etiquette in these matters, if I ask you a question which perhaps I shouldn't. Do you think there's any real chance of an acquittal?"

De Morgan said, with a smile, "That's very like the question that doctors dislike answering, when a wife says to them, 'Is my husband going to die?' All they can do is to weigh comfort against truth. The best answer I can give you is this. You no doubt remember the famous comment made by one of my predecessors, that the Devil himself knoweth not the mind of man. If I knew the minds of the twelve men and women in the jury box, I could answer your question."

When the solicitors had gone, Martin said, "You side-stepped that very neatly. Now perhaps you could tell me what you really think."

De Morgan suspended an irritable search for his favourite pipe, which seemed to have strayed, and said, "It's a David and Goliath situation, isn't it? The Crown has a truly formidable set of backers. No question about that. They've got the government machine, which has equipped them with a top pathologist and an eminent scientist, with all the resources of the Aldermaston laboratory behind them. They've got the police, both the Metropolitan Force and the Special Branch. And a well-organised clique from north London, possibly the most dangerous because they are the most unscrupulous. All backed by the massive weight of public opinion."

"Even the Church militant," said Martin gloomily. "They've rallied in support of the rector of Ucklebury Cross."

"Right. And who have *we* got? A firm of solicitors who admit that they know next to nothing about criminal work. They'll do their damnedest, I'm sure, but enthusiasm is no substitute for experience. Oh yes, and one north London newspaper."

"And nine schoolboys," said Martin. "Roger Sherman tells me that his son organised a debate at St. Paul's on the lines of 'fair play for Mullen'. Ninety-four boys voted against him, but he did get eight on his side."

Back in the office, Benson said, "It looks as though we're in for a hiding."

"It looks that way," agreed Roger. "Though I have an idea which might go some way towards levelling the odds."

"Out with it," said Benson.

An odd result of the crisis was that he was now almost the

208

keener of the two.

"De Morgan said – and I'm sure he's right – that in a case like this it's no good sitting back and scoring debating points. We've got to attack. And, as far as I can see, we've only one possible weapon – the unknown Mrs. Queen. We could afford to buy her evidence. No shortage of money now."

"All right," said Benson. "I'm inclined to agree. But I'd rather someone else made the approach. If we put him in funds, wouldn't that reporter do it for us?"

"Fred Tamplin? Yes. He's a forritsome lad. I'll ask him."

"And there is one other thing we might do. It's not my idea, it's my wife's." He explained what she had suggested.

"First-class," said Roger. "Even if they don't turn anything up, it can't do any harm."

"Subject, then, to those two points, I think we can get the brief into something like final shape. We shall need a formal proof of evidence from Dr. Thoroughgood – "

It was nearly nine o'clock when Roger got home. He had been held up, not only by the work in the office but by the fog which had come up at teatime and had been thickening ever since. Over a late supper he explained to Harriet what they had been doing.

"Tamplin's going out there now. He thinks this fog will be helpful if he has to side-step anyone who's watching. He'll have a report for me before we go to bed."

After supper they sat up talking resolutely about other things and waiting for the telephone. It rang at eleven o'clock. Roger picked up the receiver, said, "Sherman here," and listened for some time. Then he said, "Of course. I'll come straightaway."

Harriet said, "Not Tamplin?"

"That was Bart's Hospital. Tamplin's in the emergency surgical ward. A hit-and-run driver went over him. He insists on talking to me before they put him under. They'll hold off for thirty minutes, but no longer."

"Then I'd better drive," said Harriet. "I'm better in fog than you, and I can be finding somewhere to park whilst you're finding your way in."

Twenty-two minutes later she eased the car down Smith-field Street and drew up in front of the hospital. She seemed, thought Roger, as he got his breath back, to have an instinct for trouble split seconds before it happened and she had certainly driven much faster than he would have dared. He jumped out and plunged into the dark fortress.

Here he found Fred Tamplin. His head was swathed in bandages which left only his mouth and eyes visible. His right leg· was attached to a contraption of wire and wheels. The surgeon was standing, watch in hand, on the far side of the bed.

Tamplin said, "Not much time for talk." He was concentrating his bruised mind and shattered wits on what had to be said. "Never reached Mrs. Queen. Had a bit of luck though. Found that a man I play rugger with, name of Ian Malcolmson, had the house that backed on Mrs. Queen's. His garden runs down to her garden, you understand?"

Roger nodded.

"He said I could go through his house and reach Mrs. Queen that way. His wife's a bitch, but she's usually out between eight and nine. Some committee. So that's what I'd fixed to do. If you're taking it on, mention my name."

Roger saw the surgeon's hand move and got up. He said, "I'll be off. I'm sure you'll pull through all right." He doubted whether anything he said would penetrate the bandages, but Fred seemed to understand him.

When they got home, he said, "I can't go tonight. It's much too late. I'll try it tomorrow night at half past eight. I only hope the fog holds."

Harriet said nothing, but he realised that it was not the sort of silence that implied consent. Finally she said, "Do you really think it was an accident?"

"No, I don't. People don't go blinding down a side street in a fog. It was a deliberate attempt by the Orange boys to stop him talking to Mrs. Queen."

"That's what I thought. I don't want you brought home on a stretcher. Why don't you go to the police? Tell them that Mrs. Queen is a possible witness, who's being threatened."

"You don't understand," said Roger. "The police aren't on our side. They're against us. If I told them the whole story they'd insist on coming along with me. First they'd try to bully Mrs. Queen. Then they'd insist on getting a statement from her. Which is the last thing we want. She's our secret weapon. If she's going to be any use, she's got to be fired at the right time, not before. And totally untampered with."

Harriet still seemed doubtful. In the end she said, "Let's leave it. If it's a clear night, you won't have a chance. If it's foggy, you might."

"Right," said Roger. "D-day will be postponed until the weather is favourable. Does that satisfy you?"

Harriet said, "I still think you're crazy."

At seven o'clock on the following evening the fog, which had cleared at midday, was back in full force. Roger had equipped himself by drawing on his army kit. The most useful item was a pair of commando boots, tight round the ankle, rubber-soled, with steel toecaps. He wore an old pair of corduroy trousers, a roll-neck sweater and a water-proof jerkin with large pockets into one of which he had put a small Grundig tape-recorder. He planned to take the train to Hammersmith Broadway and go forward on foot. His only armament was a walking-stick which he had inherited from his grandfather. It was of the type known as a Penang Lawyer, made from thick thorn wood, with a heavy head.

The reasons he had given Harriet were sound enough. If Mrs. Queen was to be useful she had to be sprung as a surprise. But this was not the only reason for his expedition. He did not believe for a moment that what had happened to Fred Tamplin was an accident. He had been deliberately run down and left on the pavement by people who did not care whether he lived or died. On a night of fog, no one would believe that it had been anything but an accident. The fact that it was a safe crime made it somehow more despicable. Murder in intent if not in accomplishment. He thought that the driver might have been the smooth young man in the BMW Alpina, which Tamplin had told him about. A pressing reason for going to Hammersmith was the thought that he might meet him.

He expected no trouble north of the river and met none as he crossed Hammersmith Bridge. No car passed him in either direction. He had worked out his approach march carefully and now plunged into the area of small streets round the filter-beds of the reservoir. Boundary Road, where the helpful Mr. Malcolmson lived, might or might not be guarded. Boswell Road, which was the next turning, certainly would be. Plevna Street ran behind both of them. The fog was a little less dense than it had been over the river. A gleam of light could be seen from the ground-floor rooms of most of the little houses. Roger padded along quietly.

The turning from Plevna Street into Boundary Road proved to be unguarded. In the third house along on the right he found Ian Malcolmson waiting for him, a small, wiry man with the build of a scrum-half. He talked in a series of short bursts. It wasn't that he was upset. It seemed to be his natural style. He said, "You must be the lawyer. Fred told me about you. Shocking thing. I expect you heard. Happened just along the road. Bad as murder. I managed to have a word with Fred. Before the ambulance came along. He said you might be following it up. I stayed in on the off-chance. Tuesday night's our selection night. South-West London Club. I'm skipper of our 'A' team. That's where I ought to be now."

"I'm very grateful that you did stay in."

"Odd thing. I was going to suggest that Fred had a run with the first team on Saturday. He's been playing very well lately."

"I'm afraid he's had his last game for this season," said Roger.

As they were talking they had moved along the hall, through the kitchen and out at the back door. Malcolmson said, "Straight down the path and over the fence. I've cleared the wire from the top. Mrs. Queen's expecting you. One thing. If the wife comes back early you won't be able to get back through the house. She'll start screaming. Have to find some other way."

"I'll think of something," said Roger. "And thanks indeed."

Mrs Queen was waiting for him. He followed her into the back kitchen, where there was a stove, open at the front, giving out a pleasant warmth. The scene that followed stayed in Roger's memory when other, more important, things had been forgotten. Mrs. Queen, enthroned at the head of the kitchen table, under the light in its blood-red shade. Her sister and brother-in-law, ceremoniously presented, seated on either side. The flickering light from the fire, reflected from the polished coal scuttle and fire-irons, a clock on the dresser which whirred before it struck the quarters, like an old man clearing his throat; and Mrs. Queen, talking.

She had offered no objection when Roger had placed the

212

recorder on the table. She had spoken, without hesitation, hardly prompted by questions, for fifteen minutes. When she had finished she said, "Will you be asking Mr. and Mrs. Walworth to speak at the trial?"

"It will be Counsel's decision, but I rather think not. Your own account is perfectly clear."

He explained that if the Court didn't believe Mrs. Queen they wouldn't believe the Walworths. Also that when three witnesses spoke on the same matter they were apt to contradict each other and could be tripped up. His eye was on the clock, which now gave an exceptionally loud whirring as a preamble to announcing the hour. It was high time to go.

He took out an envelope, which he laid on the table and said, "I was authorised, if I thought what you had to say was particularly important, to increase our suggested offer. There is three hundred pounds in this envelope. We will pay you a further seven hundred" – he paused to let this sink in – "when you have repeated it in Court."

"Well, I'm sure that's very handsome," said Mrs. Queen. "You'd better go out the way you came. There's one or two men hanging round the front door. Up to no good, I imagine."

"If there's any trouble when it comes to the point," said Roger, "we'll send a very adequate escort to get you to Court."

"Trouble," said Mrs. Queen. "They won't make no trouble that I can't take care of."

Roger believed her. He thought that he had rarely met anyone who looked more capable of taking care of themselves. He was thinking about this when he reached the fence at the bottom of the garden and was preparing to climb over it. From the house ahead a woman was shouting. "Come inside, can't you, and shut the bloody door. Do you want us all to catch our bloody deaths of cold? What are you doing out there, anyway? Come in at once."

He heard the door slam. Mrs. Malcolmson was back.

He had said that if this happened he would think of something. There was only one way. It meant a move sideways and it involved the climbing of two garden fences and one wall. The first fence proved easy. It was made of wood, about six feet high and the wire on top of it was old and badly fixed. He jerked it out of its staples and climbed over. The next fence

213

was a different proposition. New wire, firmly fastened. His leather gloves partly protected his hands. In the end a desperate jerk brought the wire and the top board of the fence down together. He heaved himself over and landed in what felt, and sounded, like a glass frame. As he picked his way out of it he heard someone calling something from the house and sprinted for the final obstacle which was a brick wall, the top fully two feet above his head.

It was not the height that deterred him, but the fact that, as he turned into Boundary Road, he had received the distinct impression that someone was standing further along, in Plevna Street. If he climbed the wall he would land almost on top of him. But there was another possible exit. If this house was constructed on the same plan as Malcolmson's, it would have a covered passage along one side. And so it had and the door at the garden end was unfastened. He opened it as quietly as possible and found himself in a dark place which seemed to be full of obstacles. No time to waste. The householder, alerted by the noise of broken glass, would be coming out at any moment to investigate. He stumbled forward, kicked a pram out of his way, trod on something that might have been a rabbit hutch and reached the door at the far end. This was bolted, but on the inside. Ten seconds later he was back in Boundary Road.

His blood was up and he was looking for trouble.

When he turned left at the end of the road he saw that he had made no mistake. The fog had thinned a little and he could see a man standing there, with his back to the wall. As Roger came up he said, "What's up? Thought I heard someone shouting."

"That was Sam," said Roger.

"Sam who?"

"Sam Browne. You know. The man who invented the belt."

He was now perfectly placed. Holding his stick by the thin end he swung it viciously. He heard a crack. The man tumbled back against the wall with a strangled yelp.

One broken arm, thought Roger. That's a small payment on account for Fred. He ignored the man and plodded steadily on. The main opposition would be in Boswell Road.

Sure enough there were two men standing at the corner. They seemed worried, too. One of them said, "Who was that calling out?"

"It was Sam," said Roger. "Having a nightmare."

He was holding the stick, as he had been taught for close combat, in the middle. He jabbed upwards with it at the man on his right. The point landed somewhere, either in the stomach or the throat. As he went down the second man hit Roger with his clenched fist, full in the face.

This removed the last vestige of Roger's self-restraint. He used his feet, kicking the second man twice with his steel-capped shoes, first on the shin, then, as he doubled up, in the middle of the body hard enough to topple him. Other men were coming down Boswell Street, but he gave himself time to stamp hard on the first man's ankle as he lay on the pavement. He then took off down Plevna Street.

The mess he had left behind him held the opposition up, but not for long. Then they were coming after him and they were moving faster than he was. His heavy boots were fine for fighting, but not so good for running.

Decision. Take the next turning to the left. Get out of the jungle and head for civilisation. He could see the overhead lamps of Barnes Avenue ahead of him, glowing orange through the fog. There must be people there. Perhaps a patrolling policeman.

He got there, only yards ahead of the pursuit. The first buildings that he passed were shops and were shut. Next came the entrance to a block of flats. As he glanced in he saw that half a dozen youngish and athletic-looking men were coming down the stairs and had reached the hall. In that desperate moment he remembered something that Malcolmson had said. They must be – surely they could only be – the selection committee of the South-West London Rugby Football Club, who had completed their deliberations and were dispersing. As he dived into the hall he could see, over his shoulder, that his pursuers had blocked the doorway. Controlling his breathing with an effort he said, "Those people who are after me. They're the ones who knocked off Fred Tamplin."

This produced a moment of complete silence. All movement ceased in both camps.

The man who had been leading the group coming down into the hall said, "Interesting." He was huge and fair-haired, like a blond lion. After a further moment of silence he said,

"In that case, I think we'll go back to your flat, Colin. Come along with us, will you, sir?"

Nothing further was said until they were inside the second-floor flat and the door was shut.

"But if that's right, Norman," said a red-haired, red-moustached man, "mightn't it be a good idea to go down and sort them out?"

"No, Mike. It would be a bloody silly idea. With Fred out of action we're one short for Saturday already. We don't want two or three more casualties. The police are paid to deal with a shower like that. I'll ring for them to see our friend home. We haven't finished all your beer, have we, Colin? Because this bloke looks as though he could do with a drink."

"I think I ought to explain," said Roger. "I can't tell you everything, but I can put you in the picture to a certain extent."

When he had finished, the red-haired man said, "I know Mrs. Queen. Quite a girl. Boxes welter-weight."

"I hope you realise," said the blond lion seriously, "that on the whole we agreed with people who were against apartheid."

There was a murmur of assent.

"Except when they went too far," said the red-haired man, "and interfered with rugger."

"Or cricket," said Colin.

This amendment was also well received and was followed by a discussion on the rights and wrongs of apartheid which was broken up by the arrival of two police officers. There were vague explanations of unwarranted assault in the street and everyone escorted Roger to his train at Hammersmith Broadway. The opposition may have been hanging about, but made no move.

As the train started Roger relaxed in his seat and began to laugh. An elderly woman, who had been sitting next to him, edged away.

"It's all right, madam," said Roger. "I'm not drunk."

He was not drunk. He was laughing because he had just seen a great truth. Opposition to apartheid was a good thing. As long as it didn't interfere with rugby football. Or cricket.

When he got home Harriet took one look at his face and said, "Mrs. Queen seems to be a dangerous sort of woman to

216

interview."

"She boxes welter-weight," said Roger.

On the following afternoon he took the tape-recorder down to Dr. Johnson's Buildings with a typed transcript. De Morgan ignored the transcript. He put the recorder onto broadcast and they all listened to it, twice, right through.

"It opens up an interesting line," said de Morgan. "You realise that if we use it, it will mean turning our tactical scheme upside down."

"Attack instead of defence," said Roger.

"Correct. And it'll make us pretty unpopular, too. Well, we're so unpopular already that I suppose a little more won't hurt. All right. Leave it with me."

When Roger had gone he said to his junior, "Incidentally, Martin, I take back anything derogatory I may have said about Bantings." He was puffing happily at his pipe which, to the relief of everyone in Chambers, had been unearthed from behind a pile of old affidavits. "In fact, it might be a good thing if all solicitors had some army training, don't you think?"

23

The Attorney General inspected the jury with satisfaction. Twelve responsible citizens, eight male and four female, none of them under thirty.

"It was a close-run thing," said Wyvil.

The original panel for Court 1 had consisted of thirty-six persons. This was smaller than normal, but was accounted for by the fact that a fourteen-defendant City fraud in Court 2 had absorbed most of the reserves.

Two of the thirty-six had been found by the C.R.O. to have been guilty of minor criminal offences and had been removed. The Crown had exercised its right to six peremptory challenges and had got rid of two youths with long hair, one whose hair was short, but red, and three girls who looked intellectual and argumentative. The remaining twenty-eight had then been decimated by the judge's ruling that anyone who held strong views about apartheid should be exempted from service.

"Entirely a matter for their own consciences, Mr. Attorney. I have no intention of cross-examining my jurors."

This had caused something approaching panic for the jury bailiff, who knew how thin his reserves were. All concerned had breathed a sigh of relief when the very last member on the panel had proved acceptable.

"Let them be sworn," said the judge. Well timed, he thought. It was now half past twelve, so he and the jury could adjourn for their lunches. The jury would be taken by their bailiff to a private room reserved for them in a nearby hotel. He trusted that they would enjoy their meal and return refreshed.

Mr. Justice Hollebrow was a tiny man, enormously experienced in criminal matters. He was seventy years old, but as mentally alert as many men ten years his junior. The Bar recognised the soundness of his judgment and tolerated his occasional quirks.

Bonnie Parker thought he looked like a little parakeet up on his perch. In the face of considerable competition she had procured a ticket for a seat in the well of the Court. She had done this on the advice of Fred Tamplin, now convalescent, and unhappy, in Bart's. "Have a word with Mr. Crankling," he said. "Mention my name. His son and I were at the Polytechnic together and he's one of my oldest friends. The staff get an allotment of tickets. He'll let you have his if he can."

Mr. Crankling had proved obliging. He was possibly the only man who could claim seniority in the service of the law to the Attorney General's clerk, Mr. Messenger. He had started work at the Old Bailey as a boy, carrying up heavy scuttles of coal for the fires in the judges' private rooms, until the Clean Air Acts and the installation of central heating had relieved him of this back-breaking job.

Something's gone wrong, thought Bonnie.

The judge had reappeared, with all due ceremony. Counsel and solicitors were ready in their places. But there was no jury. Only the jury bailiff, in agitated conference with the clerk to the Court and, through him, with the judge. Finally the judge said, "Very well. Let them come in."

When the jury filed back into their places it was noted that there were only ten of them, and it was clear that something had upset them. One of the ladies had been crying. The judge, after a short consultation with the Attorney General and de Morgan said, "I am sorry to say that there has been an accident. Fortunately not a fatal accident, but an unpleasant one. On the jurors' way back from luncheon, a youth on a motorcycle skidded, lost control of his machine and mounted the pavement. Two jurors were injured and have been taken to hospital. Normally we might perhaps have proceeded with ten jurors, but I have decided that, in a case of this importance, a full jury is absolutely necessary. Two further jurors must be empanelled. Yes. What is it?"

The clerk and the jury bailiff were both trying to say something. The judge listened patiently and impartially to both.

When they had finished he raised his hand and said, "It seems, Mr. Attorney, that we are in some difficulty. We have exhausted our panel and there are no reserves immediately available."

The Attorney General said, "In that case, my Lord, a new panel will have to be enrolled. It will mean some days' delay I fear."

"Are you not overlooking a possible solution of the problem? Are not these the precise circumstances in which it is incumbent on you to *pray a tales*?"

The Attorney General said, "Oh." It was the sort of noise he might have made if someone had poked him unexpectedly in the stomach.

The judge, who was clearly enjoying himself, now entered into a prolonged discussion with the jury bailiff, ended by saying, "You'd better take a constable with you." When the two men had departed he said, addressing the Court, who were now in a high state of expectancy, "You are about to see an important principle demonstrated. That a jury is nothing more and nothing less than a cross-section of the public chosen, at random, to adjudicate in a criminal matter. A court official has gone out, into the street, to stop the first two appropriate persons he encounters to add them to the jury. And here, I think, they are."

The two new arrivals were a middle-aged woman dressed in well-cut country tweeds and a grey-haired, brown-faced man who wore gold-rimmed spectacles. They had been walking together, but were not, in fact, acquainted with each other. Both had arrived with the idea of getting into Court, had seen the hundred-yard queue still waiting, without much hope, outside the entrance to the public gallery and had walked round to the front of the Court where they had been seized by the jury bailiff and told to follow him.

The judge regarded his captives benevolently.

He said, "My bailiff will have explained to you that you are to join the jury. I take it you have no objection?"

Both were looking dazed, but nodded obediently.

"Very well, then, I have only two matters to ascertain. May I assume that you are both over the age of eighteen?" This produced a smile. "I see that I can. And you are both citizens of this country?"

The woman said, "In my case you can certainly assume that." Her manner of speaking underlined the status which her clothes had already announced. "I am Mrs. Gordon-Watson. I have lived all my life in this country. As also has my family before me for many hundreds of years."

The man had produced a card, which the judge studied. He said, "You are Dr. Venkata Rajami?"

"That is correct, my Lord. And I am a citizen of this country. I came here twelve years ago from South Africa. I secured naturalisation six years ago."

"Splendid. Your medical expertise will be most useful."

"Not a doctor of medicine, my Lord. A doctor of philosophy of Durban University."

"A philosophic outlook will be equally valuable," said the judge courteously.

At that point he observed that the Attorney General was on his feet. He said, "With respect, my Lord, if Dr. Rajami was recently resident in South Africa, it would surely be inappropriate for him to be a member of this particular jury."

"Are you not overlooking an important point, Mr. Attorney? When members are added to a jury under *a tales, no challenge is permitted by either side*. Let this man and this woman be sworn. Very good. Now, Mr. Attorney, we are at your disposal."

The Attorney General, who was still red in the face, said, "I do not propose to do more than outline the case for the Crown quite briefly. My witnesses will speak for themselves. The charge, members of the jury, is that the accused did, on November 1st last year, by the deliberate administration of a noxious substance, cause the death of Jack Katanga."

Not bad, thought Roger. It was a speech in the modern idiom, comprehensive, but unemphatic and dispassionate. It dealt with the acquisition of weedkiller by the accused, the opportunity he had made to use it and his reason for doing so.

"In considering this," he said, "you must bear in mind that the accused comes from a country where small offences are often punished by custodial sentences. He may well have thought that the same applied here."

There was no doubt that the jury were impressed.

"I will first show you the scene at which the events of Thursday, November 1st, took place."

A young policeman produced a plan of Katanga's house and copies were handed round. Wyvil said, "I observe that the outlines of the outside walls and most of the inside walls are drawn heavily, whilst the eastern end of the wall between the sitting-room and the kitchen is more faintly indicated. Could you tell us the significance of this?"

"As I understand it, the sitting-room was originally L-shaped. It took in not only the present space, but also the area to the north of it. When the kitchen was enlarged into a kitchen dining-room, this area was added to it and a wooden partition was put up blocking it off from the sitting-room."

"I hope that is clear," said Wyvil. The jury who were studying their copies of the plan signified that it was.

"You will find that the thinness of the dividing wall assumes some importance at a later stage in these proceedings."

She resumed her seat. Martin Bull indicated that he had no questions.

Next came a plump man with a sheaf of photographs which were handed round. Wyvil said, "It might help this witness if he had a copy of the plan. He can then explain from what point these photographs were taken."

Two had been taken from the road in front, two from the garden at the back and four inside the house. Martin Bull was particularly interested in the two taken from the garden.

He said, "Allow me to congratulate you. Compared with the photographs we sometimes see these are remarkably good and clear."

The plump man looked gratified.

"For instance, when you took this one you were standing on the lawn, I imagine."

"That's correct."

"The jury can see from it the patio which runs along outside the drawing-room and dining-room and the glass doors from both rooms which lead out onto it. I observe a small structure at the right-hand end. Can you tell us what that is? A coal bunker, perhaps?"

"As a matter of fact, I looked inside. It's a garden shed, with spades and forks and things like that."

"You're a gardener yourself?"

The witness admitted that he was.

"Then you must have noted how well kept the garden was.

222

We can see a lot of it from your second photograph."

"Yes, indeed. I always think the sign of a good garden is when the paths are nicely kept. Not that it's too difficult, nowadays, with the weedkillers they sell."

The judge said, "You mean that it is no longer a question of 'grubbing weeds from gravel paths with broken dinner knives', as Kipling puts it, in that beautiful poem, which I learned by heart when I was a boy and have never forgotten."

There was a hushed moment while the Court waited to see if the judge would recite the poem to them, but he evidently considered that this would be out of place and said sharply, "Come along. Let us get on."

"You are Dr. Alfred Moy-Williams, a licentiate of the Society of Apothecaries?"

The way in which the Attorney General said this appeared to underline the fact that this was the minimum qualification with which a doctor was entitled to practise.

Dr. Moy-Williams shifted uncomfortably and said, "Yes."

"The deceased was your patient and you were called in, when he collapsed, some time before two o'clock on November 1st. Would you tell us, in your own words, what transpired?"

Dr. Moy-Williams did his best. He described the previous accident, the scar which it had left and the arrangement he had made for the use of the bougie.

"And your certificate of death was – ?"

"Myocardial infarction caused by laryngeal spasms resulting from atresia of the trachea."

"Perhaps you would be good enough to translate that into layman's language."

"Heart failure, caused by blockage of the windpipe."

"Thank you. And subsequently, I believe, you had occasion to revise your former certificate."

After a moment for thought the doctor said, "I concluded, subsequently, that it was likely that some poisonous substance had been ingested which broke open the scar in the gullet."

"If I do not pursue this matter now," said the Attorney General, "it is because we shall be getting somewhat more – er – precise information from other witnesses."

Martin Bull said, "I have no questions for you, doctor, but considerable sympathy. We all know how easy it is to be wise

223

after the event."

Dr. Moy-Williams smiled gratefully. Dr. Thom took his place on the stand and implied that he, at least, was an old hand at the game by rattling off the oath without looking at the card.

"You are Dr. Ian Thom, M.A., B.M., B.Ch.?"

"I am."

"Can you tell us why you were called in?"

"The Will of the deceased stipulated cremation – therefore – "

"Wait a moment," said the judge. "Has the deceased's Will been proved to us?"

Martin Bull, getting up quickly, said, "If you please. The defence will be calling the solicitor who drew up the Will, which has now been probated. I can, however, assure the Court that the opening clause did enjoin cremation."

The judge said, "Thank you, Mr. Bull."

The Attorney General whispered to his junior, "Have we seen the Will?" Wyvil shook her head. "Then we'd better do so quickly."

"Yes, Dr. Thom."

"The regulations imposed on me two duties. To discuss the death with the deceased's regular medical attendant and with the nurse who had attended him. It transpired that this was his wife. I accordingly discussed the matter with her." He paused uncomfortably. He was well aware that he was not entitled to repeat what Dorothy had told him. What made it even more difficult was that it seemed uncertain whether she would herself be able to give evidence. He understood that worry and a succession of sleepless nights had brought her to a state where sedation was proving very necessary.

The Attorney General was also aware of the difficulty. He said, "Might I suggest, doctor, that you confine yourself to saying that *as a result of what she told you*, you concluded that further action was necessary."

"That is quite correct," said Dr. Thom gratefully. "I contacted Dr. Summerson, of Guy's Hospital, who was known to me, and arranged for the body to be taken to the Putney Mortuary, so that an autopsy could take place."

"Was this step also the result of your own observation?"

"Yes. I had noted significant signs of blistering at the back

224

of the mouth and tongue and in the oesophagus."

"Yes. Well Dr. Summerson will be able to tell us more about those. Thank you, doctor."

"Dr. Thom," said de Morgan, rising for the first time, "we all observed your embarrassment when you were dealing with your conversation with Mrs. Katanga. You appreciated, correctly if I may say so, that the rules of evidence prevented you from reporting what she said to you. That is the rule which excludes what we call hearsay evidence."

"Yes."

"It is a rule which, like a number of others, has been devised, for the protection of the accused, against third-party statements made in his absence and which he cannot check."

"Certainly." It seemed to him that the former Attorney General was making heavy weather of it.

"However, I am entitled, on behalf of the accused, to dispense with that protection if I wish. And I do so wish. Because I think that in this case it is essential that the truth and the whole truth should be brought out, no matter whom it harms or helps."

"What's the old goat getting at?" muttered the Attorney General. Wyvil shook her head.

"I therefore invite you to tell us what it was that Mrs. Katanga said that led you to invoke the help of Dr. Summerson."

Dr. Thom thought about this for a moment. Then he said, "Actually it was the scarring in the mouth and throat – "

"No, no, doctor. Let me correct you. That was your *second* reason for flying to Dr. Summerson. The first reason, you told us, was something Mrs. Katanga said to you."

Dr. Thom looked round the Court for inspiration. Finding none, he said, "She told me that the accused had visited the house that morning and had been left alone in the sitting-room."

"And if she had told you that the vicar had called, and had been left alone in the sitting-room, would that have caused you to insist on an autopsy?"

"Well – no."

"So what is it about the accused that his visit sent you hot-foot to Guy's Hospital?"

"Well – I knew that Katanga was a witness in that shop-lifting case – ”

"Which has, in fact, been dismissed. You know that?"

"Yes."

"Then what has the bookshop case to do with it?"

"Nothing, really, I suppose."

"Then might I suggest that your suspicions were aroused *because the accused was a South African?*"

"Certainly not. I have no prejudice against South Africans."

"I expect you will tell us that many of your best friends are South Africans," said de Morgan and resumed his seat before Dr. Thom could say anything.

The judge looked at the clock and at the usher, who intoned, "Be upstanding."

On his way home from Court that evening Dr. Moy-Williams called at the Homestead. He found Dorothy on the sofa with an untouched cup of tea beside her.

He said, "Judging from the way things are going, you will be called by the Crown to give evidence some time tomorrow. Probably not until the afternoon. I understand they are going to deal with the doctors first. Now – the one essential thing is for you to get a proper night's rest. I have brought you some pills. They are only obtainable on prescription and I should warn you that they are more powerful than the ones you have been using. You must stick exactly to the prescribed dose."

Dorothy smiled faintly. She said, "Aren't you forgetting, doctor, that I was once a nurse? I understand what pills will and won't do."

The papers next morning were muted. They were marking time. The *Sentinel* said that the interest of the defence seemed to be concentrated, for some inexplicable reason, on the garden. *The Times*, which had christened the proceedings 'The Battle of the Attorney Generals', said, 'We have had suggestions of prejudice against South Africa, but we must wait for some real indication of the line the defence proposes to take.'

They were not kept waiting long.

226

24

Inspector Blanchard of the Putney subdivision of the Metropolitan Police opened the proceedings on the following morning. He explained the very detailed search which he had made of the Homestead, its dustbins and its garden, and a later search which his men had made of the surrounding land. Searches which had not discovered anything significant.

Martin Bull said, "I imagine that your earlier search included the garden shed of which we have been told."

"Certainly. I searched it most carefully."

"What, exactly, were you looking for on that occasion?"

The Inspector was ready for this. He said, "One of my sergeants, who had come to us from Hammersmith, happened to remember the previous accident – "

"The one Dr. Moy-Williams has told us about when disinfectant was mistaken for whisky."

"Yes."

"Then you were looking for disinfectant?"

"I was looking for any dangerous substance that might have been left lying about."

"But not, specifically, for weedkiller."

"Certainly not."

"Tell me, Inspector, when did you first hear that weedkiller was suspected?"

Blanchard thought about this. He said, "I knew of it, or certainly guessed it, when I was ordered to institute a search for a certain type of tin or container."

"But that knowledge was personal to you. And, no doubt, confidential."

"Certainly. In fact I would say that there had been no public statement of any sort about weedkiller until the proceedings at the Mansion House."

"Thank you, Inspector. That was my impression, too."

Dr. Summerson, who followed, did not occupy the Court for long. He explained that he had carried out an autopsy, which confirmed Dr. Thom's observations, that he had made sections of the oesophagus, larynx, trachea and stomach and had decided that these, with the glass jar and bougie, should be despatched at once to the Home Office Laboratory. In fact, he took them up himself that evening by car.

De Morgan said, "I should be rash, indeed, doctor, to ask any questions of a man of your national – indeed international – reputation. One small point only. When you took the jar and bougie to Aldermaston you were, I imagine, very careful how you packed them?"

"As careful as I could be."

"I had in mind that you would not have wished to obliterate any fingerprints which might be on them."

"I considered it safer to make an immediate test for prints in my own laboratory."

"Of course. Much better. And you discovered – ?"

"There were several examples of the same print on the handle of the bougie. And one, very clear example of that print on the jar."

The Attorney General said, "I can, if you wish, my Lord, now call the fingerprint expert from Scotland Yard to confirm that both sets of prints came from the deceased."

"The defence concedes the point," said de Morgan.

"To be quite accurate," said Summerson, "the prints on the handle of the bougie could hardly be described as a set. There were a number of superimposed impressions. On the jar, on the other hand, there was this one set. The thumb in front and the fingers behind."

"Thank you," said the judge. "It is always well to be precise about fingerprints."

"Then I will now call Dr. Gadney."

"My name," said the black-haired man with the build of a rugby forward, "is William Gadney. I am, and have been for the last eight years, in charge of the Government Laboratory at Aldermaston. On the evening of Friday, November 2nd, certain articles were handed to me by Dr. Summerson – "

He explained, using a minimum of technical language, the tests he had made. He said, "I should add that it was fortunate indeed that the authorities moved so speedily, since the liquid which I was testing had already started to become colloidal."

Everyone tried to look as though they grasped the significance of this. Dr. Gadney said, "I mean, of course, that as it absorbed the globules of the olive oil in which it had been mixed, it became increasingly difficult to isolate the smaller components. There was, however, no doubt that one of them was paraquat."

The judge said, "We have heard a great deal about paraquat. Could you tell us what it is?"

"Certainly, my Lord. It is dimethyl sulphate of bipyridylium."

"Thank you," said the judge faintly.

"It is highly poisonous and used nowadays in many agricultural weedkillers."

"A dangerous substance to be on public sale."

"It is true, my Lord, that it is classified as dangerous in the Poisons Rules and in the Control of Pesticides Regulations. But under the Agricultural Chemicals Approval Scheme – "

"Slowly, please. I am trying to get this down. Yes. Under that scheme?"

"It could be sold across the counter provided that the seller knew that the purchaser was a farmer or that he needed it for his garden."

"You set my mind at rest. I apologise, Mr. Attorney. I interrupted you."

"Did you, Dr. Gadney, finally succeed in isolating any other substances?"

"After certain elimination tests we located chlordane. In rather smaller quantities than the paraquat. It is a liquid insecticide often found in garden weedkillers."

"And taking these facts into account, what was your conclusion?"

"I concluded that the most probable additive was Paradol."

"Which contains five per cent paraquat and three per cent chlordane?"

"Yes."

De Morgan said, "Dr. Gadney, would you first be good enough to explain exactly what you mean by elimination tests?"

"Certainly. When a liquid is subjected to chromatography the instrument produces its result in the form of a graph, running roughly level, but with distinct peaks. It is these peaks which indicate the presence of different substances. We identify them by the size of the peak and its relative position in the graph. The larger ones can be identified easily. The presence of five per cent of paraquat was unquestionable. In the case of smaller peaks what we had to do – speaking roughly – was to surmise what they *might* be and then to rule out possible competitors by a series of elimination tests."

"Thank you, doctor. Might I put what you have told us even more crudely? You had to guess what these other components might be and then prove most of your guesses wrong."

"If you wish to put it that way."

"Then suppose that there was an even smaller peak – as you call it – or a number of peaks, am I right in thinking that it would have become increasingly difficult to identify them?"

"By now, almost impossible."

"So if I suggested that one of them might be parathion – a phosphorous insecticide, my Lord, often added to garden sprays – you would not regard this as impossible?"

"No. Not impossible."

"So that the added liquid might – just as an example – have been Killblane which contains five per cent paraquat, three per cent chlordane and two per cent parathion?"

"Killblane could not be ruled out. Others, too."

"But equally," said the Attorney General in re-examination, "there was nothing in your tests to show that it was not Paradol?"

"Certainly not."

"Then I think," said the judge, "that this would be a suitable moment to adjourn for lunch. And might I urge the jury to be very careful in crossing the streets."

First after lunch came Lionel Luck. He took the oath perkily, introduced himself and identified a tin of Paradol.

"Exhibit P.1," said Wyvil. "Not the one that was sold, but an identical one from Mr. Luck's shop."

Mr. Luck said that he had recognised Mullen, from numerous photographs in the press, and had thought it his duty to report immediately to the police his purchase of a tin of

Paradol garden weedkiller.

Martin Bull, rising slowly, said, "I understand that you might well recognise the accused from pictures you had seen. These would mostly, I think, have been in connection with an alleged charge of shop-lifting, which has now been dropped."

"That sort of thing."

"My first question is why you should have sold a tin of Paradol to the accused at all. Did you know him as a gardener?"

"Not exactly, no."

"Then under the Poisons Rules you should not have sold it to him."

"I'm afraid we shopkeepers don't take those rules very seriously."

"Then I advise you to change your habits," said the judge sharply.

"Yes, sir. I mean, my Lord."

"My next point, Mr. Luck, is this. Why should the purchase have excited you? If the accused had purchased a tin of washing-powder, would you have hurried round to the police station?"

"Of course not. But it wasn't washing-powder, was it? It was weedkiller."

"And what was so suspicious about that?"

"Well, I'd heard that he might be accused of poisoning Mr. Katanga – "

"What!" Bull barked this out so sharply that everyone jumped. He said, "This purchase in your shop was made on Wednesday, October 31st."

"Well – "

"Inspector Blanchard also told us, this morning, that so far as he knew there had been *no* public statement about this matter until the hearing at the Mansion House."

"Well," said Luck, who had got his breath back, "someone must have come into the shop and told me."

"His name, please."

"I can't exactly remember. And if I did happen to remember, I wouldn't want to involve anyone else."

"Mr. Luck," said the judge, "please understand this. There is no question of *you* involving anyone. If this person has evidence to give, he can be brought here, subpoenaed to give

231

that evidence."

"I am sorry, my Lord. But I can't remember who it was who told me. Not exactly. I have so many customers. And I've got no help. I'm at my wits' end sometimes – "

"I see," said the judge. There was silence while he made a lengthy note. "Yes, Mr. Bull."

"I suggested, Mr. Luck, that you *hurried* round to the police station. You did not contradict me. Of course, as an old enthusiast for anti-apartheid activity, you had every reason to get Mullen into trouble, had you not?"

"Who says I'm keen on – what did you call it – anti-apartheid activity? I don't take any interest in things like that. None at all."

"Then why did you rush out of your shop, leaving it unattended, and join the gang who were mobbing Mullen?"

"I didn't – I don't know what you're talking about – I can't remember – "

"Of course you remember. It happened within fifty yards of your shop."

"Oh, that time. Yes. Now you mention it, I do recall the incident."

"I didn't ask whether you recalled it. I asked why you joined in."

As Bull spoke he seemed to be examining a number of photographs. Luck watched him nervously for a moment. Then said, "I might have come down to the end of Pipe Street to see what was going on."

"Further than that, surely. Didn't you cross Cheapside and push into the crowd in Axe Lane?"

"I – well – no. I don't think I did anything like that."

"I have here, my Lord, certain photographs: Exhibits M.1–4. We shall be calling the photographer in due course. But in view of the answer given by this witness I think you should see them now. Two of them were taken, as you will see, on the occasion of the riot. Two were taken at a later date, from a point opposite Mr. Luck's shop."

The judge studied the photographs, looked at the witness and then back at the photographs again. He said, "I take it you are aware, Mr. Luck, that telling a lie, when you are on oath, constitutes the crime of perjury and can be visited by severe penalties. Let me, therefore, put to you once again the

232

question you have already been asked. Did you thrust yourself
into the crowd that was harassing the accused?"

"I may have done, my Lord. I am so confused these days
with worries about my business that my memory lets me
down."

The judge looked at Bull, who said, "We must, I suppose,
accept that very qualified explanation."

The judge made a further note in a silence that had become
embarrassing.

"No further questions," said the Attorney General. He
seemed as keen to get Mr. Luck out of the box as Mr. Luck
was to leave it. He said, "My witnesses have been dealing, so
far, with the questions of opportunity and means. We now
have to consider motive. As my Lord will instruct you, it is not
strictly necessary, in a charge of murder, to prove motive. But
where motive clearly exists, it is our duty to bring it to your
attention."

De Morgan had been studying the witness list. He said to
Bull, "Harold Ratter, Mavis Widdicombe – she'll be the girl
from the limited editions department – and Sebastian Lucius
Snow – presumably the manager. We're not disputing what
took place in the bookshop, so we can leave the first two alone,
but you could heckle Snow. If it does nothing else, it'll
strengthen the idea that we're relying on prejudice – which
may take their eyes off the ball."

Accordingly, the stout detective and the nervous Miss
Widdicombe came and departed unquestioned. To Mr. Snow,
when he had given his evidence, Martin Bull said, "I imagine
that you have experienced a good many cases of shop-lifting
in your well-known shop?"

"Alas, yes. In the ten years that I have been in charge, no
fewer than twenty-nine such cases."

"Then you must have devised what one might call a standard procedure for dealing with them?"

"Indeed, yes. If the delinquent is very young I can usually
frighten him enough to make it unlikely that he will try it
again. If he is a more hardened character I obtain his name
and address and warn him that he will receive a summons."

"But in this case, although you had incontrovertible evidence of his identity, you had the accused marched off to the
police station. In what way was this accused different from the

233

other twenty-eight?"

Mr. Snow took a deep breath, squared his shoulders and said, "He was a South African policeman. I considered that the experience would be good for him."

"A useful experience of British impartiality?" suggested the judge.

Mr. Snow looked baffled, but managed to say 'yes' before turning round for further questions. But Bull had sat down.

Whilst this was going on Anna and Dorothy Katanga had appeared at the door leading into the Court from the witness room. Before the Attorney General could speak de Morgan rose and said, "I understand from the list I have been given that Miss Macheli" – he nodded at the girl – "will be giving evidence next. Might I therefore ask that Mrs. Katanga, who will be following her, leaves the Court?"

"Yes," said the judge.

Dorothy was led out and Anna entered the witness-box looking, thought Roger, exactly like a small girl who had been taken to a party by her mother and deserted.

"Your name," said the Attorney General, "appears in these proceedings as Anna Macheli. It is, in fact, Anna Masai, is it not?"

"Yes, sir."

"I am not taking the point against you. We all understand that you have, for many years, regarded yourself as the adopted daughter of Professor Macheli."

"Yes, sir."

"And when you first came over here, the Professor – this was in connection with his residence permit – showed you as his daughter?"

"Yes, sir."

"A small irregularity which certain officials of the South African government unearthed and which they threatened to report, unless you were willing to help them. In particular, they used you to ferret out all possible details of Jack Katanga's life. Including the earlier accident – it happened before your time, of course – and the use of the bougie."

"Yes, sir."

"Thank you. I wanted the jury to understand that."

They understood it, all right, thought Roger. And they didn't like it much.

"Might we return then to what I will call the fatal Thursday? The accused telephoned your house. You remember? Yes. What I want to be quite clear about is what you said to him."

"I told him that Mr. and Mrs. Katanga were out and wouldn't be back until around midday."

"Midday. Not eleven thirty or midday?"

"No, sir. Midday."

"So when the accused arrived, you had to show him into the drawing-room and leave him there. Now we have been told that the partition between the kitchen and the drawing-room is very thin. Was it thin enough for you to hear the accused if he moved about?"

"Yes, sir."

"For instance, you would, I suppose, have heard if – "

De Morgan was starting to get up, but it was the judge who intervened.

"I don't think you should put words into the witness's mouth."

Anna said, suddenly and loudly, "I wasn't listening all that much. I was getting lunch."

"Very well," said the Attorney General sourly. "Tell us what happened next."

"Mr. Katanga came back. He must have seen the car outside because he went straight to the drawing-room. Then Mrs. Katanga came back. She was in the kitchen with me. We could hear them arguing next door. They were almost shouting."

"Then you can tell us what the accused said."

"He was saying that Mr. Katanga's mother and his sisters had been arrested and unless Mr. Katanga changed what he was going to say, about the bookshop, they'd be questioned. The way he said it, it sounded like – tortured."

The Attorney General waited for nearly half a minute, making a pretence of examining his brief. He was well aware of the effect the last answer had made on the jury.

"And what did Mr. Katanga say?"

"He said, 'Do what you like and be damned with you.' And I could hear the scrape of his chair as he got up, so I guessed the interview was over and went to open the front door. They came out and went down the path, stopping to argue, and then Mr. Mullen got into his car and drove off and Mr.

Katanga came back."

"That's very clear. Thank you."

"Miss Macheli," said de Morgan, speaking so quietly that the witness had to lean forward to hear him. "You were two years in that house at Putney, helping the Katangas. I believe that Mrs. Katanga was often out in the morning, shopping, in the West End, whilst Mr. Katanga stayed behind to get on with his literary work. Is that right?"

"Yes, sir."

"So that you were alone in the house with him."

"Yes, sir."

"On some such occasions, did he try to take advantage of you?"

Anna stared at him, her eyes wide open. Then she said, "I don't understand you."

De Morgan, speaking now quite sharply, said, "I will put it in any way you like. Did he try to seduce you?"

The gallery was starting to murmur. They didn't like this line of questioning. The judge sat like a graven image.

Anna, at last, said, "No – no." She had something else she wanted to say. It came almost in a whisper. "He was a gentleman."

"Very well," said de Morgan. "We'll leave it there. Tell me, have you ever seen this before?"

He had in his hand the tin of Paradol.

"No," said Anna. "I'm sure I haven't seen anything like that." She was so relieved at the change of topic that she spoke easily and clearly.

Good technique, thought Roger. First upset her, then ask her an innocent-seeming question.

"Or like this?" He had produced a squat black plastic bottle. "I shall be identifying this shortly, my Lord. It is a garden weedkiller, called Killblane."

"Yes, I think so. I'm not quite sure. I think I've seen something like that. In the tool shed."

"The shed we have been told was at the end of the patio?"

"Yes."

"Thank you. This will be S.B.1, my Lord."

Wyvil was looking at the witness list which the defence had produced. S.B. must be the mysterious Sophie Burnett.

"Almost finished, Miss Macheli. Just one thing more. You

236

stood at the door and watched the two men going down the path, stopping to argue and then going on and the accused driving off and Mr. Katanga coming back. How long did all this take – roughly?"

"Well, it might have been five minutes – or a little more."

"Thank you."

It was nearly four o'clock when Dorothy followed Anna onto the witness stand. The dusk of a January evening had been closing in on the Court and now the additional lights came on.

"Mrs. Katanga," said the Attorney General, "I will trouble you as little as possible."

Roger was staring at Dorothy, fascinated and horrified. He thought he had never seen such a frightening change in a woman. In the weeks since he had observed her at the inquest she seemed to have aged ten years. Her eyes were haunted and the deep pits under them seemed to tighten the whole face against the bones of the skull.

"First a question about the visit which the accused paid you on that Thursday. When had you told your girl that you would be back?"

"Around midday."

"You're sure of that?"

"Yes. I always liked to get back from the shops about midday. That gave me time to see about the lunch."

"I quite follow. When you did get back and were with Anna in the kitchen, did you overhear what passed between your husband and the accused?"

"You mean the threat he made about my mother-in-law and her children? Yes. I heard that. And I heard my husband refuse to withdraw his evidence."

"We have been told about that. But I am glad of your confirmation. There are a few further points of timing in which you can help us. Your husband had finished seeing off the accused by when?"

"It would have been about a quarter to one when he came back into the house."

"And he refused to join you at lunch – when would that have been?"

"Perhaps half an hour later. Or a bit more."

"And the first indication of trouble – choking and so on – ?"

237

"About a quarter of an hour after that."

"Your husband had, I believe, recently taken to using the bougie every day?"

"Yes. Every day at around one o'clock."

"That's very clear. Thank you. I have no further questions."

"Mrs. Katanga," said de Morgan, "I, too, will be as quick as I can, but I have more ground to cover than my learned friend. Would you first think back to the time when your father deserted you. Would it be right to say that your husband's family – his mother and his sisters – rallied round you?"

"They were kind to me."

"I believe that you wrote more than once to your father – when you finally managed to secure his address in England."

"Yes. I can remember writing – yes."

"And in those letters you spoke *very* warmly indeed of Mrs. Katanga. You referred to her as being a second mother to you."

"I'm afraid I can't remember details like that."

"Well, the letters will be produced in due course. For the moment, might I say that you had a very warm place in your heart for those three women?"

"Yes. You could say so."

"Then what were your feelings on that Thursday, when you learned that your husband was prepared to allow them to be tortured?"

After a pause the witness muttered something. The judge leaned forward and said, "I'm afraid I missed that."

"She said, my Lord, that she was upset."

"Thank you."

"Tell me, Mrs. Katanga, why did you leave Hammersmith?"

Shock tactics again, thought Roger.

"Why – ? It would be because we were offered a better house."

"Was that the only reason? Was it not also because your neighbours were starting to spread unpleasant rumours about you and your husband?"

"I don't understand you. Rumours? What rumours?"

"Suggestions, for instance, that when the first unfortunate accident with the disinfectant took place, you were in no hurry to summon assistance."

"Oh! Oh! It's not true."

238

"In fact, that you deliberately delayed summoning the doctor."

"I had trouble with the car. It wouldn't start."

"And what was wrong with the telephone?"

A pause. And then – "There might have been no one at the surgery."

"At eleven o'clock in the morning?"

The public gallery was beginning to boil and the Attorney General was on his feet. He said, in tones of outrage, "Unless my friend intends to produce some evidence of what he is putting to this witness – "

"Such is my intention," said de Morgan stonily. He was looking neither at the jury nor the judge, but at a point just above the witness's head. He stood, in silence, until the Attorney General had subsided and the Court was quiet. Then he said, "There was another rumour, was there not? That on certain occasions your husband behaved brutally to you?"

"If there was such a rumour," said Dorothy slowly, "I know of no foundation for it."

"I shall be doing my best to supply that foundation in due course. One last question, then. After leaving Hammersmith and during the time you have been living in Putney, did you and your husband sleep in separate rooms?"

This was too much for the gallery and any reply Dorothy may have made was drowned in a roar of protest. In the well of the Court no one moved until the shouting faltered and died. Then the judge said, "I was, in any event, about to rise. Before I do so, let me give you a warning. If, tomorrow, there is the slightest repetition of that disgraceful behaviour, the Court will be cleared."

"We had the gallery pretty well packed," said Boyo Sesolo. "Tomorrow we should be able to do even better. We've taken the head of the queue already and a little bit of money or muscle should get us all the other places."

"Good," said Hartshorn. "And outside?"

"It's under control. We've enough people to block the Old Bailey and Newgate Street. And if they divert into Giltspur Street or Snow Hill we can hold these two. They can't run us down. We're well supplied with metal jacks that'll blow their tyres. Probably overturn the vehicle if they came too fast. And if *that* happens, the crowd won't interfere. Nine-tenths of them are on our side. If that bastard gets less than a full life sentence, he'll be a badly damaged man before he gets to prison, I promise you that."

Oddly enough, the person who had the most reason to be triumphant was the most worried. After the meeting Rosemary said to Mkeba, "I've been in this from the start. And it's been a long trail, with a lot of twists and turns. Now that we're in sight of the end don't you think, Andrew, really, that we might leave Mullen to the law?"

"Personally, I'd like to. But we daren't. All eyes in South Africa are on us. We *must* demonstrate what the people of England think of a sadistic crook." When Rosemary said nothing, he added, "We're winning. Sure, we're winning. But we haven't won yet."

Martin Bull said, "We shan't get a very good press tomorrow, I guess."

He, John Benson and Roger were in de Morgan's room, to which they had fought their way, helped by a strong posse of police. The former Attorney General seemed unworried.

"I only wish," he said, "that I was twenty years younger. At the start of your career, unpopularity can be a great help. Pat Hastings made his name by defending a German businessman at a moment when the sinking of the *Lusitania* had raised anti-German feeling to hysterical heights. Excuse me."

He listened to the telephone for some minutes, then said, "I don't fancy dining in a draught. Why don't we have dinner at my Club?"

The telephone seemed to agree with this. De Morgan said, "That was my wife. Someone has been throwing bricks through our dining-room window."

240

25

"My witnesses," said de Morgan, opening the proceedings on the following morning, "are being called with one object only. That the jury may be in a position, at the end of the day, to arrive at a balanced verdict. I trust that they will be allowed to give their evidence" – he glanced up at the gallery – "undisturbed."

Sesolo's promise had been fulfilled. By force or by fraud the gallery had been packed with fighting members of the Consortium. But they were not there alone. When they were allowed in they had found, to their surprise, a number of men already seated, at carefully spaced intervals, on the benches. They were all large and all had proved uncommunicative.

Dr. Thoroughgood, of the London Laboratory, opened for the defence. He explained that he had analysed both Paradol and Killblane, bought from shops. He agreed that the only difference between them was two per cent of parathion in the Killblane. He had also examined the black plastic bottle S.B.1 and had found it to be three-quarters full of neat Killblane.

He was followed by the Reverend Simon Ramsay who produced, with deep resentment, letters which his daughter had written to him from Africa. It appeared that when he had become nationally famous over the bail proceedings he had been much plagued by journalists and had incautiously revealed the existence of the letters to one of them.

"I much regret having done so," he said. "And I am producing them under protest."

"We appreciate that," said de Morgan and proceeded to read a number of passages to the jury which fully bore out his statement about Dorothy's affection for her mother and sisters-in-law.

The next witness was Sophie Burnett, a self-possessed girl of twelve, in neat school uniform. With a gap-toothed grin which entranced the Court she told them, in detail, about the nature ramble and treasure hunt which had resulted in her turning up the Killblane container from under a pile of leaves on Putney Common. The Attorney General, who knew that cross-examination of children was a self-defeating exercise, smiled at her and let her depart.

The next witness, a white-haired, rosy-cheeked man introduced himself as Charles Piggott. He had been, he explained, until five years ago, Clerk to the Oxford Magistrates. He had with him certain court records. These showed that, twenty-one years ago, one Charles Mullen, whom he identified as the present accused, had pleaded guilty to the theft of a book from Harmsworths, the Oxford booksellers. He had been bound over for one year.

Having produced this totally unexpected evidence, which had set the reporters' pencils scurrying, he looked at the Attorney General, who could find no questions for him.

"What the hell's he playing at?" he said to Wyvil.

"I think I'm beginning to see," said Wyvil. "And I don't like it."

She liked the next one even less. It was Arthur Pauling, a partner in the firm of Pauling and Blackett, solicitors. He produced, with copies for all concerned, the Will of Jack Katanga.

"There are only two clauses, I think, that will interest you. The first is the one which called for cremation. A wish which could not, as you will have heard, be carried out. The other" – everyone had been reading fast and had got there ahead of him – "is a specific legacy of one thousand pounds to Anna Masai, known as Macheli. The residue of his estate goes to his wife."

"Can you give us an estimate of what that residue will amount to?"

"It's difficult to be precise. The unknown factor is the value of the copyright in his books. I should be surprised if his total estate, less liabilities, amounted to more than three thousand pounds."

"So that Anna has been left a third of his estate. Can you

242

suggest any reason for this beneficence?"

"We can only go by the Will. It says, 'for the help she has been to me'."

De Morgan sat down. The Attorney General could find no questions to ask him, either. The next witness was a cheerful-looking youngster who answered to the name of Hugh Marshment and identified photographs M.1–4 as having been taken by him. When Wyvil rose to cross-examine him, it was seen that she had, in her hand, a copy of the *Highgate Times and Journal.*

She said, "Tell us, Mr. Marshment, are you a player of volley-ball and do you," she examined the paper, "perform for the Highside Harriers?"

"That's right."

"Then you will have been involved in the disagreeable incident when certain anti-apartheid enthusiasts broke up the game."

"I'll say I was involved. I got a black eye."

"And this, no doubt, prejudiced you against anti-apartheid activities."

"It may have prejudiced me. I don't think it prejudiced my camera."

"The camera cannot lie," agreed Wyvil smoothly, "but the pictures which it takes can be carefully slanted."

Since this was not a question Mr. Marshment wisely made no attempt to answer it.

"My last witness," said de Morgan, "is Mrs. Prudence Queen."

The judge looked at his watch. Not yet twelve o'clock. Excellent. They should finish that day.

"Mrs. Queen, I understand that you, your sister and your brother-in-law, Mr. and Mrs. Walworth, live at No. 9 Boswell Road, Hammersmith, and were living there a little more than two years ago, when the Katangas were living at No. 7."

"That's right, sir, next-door neighbours. Very close. And what with helping them with jobs round the house, I was in and out most days."

"Then I'd like to direct your attention to an incident which took place in June of the year in which the Katangas left Hammersmith. I am referring to the time when Mr Katanga accidentally swallowed a quantity of disinfectant."

243

"That's right, sir. The first we knew about it was when Mrs. Katanga came running out into the street. We're not a posh neighbourhood. We don't have our own garages. People who have cars park them on the far side of the road."

"A most inconvenient habit for everyone else," said the judge. "But please continue."

"Well, sir, we saw her jump into the car and start grinding the self-starter. This went on and on. Being Saturday morning most people were at home and by this time a lot of them were looking out of their windows. One man shouted, 'Have you switched on?' Mrs. Katanga must have heard, because she did something and the car spluttered and then stopped. The man, who had come out into the street, said, 'You must have oiled up the plugs grinding away like that. You'll never start her now. If it's urgent, I'd better take you.' So in the end, she went round to the doctor's in his car."

"In the end," said de Morgan thoughtfully. "How much time would you suggest she had wasted by messing about with the car instead of telephoning?"

"Might have been ten minutes. We all asked her why she didn't telephone. She said she was too worried. Of course, it made people talk. That, and other things."

"Other things?"

"Like him beating her."

This produced a pin-drop silence. The judge had leaned forward, as though to hear the witness more clearly. He said, "Mr. de Morgan, I must ask you to ask your witness, please, to be quite explicit."

"I will do so, my Lord, but did not wish to appear to lead her."

But this was a witness who needed no prompting. She said, "Well, sir, living as you might say, right on top of them we couldn't help hearing things."

"What sort of things?"

"Like Mrs. Katanga, up in her bedroom, sobbing her heart out, poor soul. Mostly in the afternoon, that would be."

"Was her husband at home?"

"Oh, yes, sir. Not having a regular job, he was often home afternoons."

The gallery was seething, furious at what was being suggested. Frustrated by the fear of being thrown out if they gave

244

the least expression to their fury.

"Anything else? Not to hear, not really. They kept the bedroom windows shut when this was going on. But we couldn't help seeing things. Marks round her wrists, as though she'd been tied up. And once, I remember, we were in the chemist's, waiting for the man to attend to us. Coming in first I'd grabbed the only chair, so I got up and offered it to her. She said, 'No. Thank you, I'll stand.' Just as though" – the thought seemed to amuse Mrs. Queen – "she was a boy who'd been caned and was too sore to sit down."

De Morgan said, "Thank you. No, you must stay where you are. I think my friend has some questions for you."

When the Attorney General got up, it was clear that he was angry. Too angry to deal effectively with Mrs. Queen, thought Wyvil; though she added the rider – if such a feat were possible.

He said, "You have given us your name as Mrs. Queen. Might I ask if your husband is still alive?"

"I wouldn't hardly call that a vital matter, sir. But in fact I never had a husband."

"Then why do you call yourself Mrs. Queen?"

"It seemed more suitable at my age."

"But it was a lie?"

"If you wish to call it so." There was a flush along the top of her cheeks. Does he realise, thought Roger, that he's handling a Mills bomb and has just withdrawn the pin?

"Very well. Now as to the extraordinary story you've told us. You said 'we noticed' and 'we heard'. Were the other people your sister and brother-in-law?"

"Yes, sir. Other people too, sometimes."

"Then why are they not here supporting your extraordinary – I nearly said ridiculous – statements?"

"Well, sir, I did suggest it to our lawyer. But he said, 'No, just give them the plain facts yourself. If you bring along other people to tell the same story the lawyer on the other side will only try to make you contradict each other.'"

The laugh which this produced did nothing to calm down the Attorney General. Wyvil had her hand within inches of his sleeve. She knew that he was about to make the fatal mistake of asking a question at large, without any idea of what the answer would be. He said, "You've given us an unconvincing account of marks on Mrs. Katanga's wrists which might have been caused in many ways and a story of her not accepting the offer of a seat – natural, surely, as you were a much older woman. Was that all you saw?"

"Well, sir, once when they hadn't drawn the bedroom curtains right across, we did see that he'd tied her to the end of the bed." Before the Attorney General could make any comment, she added, in her most reasonable tones, "You know how it is, sir. When a man's wife gets a bit older and she doesn't set him off like she used to, he does things to her – spanks her or ties her up – just to work himself up. Of course, I suppose that being a bachelor you mightn't understand about things like that."

Looking down on the Court, the judge could see that some of the people were shocked, but more were trying not to laugh. He said to the official shorthand writer, "That last comment will *not* form part of your report." And to the Attorney General, "Please proceed."

"I can see no object, my Lord, in prolonging this farce."

"In that case, since I understand that this is the final defence witness – no re-examination? Very well, Mr. Attorney, the floor is yours."

It was twenty past twelve and the Attorney General had been hoping for the respite of a lunch interval to gather his thoughts together. Discussing matters with Wyvil on the previous evening he had said, "If ever there was a case in which the old rule would have operated more fairly, I mean the rule which gave the Crown the last word, it's this one. I've still no real idea what line de Morgan's going to take." And when Wyvil had pointed out that it would be the judge who had the last word he had growled, "Old Hollebrow is getting near retirement. He doesn't want to be guyed by the Court of Appeal. He'll keep a foot on both sides of the fence, you'll see."

He now demonstrated his professionalism by moving smoothly into the attack. "I imagine, members of the jury, that you were as amazed as I was by the last witness, both at what she said and *why* she said it. Why, in the world, should we have had to listen to a supposed account of the late Jack Katanga's relations with his wife? An account which, being dead, he can no longer contradict. It is not he who is on trial.

246

The object, and the only object of these proceedings, is to determine whether the accused murdered Mr. Katanga."

Motive, means, opportunity. They had heard it all before, but it did no harm to have it hammered out again. He made an excellent point about the fingerprints. He said, "As you have heard from Dr. Summerson, although there were, as would be expected, numerous and over-lapping examples of the deceased's fingerprints on the *handle* of the bougie, there was only one clear set on the jar itself. No doubt they came there when he moved the jar out and used the bougie – with such fatal results – that day. But why only *one* set? Surely because the murderer, when he added paraquat to the oil, had been careful to wipe the jar in case he had left prints of his own on it. And who would be more likely to take such a precaution than an experienced policeman?"

He made another good point, about the Will ("Sprung on us at the last moment, like much of the defence evidence.") "No one when making a Will assumes that he is going to die the next day. The deceased was at the start of what looked like being a very successful career. By the time he died a thousand pounds might not be a third – might not even be a thirtieth – of his estate."

Roger could find only one fault in the speech. It went on a little too long,. As the time passed one matter was exercising the minds of the jury to the exclusion of all others. When were they going to get their lunch? It was a quarter past one when the Attorney General concluded his careful summary and it was twenty past two when de Morgan rose to address them. His opening was unexpected.

He said, "I wonder how many of you remember the cases of Evans and Christie which were heard nearly forty years ago in this Court. In fact, members of the jury, it would help me if you would indicate."

Five hands went up at once, after a pause two more.

"Well, it's a majority." Hearing a laugh, he swung round. The judge had his hand up.

"Thank you, my Lord. Let me explain. Evans was charged with the murder of his wife and child. It seemed an open-and-shut case. But Counsel for the defence had come to the conclusion – it's far from clear how he did so – that one of the Crown witnesses, a man called Christie, was the real murderer. The subsequent discovery of the bodies of five young ladies concealed in Christie's flat certainly lent support to this theory. But that is not the point. What is clear is that once he had reached this conclusion Counsel was bound, by the rules of advocacy, to put it to Christie when he was giving evidence. And so he did. His exact words were, 'Mr. Christie, I have got to suggest to you – I do not wish there to be any misapprehension about it – that you are responsible for the deaths of Mrs. Evans and the little girl.' Now please note, and note carefully, members of the jury, *that I made no such suggestion to Mrs. Katanga when she was giving evidence.*"

"Ah," said Wyvil softly, "I thought that was where we were going."

The implication dawned more slowly on the rest of the Court. As it did so there was a collective sigh, like the wind moving in the tops of the trees, a gentle forerunner of storm.

"Although the more hysterical of our daily papers will no doubt think otherwise, it should be clear that I am *not* accusing Mrs. Katanga of killing her husband. My object is very different. As the Crown has admitted, the evidence in this case is circumstantial. Such evidence can be impressive, but it needs to be examined, with great care, to see that it leads to the conclusion which the Crown desires – and to no other conclusion. So let us examine it, to see whether, in each of its three compartments, an alternative theory might present itself.

"First, as to means. Or, in other words, the availability of weedkiller. I do not know if you were as little impressed as I was by Mr. Luck's evidence. I think he told a number of lies. But in a sense this is not important, since I am going to suggest that Paradol, the tin which he told us he remembers selling, does not really come into the matter at all. It is on the alternative and, according to Dr. Gadney, the equally likely product, called Killblane, that your attention must be fixed. The girl Anna did not see any signs of Paradol – and it is a container which does not hide its light under a bushel – but she did think she had seen a container of the more modestly packaged Killblane in the garden shed. Now it is clear, from the evidence of Inspector Blanchard, who made an immediate search, that by the following day it was no longer there. So what had happened to it? You will find a very possible answer

in the evidence of young Sophie Burnett, who found it concealed under leaves, on Putney Common, not far from
Katanga's house. And if you imagine that it might have been
any old container thrown away there, think again. Dr.
Thoroughgood has told us that it was three-quarters full of
neat Killblane, which retails at eleven pounds a bottle. An
expensive thing to jettison, don't you think?

"So, if Killblane was the fatal additive – and I can't help
thinking that the Crown's case would have been much better
founded if it had proceeded on that assumption – let us turn
to opportunity. The Killblane is in the shed. The accused
could not have reached it without passing in front of the
kitchen window and glass door which gave on to the patio –
look at the plans and photographs, please – thank you. Of
course the accused might have brought Killblane with him,
intending to use it whether he was successful in getting the
deceased to withdraw his evidence or not. He had half an
hour to use it. On the alternative theory, Mrs. Katanga had
the period – five minutes or more according to Anna – when
she was alone in the kitchen and Mullen was being shown out.
Five minutes, to step out onto the patio, take the Killblane
from the shed, enter the sitting-room, use it and conceal it for
subsequent disposal. So which theory do we believe? I should
not, I think, be guilty of exaggeration if I said that at this
point the two theories were running level.

"But when we come to motive, does not the balance tilt
decisively in favour of the alternative theory? For what was
the suggested motive of the accused? To save himself from
the consequences of a charge of attempted shop-lifting. For
which, even if found guilty – and the case was far from strong
– the maximum penalty would have been a fine. The prosecution has attempted to bolster the point by suggesting that,
coming from a country in which people, black people in
particular, get imprisoned for trivial offences, he might have
been so ignorant of the practice here that he feared like
treatment. But how can he, of all people, have thought this?
As you have heard, in a case of actual shop-lifting he had been
bound over. Why should he suppose that the law would be
more severe on the lesser offence of attempted shop-lifting?
That is nonsense, is it not?

"Turn, now, to Dorothy Katanga. In her previous house,

maltreated and humiliated. In her new house, more humiliated still, by the substitution of the hired help to relieve her of her duties in bed. A smouldering resentment, which needed only the smallest provocation to fan it into flames. And what a provocation it was! She learned that her husband was callously ready to hand over three women to whom she was devoted, to imprisonment and torture. I ask you to judge for yourself which was the more powerful motive.

"If you are thinking that the alternative possibility which I have outlined is every bit as theoretical as the case propounded by the Crown, I accept that. I accept it willingly. They are both theories. All I ask you to do is to balance one against the other. And when you have done so let me remind you of something said by Mr. Justice Humphreys, the greatest criminal lawyer of this century: 'Circumstantial evidence *must* be strong enough to exclude all reasonable alternatives.'"

De Morgan had been listened to in a silence unbroken by word or movement; by the gallery in unremitting hostility; by the body of the Court in appreciation of a remarkable forensic effort; and by the jury? Difficult to say. Certainly the summing-up of Mr. Justice Hollebrow did nothing to help them make up their minds. He spoke for half an hour, scrupulously repeating the points made by both sides, but giving no hint of his own opinion. After which, he dismissed them to their room and disappeared to his.

Normally, the Court would have emptied, but no one seemed anxious to lose their place. De Morgan went down to have a word with Mullen, whom he found in a sour temper at not having been allowed to give evidence. He could only say to him. "I thought it best." On his return, Bull said, "If the jury makes up its mind quickly, it'll mean they're against us."

"You might be right," said de Morgan. He was too drained of emotion to argue.

It was quicker than anyone had expected. Just before four o'clock the word went round that the jury were returning. Counsel squeezed back into their places and the judge reappeared. The jury filed in and reseated themselves. Only Dr. Rajami remained standing.

The Clerk of the Court said, "Members of the jury. Have you agreed upon your verdict?"

"We have, sir," said the Doctor. "We are unanimous."

250

"Do you find the prisoner guilty, or not guilty?"

"We are unable to say that the evidence conclusively proves the prisoner to be guilty."

The judge said, "Then your verdict is 'Not guilty'?"

"Yes, sir."

The explosion from the public gallery was, in part, a pre-arranged demonstration, but in part also a genuine outburst of rage, frustration and disbelief. As they rose, the policemen among them moved also, making for the place where they should have been stationed originally, the internal exit from the gallery. Here they formed an unbreakable barrier – ten seconds too late.

At least fifteen men had escaped. Led by one who clearly knew the way they stormed along the passage and hurled themselves against the door at the far end. This demonstration of force was unnecessary. The police had left this door unlocked, as access for their own reinforcements; a second, and a bad mistake. The door led into a robing room where a barrister, who was changing into Court dress, standing with his trousers in one hand, gaped at them. They had no time for him. Their object was to reach the bottom of the stairs before the police started to come up. They were in time, but only just. The collision took place on the bottom steps where they emerged into the lobby.

Impetus and numbers were on the side of the intruders. Their weight carried them down the last few steps and their fury carved a path through the opposition. The encounter left three of each side wounded on the ground. The remaining dozen stormed across the lobby, brushed aside a protesting official and erupted into the Court.

It was a bitter confrontation with the law; the law which had frustrated them. And there it was, before their eyes. The smug lawyers, their pompous officers and the furnishings of their mystery. They would do as much damage as possible before they were stopped.

The judge had retired through a door at the back. The leaders of the mob climbed onto the rostrum and succeeded in upending the great double desk, which fell with a splintering crash into the well of the Court. Benches were torn up and used as battering rams. Counsels' lecterns and anything else that was loose became missiles.

251

The encounter was not entirely one-sided. After a moment of shock and incredulity the more robust members of the Court started to fight back. A volume of *Archbold's Practice*, the heaviest book known to the law, had been picked up and slung across the room. It hit John Benson on the leg. Two inches higher and it would have fractured his knee-cap. With a roar of rage and pain he grabbed one of the loose chairs from the well and launched himself into battle. Seeing him go, Roger and Martin hurled themselves after him and the three of them fought their corner with considerable effect as the police reinforcements poured in.

These concentrated on seizing the intruders, one at a time and dragging them into the lobby, where they were hand-cuffed and herded into Court 2, which was empty, having finished business early.

Whilst this was going on the remaining men in the gallery, after howling insults and hurling a few missiles into the Court, were shepherded through the public entrance and out into the street. Here they soon informed and infected the crowd who were round the Court in numbers that defied all attempts at control.

At the end of ten minutes the last of the intruders had been captured, a casualty station had been set up and all the doors of the building had been barred. No one could get in, but no one could get out.

Mullen had been taken straight down by the stairs inside the dock and his fate was being discussed by three men. Chief Superintendent Baron of Special Branch, the Assistant Commissioner of City Police, and Major Dann, the head of Court security. They were being kept abreast of the situation by messages from those who had the crowd under observation.

"It'll be dark in an hour," said the Assistant Commissioner. "We could put him in one of the vans in the underground garage and try to rush him out."

Baron said, "It wouldn't work. They've got the roads carpeted with sharpened jacks. You'd burst all the tyres and the crowd would upset the van."

The three men contemplated this possibility unhappily. "Then we may have to ask the army to get him away," said Dann. "An armoured half-track wouldn't be stopped by the jacks and it wouldn't be an easy vehicle to stop or turn over.

Not that we want to call in the army unless we have to."

It was at this point that Mr. Crankling, who had attached himself to the discussion, coughed. It was a cough that announced that he had a contribution to make. He said, "In the old days it was my job to bring up coal for the judges' fires, from the cellar at the back of the building. In fact, there's a bit of coal still there. The coalmen didn't tip it in loose. It was delivered in sacks, through a trap in the pavement. In Warwick Square, that is."

Comprehension was starting to dawn.

"Where a hundred-weight sack can come in, a man can get out. So I thought – "

"Brilliant," said Dann. "See if you can get the trap open. It'll be rusted up and you may need tools to do it."

"I'll get her open," said Mr. Crankling. "Don't you worry."

"I'll telephone those publishers – the ones who have offices in the Square. Their senior partner's a friend of mine. I'll ask him to send for a taxi. As soon as it's standing outside his door I'll give the signal."

Baron said, "It can take him straight to Battersea Heliport. I'll have a police helicopter waiting for him."

The only person who did not seem to appreciate what was being done for him was Mullen. He was not frightened of the crowd. With a moderate use of live ammunition his police had dispersed many more formidable gatherings. He couldn't understand the difficulty.

He was led, protesting, to the cellar where Mr. Crankling, perched on two sacks of coal, had levered open the trap. He took a look outside and reported that it was all clear and the taxi was in position.

"Just a woman on the pavement," he said. "She doesn't look hostile."

Mullen was hoisted up, his face smeared with the coal dust that had come down from the ceiling, and was propelled through the trap, landing on hands and knees on the pavement. As he appeared Bonnie Parker, tipped off by Mr. Crankling, secured two photographs.

At nine o'clock that night a news flash announcing the arrival of Mullen in Brussels dispersed the crowd more efficiently than any number of policemen could have done.

26

Two weeks later three men were talking in de Morgan's room in Dr. Johnson's Buildings. The damage to Court No. 1 had been repaired; the upset feelings of some of its staider occupants were going to take longer to heal.

Martin Bull said, "With all respect to your admirable closing, sir, weren't you surprised at the speed of the jury's verdict?"

Roger had come to collect back the mountains of papers, countless copies of every document, important and unimportant, that Counsel seemed to delight in. For him the sun was shining. He had been offered and had gratefully accepted a partnership in Bantings. He said, "As a matter of fact, I can tell you something about that."

"Gossip from the jury room?"

"Not gossip, Martin. First-hand evidence. That lady who was co-opted onto the jury, Mrs. Gordon-Watson – "

"Don't tell me. She was your aunt."

"No. No relation. But a family friend. Godmother of one of my sister's children."

"Excellent," said de Morgan. "Proceed."

"Well, what she said was that she'd never conceived that a jury could be as intelligent as this one. She'd always imagined that they contained an element of riff-raff. Not so in this case. Sensible, solid, intelligent folk. When Dr. Rajami put it to them, they saw his point at once. *They didn't have to choose between the two theories.* All they had to decide was whether both of them were equally possible. If that was their conclusion they *couldn't* convict. It didn't take them long to make up their minds."

"It's a pity the general public weren't as quick on the up-take," said Martin.

"The public mind," said de Morgan, "moves in a mysterious way. In some inexplicable way Dorothy Katanga's suicide has led them to believe in Mullen's innocence."

"Actually – " said Roger.

"That belief seems to have taken the heat out of any personal hostility to myself – and others on our side, of course."

"In fact – " said Roger.

"The only loser has been my wife. She much regrets the removal of two agreeable young policemen who were a great help with the washing-up."

"Actually," said Roger, "the verdict at the inquest wasn't suicide. It was death resulting from an accidental overdose of sleeping pills."

"And a very proper verdict too. Nobody believed it."

"They'd have believed it even less," said Martin, "if the jury had been told that Dorothy was a trained nurse and well capable of judging the correct dose."

"Never tell a coroner's jury more than you have to," said de Morgan. "But you still look unhappy, Mr. Sherman. Is something worrying you?"

"I must confess that I was disappointed. I was under the impression that one of the objects of a trial was to arrive at the truth."

Both barristers laughed tolerantly at this naïve idea. "A criminal trial," said de Morgan – his pipe was performing so happily that he spoke, like the oracle of old, out of a cloud – "has only one objective. To demonstrate whether convincing proof can be adduced of the guilt of the man charged. Mind you, I'm not saying that a case which is properly argued in Court may not have *results*. Quite apart from the death of Mrs. Katanga, this one, when you think of it, has been singularly productive of results."

He held up his right hand and ticked them off on his thumb and fingers.

"First, I understand that Mullen is in disgrace. He has been publicly stripped of all his posts. Oddly enough this doesn't seem to be due to the two charges against him – of both of which, incidentally, he was cleared. No. It was the publication in every newspaper here and abroad of the photograph of

255

him crawling out of the hole with coal dust all over his face. Autocracies can weather any amount of criticism. The one thing they cannot stand is being laughed at. A second, and connected, result is that the helpful editor – what was his name – ?"

"Gilbert Glaister."

"Right. I gather that he has made a considerable killing by selling world rights in that photograph and has retired and handed over the paper to young Tamplin. A third person" – he held up his middle finger – "who has come less happily out of it, is Mr. Luck. The Director has still not decided whether to charge him with perjury. It now seems that he may offer him a way out. On condition that he co-operates with the authorities and reveals where the bribe, which had clearly been paid to him, came from. If he does so it may cause a lot of trouble to a solicitor known to me who practises in Basinghall Street. Yes. That would be a definite plus.

"Fourthly, the attention of the authorities has been drawn to the activities of that gang in Mornington Square. Some of the young men, who are now faced with stiff sentences for criminal damage and obstructing the administration of justice, may feel inclined to lay the blame on the central organisation, thus making them accessories to the offence. Excellent.

"Fifthly – " Here he held up his little finger, which carried a thick gold signet ring. It reflected the bleak January light over the Temple Church which Roger had visited four months before. Was Marshall Fitzhugh looking down kindly on what they had done?

"Fifthly and lastly, a poke in the eye like this could be effective to swing the next election against the Government. It's bound to be close."

"If it did," said Martin, "you might find yourself back in Sir Humphrey Belling's shoes."

De Morgan laughed so heartily at the idea that Roger could not decide whether it amused him or not.